MONTANA MAVERICKS

Welcome to Big Sky Country, home of the Montana Mavericks! Where free-spirited men and women discover love on the range.

LASSOING LOVE

After years away, some of Bronco's most memorable sons and daughters have returned to the ranch seeking a fresh start. But there are some bumps along the road to redemption. Expect the unexpected as lonesome cowboys (and cowgirls) discover if they've got what it takes to grab that second chance!

Eloise Taylor fled her wealthy, judgmental family years ago. Now, pregnant and alone, she reluctantly returns to the Taylors' prickly embrace. The *last* thing she needs is a new relationship, especially with a notoriously commitment-phobic schoolteacher. But as the holidays approach, she can't help but long for things she shouldn't...

Dear Reader,

I might have mentioned in past letters that I have four brothers, which means I love writing about big families. When I first wrote about the Sanchezes, I used the Duarte side of my own family as inspiration for their Sunday dinners—lots of people, lots of opinions and lots of food. In fact, my baby brother came home for a visit recently and schedules were tight. When I suggested hosting dinner on Saturday, he was almost offended and immediately asked, "Why not Sunday?"

Family dinners look different for everyone, but the best ones involve sharing good food and even better memories. That's why having the opportunity to write about the Sanchez family again is like being welcomed home for a Sunday dinner. I'm so excited to be back in Bronco, Montana, for their next story.

In *The Maverick's Holiday Delivery*, teacher Dante Sanchez loves his students, but isn't quite ready for children of his own. So then why is he spending so much time with soon-to-be mom Eloise Taylor, who just returned to town unexpectedly? The unlikely pair are causing quite the gossip, but all that will surely change once the baby gets here—won't it?

For more information on my other Harlequin Special Edition books, visit my website at christyjeffries.com, or chat with me on Twitter @ChristyJeffries. You can also find me on Facebook (Facebook.com/authorchristyjeffries) and Instagram @christy_jeffries. I'd love to hear from you.

Enjoy,

Christy Jeffries

The Maverick's Holiday Delivery

CHRISTY JEFFRIES

HARLEQUIN
SPECIAL
EDITION

Special thanks and acknowledgment are given to
Christy Jeffries for her contribution to the
Montana Mavericks: Lassoing Love miniseries.

HARLEQUIN®
SPECIAL EDITION™

Recycling programs
for this product may
not exist in your area.

ISBN-13: 978-1-335-59432-7

The Maverick's Holiday Delivery

Copyright © 2023 by Harlequin Enterprises ULC

For questions and comments about the quality of this book,
please contact us at CustomerService@Harlequin.com.

Harlequin Enterprises ULC
22 Adelaide St. West, 41st Floor
Toronto, Ontario M5H 4E3, Canada
www.Harlequin.com

Printed in U.S.A.

Christy Jeffries graduated from the University of California, Irvine, with a degree in criminology and received her Juris Doctor from California Western School of Law. But drafting court documents and working in law enforcement was merely an apprenticeship for her current career in the dynamic field of mommyhood and romance writing. Christy lives in Southern California with her patient husband, two sarcastic sons and a sweet husky who sheds appreciation all over her car and house.

Books by Christy Jeffries

Harlequin Special Edition

Montana Mavericks: Lassoing Love

The Maverick's Holiday Delivery

Furever Yours

It Started with a Pregnancy
It Started with a Puppy

Twin Kings Ranch

What Happens at the Ranch...
Making Room for the Rancher
Not Their First Rodeo

Montana Mavericks: What Happened to Beatrix?

His Christmas Cinderella

Montana Mavericks: The Lonelyhearts Ranch

The Maverick's Christmas to Remember

Visit the Author Profile page
at Harlequin.com for more titles.

To Charles Duarte, the oldest baby brother anyone could ever have. I'm sorry we nicknamed you "senior citizen" when you were little. I should've appreciated back then that you were an old soul with wisdom beyond your years. Although, I'm not exactly sure how you can miraculously become so immature when you're chopping it up with your nieces and nephews. There's nobody I'd rather have Sunday dinner with than you...

Chapter One

Dante Sanchez stared longingly at the cast-iron baking dish cooling at the opposite end of his parents' dining room table. At this rate, the hot apple crumble was going to be room-temperature apple crumble if his sister kept going on and on about some party her in-laws were hosting at her restaurant here in Bronco.

It didn't help that everyone in the Sanchez family had a tendency to talk over each other at their weekly Sunday dinners. Right now, most of them were coming up with excuses for why they wouldn't be able to make the event at Camilla's restaurant on Friday night. What *wasn't* being said, at least out loud, was that none of the Sanchezes wanted to go because the wealthy Taylor family was pretentious and unwelcoming and, to be honest, pretty full of themselves. Minus Camilla's husband, Jordan, of course.

Dante glanced at his mother's antique clock on the

wall and calculated how much of the Bulls' game he was going to miss. He excused himself from the table to grab the vanilla ice cream from the kitchen freezer. Maybe the sight of the dessert topping would remind everyone that they had more important things going on than which Taylor was celebrating which minor accomplishment.

"Come on, you guys," Camilla said when Dante returned to the table with the ice cream and a mismatched stack of bowls. "Jordan's stepmom is insisting on a pre-holiday party this year to ease some of the family tensions and asked if I'd be willing to host a private event at The Library since it's neutral territory. All the older generation Taylors are going to be there with their extended families and I'm going to be outnumbered on my own turf."

Their dad, still wearing his referee jersey from officiating a rec league earlier today, tsked. "Sounds like you *gave up* the home field advantage."

Their mom, still wearing her Hairdressers Tease to Please apron, tsked. "Not those old plastic bowls, Dante. You're all grown adults now and can be trusted with the breakable stuff."

"But then all the servings will be the same and my siblings won't complain about me getting the biggest size." Dante slapped Dylan's hand away when his older brother reached for the always coveted, and somewhat misshapen, blue bowl with soccer ball decals decorating the rim.

"Can we focus on this party," Camilla reminded them, "and not on that ugly old bowl that Dad uses to feed the stray orange tabby when it shows up on the back porch every night?"

Dante shuddered and dropped the bowl into Dylan's lap. "It's all yours, man."

Dylan shrugged and scooped a large helping of apple crisp into it while their sister continued pleading with them.

"I just need some normal people there so I'm not bombarded by all the Taylors. No offense, babe." Camilla paused long enough to affectionately pat her husband's back and smile sweetly at him. "I love you and I love being a Taylor—"

"A Sanchez-Taylor," their dad interrupted.

"Yes, a *Sanchez*-Taylor," Camilla corrected herself, then spoke to her husband. "It's just that your family—well, mostly your dad and his brothers—can be a little much when they all get together. And since the party is at my restaurant, there's this added pressure for me to be on top of my game and I'd just feel more comfortable having some familiar faces around."

"You don't have to explain it to me. I used to give myself the exact same pep talk every time I walked into a board meeting at Taylor Beef." Jordan Taylor, a successful businessman and a doting husband—a bit too doting if you asked Dante—squared his shoulders and looked around the table. "So what will it take to get at least one of you to attend?"

Dante didn't bother hiding an amused grin. "Are you seriously resorting to bribery, Jordan?"

"He shouldn't have to," Camilla pointed out. "You should be willing to support your sister and her fledging business while expecting nothing in return."

"First of all," Dante said as he pointed the serving spoon at his sister, who had converted the old building that once housed the city's library into an actual restaurant while keeping the name the same. "The Library is one of the trendiest places in Montana and I couldn't even get a reservation there last week. And that was on a Tuesday night."

"Why did you need a reservation on a Tuesday night?" his mom asked. "Nobody told me you were dating someone new."

Denise Sanchez, who heard all the latest Bronco gossip at her beauty salon, was one of the reasons Dante never went out with anyone from their small hometown. Now that two of her five kids were married and one was engaged, she was always throwing out hints about wanting grandchildren next. Dante wasn't ready for any of that.

"We're talking about Camilla's very *successful* and not at all fledgling business, Mom. Not my dating life," Dante reminded her, then turned to his sister. "Second of all, I am always willing to support you free of charge. But if your husband is offering to provide some incentive to get me to go to his family's party and miss out on poker night with my buddies, then all I'm saying is that my classroom is down two computers and Bronco Valley Elementary doesn't have the budget for replacements."

"Done," Jordan said a little too easily.

"But…" Dante narrowed his eyes, suddenly curious as to how far his brother-in-law would go to keep Camilla happy. "That's only going to help my third graders. I was also hoping to fund an after-school basketball program for more of the kids here in the Valley. You know, with new uniforms and equipment and maybe even an assistant coach?"

Jordan offered an amount that would probably fund

several after-school teams, then added, "Although, I'm only available for assistant coaching on Wednesdays since I know that's going to be your next demand, Dante. And if Dylan is going to be one of your referees, I'm available less than that. He always calls me out for my three-point shot."

"That's because your foot always crosses the line," Dylan said around a mouthful of dessert.

Several voices rose at once and Dante spent the rest of dinner enjoying his room-temperature apple crisp with a big scoop of ice cream and a healthy serving of trash talk amongst his favorite people.

Five days later, when he walked into his sister's restaurant, Dante felt the first twinge of guilt for letting his brother-in law bribe him into coming. Not that he was going to return the check Jordan dropped off at the school this morning. Dante had already placed the order for the new Chromebooks and charging stations.

Still.

A loyal brother would've volunteered to support his sister with no strings attached. Even if there were a lot of other places he'd rather be on a Friday night. Like grading spelling tests or icing his knee after a few rounds of pickup basketball at the high school gym. Or even returning several overdue books to the new public library, which was moved to the fancy civic center complex in Bronco Heights thanks to yet another donation by the Taylor family.

Man, there really was no way to escape the town's elite. He scanned the crowd of guests and wasn't surprised to only see a few friendly faces. Oh, well. At least the food would be good and the drinks would be cold at this Library.

Dante made his way over to the bar and fist bumped the bartender. Gary was actually the middle school PE teacher, but picked up a few night shifts.

"Nice to see someone else from the Valley here tonight." Without having to ask, Gary reached for a chilled pint glass from under the bar and began filling it with Big Sky Blonde, Dante's favorite ale.

"Yeah, well, the Heights may have gotten the new city buildings and infrastructure budget, but the Valley still has the best food." Dante reached for a chorizo-stuffed mushroom off a server's tray as she passed.

Camilla was right behind the server with a stack of tiny white plates for the buffet line and a warning look for Dante and Gary. "You two knock it off with that Heights versus Valley talk," she scolded in a hushed voice. "We're all one big happy town tonight."

Gary shrugged. "As long as your father-in-law's wife keeps tipping me twenty dollars every time I refill her wine glass, we will all be happy, indeed."

"Could you at least try to mingle a little, Dante?" His sister nodded toward the guests filling up the seating areas. "You're supposed to be here for emotional support. Not to distract my best bartender."

"Distracting? I was emotionally supporting Gary, who is emotionally supporting *me* with this perfectly chilled lager." Dante lifted his glass and tried not to smirk at his sister's death glare. It was the same one she'd been using on him and their brothers since she was four years old. "Oh, relax, Camilla. I was just about to make my way over to your father-in-law and ask ol' Cornelius and his brothers if they have any stock market tips for me."

"Just so you know, telling a woman to *relax* certainly

explains why you're still single, Dante." Camilla blew a strand of brown hair away from her face and shifted her stack of plates. "Also, Dylan already tried that icebreaker at my wedding and they thought he was trying to get them to invest in a pyramid scheme. So consider yourself warned."

Of course, men like the Taylors assumed everyone was after their money. Dante rolled his eyes. "Here, let me help you set up the—"

"I got this." Camilla rejected his offer to take the dishes from her arms before he could finish making it. "You can help by being friendly to all my guests."

His sister whirled away, doing what she always did—making sure things ran smoothly while effortlessly sipping champagne and blending in with the rest of the guests.

As Dante took another drink of his beer and looked around the clusters of well-dressed people shoving their faces full of appetizers, he couldn't quite figure out what she was so concerned about. The Taylors may dress like a million bucks and the older generation might act like they owned the town, but times were changing in Bronco. In fact, the latest generation, like Camilla's husband and his sister Daphne, who owned Happy Hearts sanctuary, were actually pretty down to earth. Dante even had one of the cousin's kids in his class this year, which meant at least some members of the family were willing to live outside the affluent bubble of the Heights. Besides, everyone in town liked Camilla and they all loved her restaurant.

Sure, the patriarchs of the Taylor family—four snobby brothers including Jordan's stuffy and opinionated father—could be hard to take. But that was only if someone cared what the filthy rich Taylors thought. And Dante most definitely did not care.

A sudden hush fell over the crowded restaurant and several heads pivoted to the entrance. Okay, so maybe Dante was a little curious about what they thought because he took a few steps away from the bar to see why everyone else had grown so quiet.

The pint glass paused halfway to his lips as he watched a brunette wearing a long faux fur coat and a defiant attitude stride past several stunned expressions. Interest hummed through him when he finally caught sight of her beautiful profile. Dante had a strict rule about not dating anyone who lived within a twenty-mile radius of the Bronco town limits, and this woman definitely wasn't from around here.

Smiling to himself, he decided the evening might turn out to be more promising than he'd originally thought.

Something nudged his back and he turned around to see Camilla holding a plate of the most delicious smelling empanadas he'd ever wanted to eat. Instead of offering him one, his sister pulled her food out of reach while keeping her wide eyes focused on the newcomer. Camilla's voice was low and came out in a near hiss. "Nobody mentioned Eloise was coming."

"Am I supposed to recognize the name?" He lowered his own voice so that he could take better advantage of his sister's distress to snatch an empanada and pop it into his mouth.

"Eloise Taylor. She's my husband's cousin."

"Your husband has lots of cousins." This time when Dante tried to grab a second shrimp-filled pastry, his sister proved to be much faster.

"Her dad is Thaddeus." Camilla jerked her chin toward one of the Taylor patriarchs whose permanent frown only shifted slightly at the appearance of his daughter. "She had some big fight with her parents after college, but nobody seems too sure of the details. All I know is that she hasn't been home to Bronco in at least seven years."

Dante did the math in his head and realized they were likely close to the same age. Which meant Eloise must've gone to a private school instead of Bronco High since he'd known everyone in his graduating class. Trying not to be too obvious, he lifted his beer for a long drink while he studied her.

There was no way he'd forget someone who looked like that. Eloise Taylor was stunning, with big brown eyes framed by lush lashes, long flowing dark hair and a glowing complexion. He couldn't see her exact figure in that big coat, but she walked with the grace of someone who did Pilates regularly and the confidence of someone who knew exactly how good she looked.

"I have to let the chef know it's time to plate the entrées." Camilla didn't bother whispering because the noise around them returned just as quickly as it had left. In fact, the voices closest to Dante sounded even louder and more animated as people tried to pretend that they were engaged in deep conversations while casting covert glances in Eloise's direction. "Keep an eye out for any drama and make sure nobody causes a scene."

"I think it's a little too late for that," Dante said, unable to take his own eyes off the beautiful woman who'd been intercepted a few feet away from him by a relative who'd maybe had a bit too much wine. The woman raved about how lustrous and shiny Eloise's hair looked.

Dante didn't think people used the word *lustrous* unless they were in shampoo commercials. He asked his sister, "What do you want me to do if things get out of hand? I didn't bring Dad's or Dylan's referee whistles."

"Just pretend they're your students and, I don't know, quiz them on state capitals or start up a game of dodgeball or something." A server passed balancing a stack of empty glasses. "Maybe skip the dodgeball. I don't need any broken dishes tonight."

By the time Dante finished his beer, Eloise had finally made her way across the restaurant to her parents. At least, he assumed that was her mom. He'd heard that some of the older Taylor men went through wives the same way they went through luxury cars.

Dante had mixed feelings about listening to the gossip. As a single man whose relationship status was often discussed, he hated being the subject of drama and rumors. As a teacher, though, he wanted to know which students might not be able to afford school lunch because they had a parent out of work. Or which student had a relative in the hospital or a cat who'd run away from home. As a brother, he wanted to make sure that nobody was going to cause problems at his sister's restaurant. And whatever was about to go down tonight would probably be the talk of the town for the next few days.

He was too far away to hear the substance of Eloise's greeting with her parents, but so far everyone's polite smiles were still in place. Thaddeus gave Eloise a brief kiss on the cheek, which had to mean he was at least glad to see his daughter. On the other hand, that could only be for show since some families cared more about appearances than affection. The mom's hug seemed a bit more natural, but Mrs. Taylor kept glancing at her husband, as though she were gauging his reaction. Unfortunately, Thaddeus's expression changed when his daughter finally took off her coat.

Eloise Taylor was pregnant. Very pregnant.

There were several gasps, and even Dante couldn't stop his eyes from blinking a few times at what he was seeing. His brain was slow to process the fact that the beautiful woman obviously wasn't for him. Probably because he was simultaneously fighting some unexpected impulse to walk over and introduce himself.

Finally, his brain won the struggle and he shook off the urge, as well as the disappointment sinking in his chest. For his sister's sake, though, he did watch for a couple more beats to make sure that Eloise's surprising announcement was the only drama unfolding.

For the most part, her siblings and cousins—or at least the people who appeared to be from their generation—formed a circle around her and seemed to be making congratulatory statements. Most of the older generation, though, stood rigid, their glances solidly on Thaddeus. Dante curled a lip in disgust. He couldn't believe that they were seriously awaiting some dour guy's cue on how they should respond.

Unfortunately, Thaddeus responded by pivoting and marching straight to the men's restroom. His abrupt exit wouldn't have caused such a scene if his brothers hadn't followed right behind him, like uptight little soldiers. Eloise's mother recovered with a bit more grace than her husband and pulled her daughter in for another stiff and awkward hug.

Dante shook his head and turned his attention to the NBA game on the TV near the bar. If he or any of his siblings announced that they were having a baby, his parents would've been jumping up and down with joy. In fact, most of the people in this restaurant tonight were either Taylors by birth or by marriage. Clearly, their huge family must've had its share of birth announcements in the past. So what was the big deal if one more baby was added to the brood? He'd never understand rich people.

Dante ordered a second beer and looked for more appetizers. Just because the dramatic scene was over, though, didn't mean the tongues were done wagging.

"How's it going?" Dante asked Jordan's brother Brandon when they ran into each other at the hors d'oeuvre table.

Before Brandon could answer, his wife Cassidy appeared by his side. "Your cousin Ryan accidentally left his phone in the men's room and wants to know if you'll go get it for him."

"Not as long as my uncles are huddled in there trying to strategize the best way to get Eloise married off before her due date."

So Eloise was still single? An unexplainable thrill shot through Dante before he reminded himself that she could still be engaged or in a long term relationship.

"That's the same reason your cousins Seth and Daniel told him no," Cassidy said before taking a mini birria tostada from her husband's plate.

"Are there any more of those empanadas left?" Mac, Jordan's opinionated assistant and Camilla's silent partner who'd help her buy The Library, surveyed the appetizers. "I've got my bowling league tonight and can't stay for dinner."

Dante begrudgingly let the silver-haired woman

take the last one. But only because he knew Mac was a wealth of information when it came to the tight-lipped Taylors, and he needed to report back to Camilla any snippets of information he'd overheard.

"Where's your sister?" Mac asked Dante. "I hope she's not telling the chef to wait on serving the main course just 'cause Thaddeus Taylor is throwing a fit about lil' Eloise showing up unexpectedly. You'd think a grown man with a multibillion dollar business would have more important things to worry about than what a bunch of local gossips are saying."

"People are already gossiping?" Dante asked as casually as possible. As though, he hadn't been raised in Bronco and knew first-hand how fast a rumor could spread.

Mac shook her head, but her steel curls didn't move. "Of course, it's all just speculation at this point. But if you ask me, it's nobody's business who the father of Eloise's baby is. She'll let people know when and if she wants them to know."

Dante took another swig of beer, trying to wash away the taste of guilt still lingering on his tongue for asking a follow-up question he knew would get a response. Mac's answer immediately reminded Dante why he avoided being the subject of gossip himself. It was one thing to be curious about someone's situation. It was quite another for people to be judgmental as hell—especially when there was an innocent baby involved.

When Mac left, Daphne and Evan Cruise invited Dante to join them at their table, but he preferred his seat at the bar. Not only could he keep an eye on the basketball score, he also had a better view of the restaurant from over here. Plus, if Gary got a free second from filling drink orders, Dante could hit him up about volunteering with his new after-school league.

Every time Dante caught sight of Eloise, though, he experienced a tug of remorse for his inability to quell his curiosity in her family life. Actually, he wasn't interested so much in her family as he was in her. Despite his magnetic draw to the beautiful woman, Dante kept telling himself that the soon-to-be mom was not his business. His business was making sure Camilla's night went off without a hitch. And judging by the empty plates the staff whisked to the kitchen between courses, everyone was certainly enjoying the food.

The first time he caught Eloise looking in his direction after dinner, Dante experienced that pulling sensation again and glanced away quickly. Not only was he fighting against an unusually strong physical reaction to her, he was unable to ignore the fact that she was already the focus of so much attention. The last thing he wanted to do was make her feel like some sort of spectacle. The second time she looked his way, though, he held her gaze long enough to give her a reassuring smile. Then he kicked himself for the patronizing assumption that she needed assurance from anyone, let alone from some random dude sitting at the bar.

The third time they locked eyes, Dante returned the stare with bold curiosity. After all, if she was going to keep looking in his direction, it only seemed fair. This time, Eloise looked away first. But not before he saw a flush of color on her high cheekbones.

"She's not for you, man," he mumbled into his glass before taking a huge gulp. He'd switched over to water after his second beer despite the fact that it wasn't a school night. Dante was used to being held to a different standard because of his job, which was sometimes an inconvenience. On the bright side, being a teacher also gave him a built-in excuse for leaving parties like this one. All he had to say was that he had to go work on his lesson plans. Nobody ever tried to convince him to stay later when they knew his job entailed enlightening the young minds of a future generation.

He went to the kitchen where his sister already had to-go containers waiting for him. Camilla passed him the fancy paper bag with The Library's logo stamped on the front. "You lasted longer than I thought you would."

"I think the words you're looking for are *thank you, Dante, for being my favorite brother and for taking one for the team tonight.*"

Camilla laughed. "Thank you, Dante, for being *one of* my favorite brothers. And you're welcome for all the free food I give you every single time you show up here with the appetite of an entire offensive line of football players."

"Me and my appetite will see you on Sunday for dinner." He hefted the bag and gave her a playful nudge. "I'll need more empanadas by then."

Heading toward the exit, Dante scanned the restaurant for a last view of Eloise Taylor but was only rewarded with the steely—and slightly suspicious—glare from her father, Thaddeus. The older man, who'd finally rejoined the party after presumably pouting in the men's room for the first half of dinner, was probably wondering how someone like Dante had made the invite list. With a rebellious smirk, Dante threw him a wave goodbye.

He was standing in the parking lot, waiting for the valet attendant to bring his car when Eloise stormed around the corner of the building, her open coat blowing behind her in the cold breeze. It was on the tip of Dante's tongue to ask her how long she'd been out here, but he soon had his answer.

"I've been waiting on a rideshare for the past twenty minutes, but this town has never been known for its thriving public transportation system." She nodded at the headlights pulling up. "Please tell me this is your car. If I can't get away from my father this very second, I'm going to scream."

Crap.

Dante looked wistfully at the entrance of the restaurant. It was a shame that Camilla had come so close to pulling off a successful night for her in-laws' party. Sure, there'd been that little scene earlier, but everyone had quickly recovered. Judging by Eloise's current tone and clenched jaw, though, things could go sideways real quick. "No need to scream. I'm sure we can figure—"

Eloise was in the passenger seat of Dante's SUV before he could finish his suggestion. Whoa. She moved fairly quickly for a pregnant person.

Apparently, she wasn't used to waiting for an invitation. Had this woman never heard of stranger danger? Had *he*? Dante would never let one of his sisters get into a car with a person they didn't know. But it wasn't like he could just leave Eloise stranded outside in the cold. And could he really blame her for wanting to get away from her father? Dante had gone out of his way to avoid all the older Taylors tonight.

The valet attendant cleared his throat and Dante realized he couldn't leave the young man standing by the driver's door forever.

Not wanting to give anyone the impression that he

was some sort of hired taxi, Dante climbed behind the wheel and purposely handed Eloise the to-go bag. Then he asked, "Where are *we* going?"

Not missing a beat, Eloise twisted in her seat and set the carryout bag on the floor of the back seat. "We're going to the Heights Hotel and asking for an upgrade to a room with a tub big enough for two."

Chapter Two

Eloise watched the man's face go from sexy and smug to wary and surprised in a matter of seconds. She would have laughed if he hadn't been so ridiculously attractive, with a compelling stare that made her blush every time their gazes had met tonight. His boldness had drawn her in, especially when he hadn't even bothered to pretend to look away when she caught him staring. As if he hadn't noticed that she was not only seven and a half months pregnant, but also a source of shame to her uptight parents.

Eloise had already caused enough scandal this evening with her dramatic entrance at the party. Her parents had deserved the shock. This guy with the sultry brown bedroom eyes and the smooth dark tan complexion didn't ask for any of this.

"I'm sorry." She smothered an exhausted groan. She was too emotionally drained and too desperate to get away from all the prying eyes; she didn't want to waste time or headspace sitting in this idling car just to hear his polite rejection of her. "I didn't mean for that to sound like an invitation. I'm already staying at the Heights Hotel. And since I can't have a glass of wine right now to calm me down," she said as she rubbed her hand along her baby bump, "I need to soak in a steamy bubble bath that can accommodate me and my plus-one."

Instead of asking all the not-so-subtle questions everyone else had already asked tonight, the man nodded and pulled out of the driveway in silence. She closed her eyes and took a deep breath. The interior of his car smelled like leather and one of Eloise's favorite colognes. Taylor Marketing, the company she'd founded, had done the launch for the new scent and she'd given Wade a bottle last year for Christmas. However, her ex had preferred his tried-and-true brand that he'd been using since college. Eloise should've taken that as her first sign that they weren't compatible. Maybe if she would've broken up with him back then instead of waiting to find out the hard way that he wasn't cut out to be a husband and father...

No. She wasn't going to think of all the red flags she'd ignored. She was moving to Bronco, Montana, to focus on her future. Not to dwell on her past. Instead, she'd been reminded of why she'd once left this small town in the first place. And she'd only been here a couple of hours.

Eloise had missed so much in the years she'd been gone. Most notably, her siblings and her cousins and some of her childhood friends. She'd been expecting to walk into the same old stodgy Taylor affair tonight and liven things up with her big announcement.

What she hadn't expected was how many of her family members—the ones closer to her own age—would be in attendance with their own significant others, clearly in love. She was happy for them, obviously, but somehow the new additions to the Taylor family had shifted the vibe ever so slightly.

Of course, she should have realized things would change since the world hadn't stopped when she left town. She'd gotten the engagement announcements and the wedding invites and all the updates on social media. Seeing it all in person, though, suddenly made her feel as if *she'd* been the one left behind.

"Thank you for giving me a ride," she said when they pulled up to the front of the newer hotel several minutes later. The Taylor family dynamic wasn't the only thing that had changed since she'd been gone. With several trendy restaurants, bars and shops, the downtown area was livelier than she'd been anticipating. "You probably didn't expect to deal with an emotional pregnant woman on your Friday night."

"No, I usually save that for Saturday nights."

The guy had a good sense of humor, which only made her feel worse about ruining his evening. Like she'd ruined everyone else's evening. Nothing was going as planned. She rubbed her temples, scrunching her eyes closed before the tears of frustration started flowing. Lately, she tended to get weepy at the most inopportune moments.

"Hey, are you going to be okay?" He put the car in Park and turned toward her. "I can walk you up to your room if you're not feeling well."

"No," she said a bit too quickly. It used to be that when a man offered to see her upstairs, it meant he wanted to

stay the night. Being pregnant, though, meant she no longer had to worry about a guy's ulterior motives when it
came to that. The concern on his face made it clear he
had no intention of putting the moves on her.

But Eloise's nerves and emotions were too raw and
she had enjoyed the soothing quiet of his car a little too
much. Plus, she couldn't explain it, but there was something about the guy that made her feel...secure.

"Yes," she said, changing her mind. "I mean, you
don't have to. But I guess... Maybe. If you want."

Eloise negotiated million-dollar deals and talked to
her clients in rational terms when they were indecisive about their marketing campaigns. She'd practically
raised herself and had been making her own decisions
since she was a teenager. So why couldn't she decide
whether or not to be alone tonight?

Because sometimes it was nice to have someone else
calling the shots for a change. To have someone else
take care of her instead of the other way around. Even
if the guy was a handsome stranger who never asked
for any of this to be dumped in his lap.

And wow was he handsome.

Her mouth went dry as he opened the car door for
her. He was at least six feet tall with broad shoulders
and probably an athletic build under that brown suede
jacket. His dark hair was short, yet professionally styled,
as if he went to an actual salon rather than a chain
barbershop. His jawline was sharp with just a hint of
matching dimples in his cheeks to soften his expression. His rich brown eyes held the slightest mischie-
vous glint that made him seem more approachable and
his wide smile was bright against his complexion that
suggested a Mexican-American heritage.

She hadn't recognized him back at the restaurant, yet there was also something strangely familiar about him. It was possible that he worked for her family, but he'd also kept himself apart from the other guests at the party. There had to be a story there.

As they entered the lobby, he nodded toward the reception desk. "I'm guessing you already checked in and weren't planning to stay at the Triple T?"

Clearly, he knew who she was and that her family was not only the richest in Bronco but owned one of the biggest ranches in the entire state. It wouldn't be the first time someone went out of their way to be nice to her once they found out her last name. She should probably remind him that she wasn't exactly on good terms with the rest of the Taylors or their trust funds.

"My father's ranch?" Eloise snorted back a laugh as she cradled her stomach. "Isn't the answer obvious?"

"Not really when you're wearing that large coat." He shrugged. "Besides, is it really that big of deal that you're expecting? I mean, it's not like we're living in the Middle Ages."

"You must not know my family very well."

"Actually, I know them better than you might think." He smiled. "My sister is married to one. That was her restaurant where the party was held."

"Right." Eloise nodded as it all clicked into place. That must be why she'd been drawn to him. Why she felt like she could trust him. His smile was kind, approachable. Nothing like her father's unwelcoming scowl. She cleared her throat. "Jordan's my cousin. I knew he'd gotten married and I meant to introduce myself to his wife—your sister—but then I'd gotten so annoyed with my parents, and she was busy hostessing. I left before I got the chance. What's her name again?"

"Camilla Sanchez. I'm Dante Sanchez." He extended his hand. "Nice to officially meet you."

The second her palm touched his, an electric current sizzled all the way up her arm. He must have felt it, too, because he immediately pulled back from the handshake and crossed his arms in front of his chest.

Besides, who cared if there were sparks or even fireworks going off between them? Dante Sanchez seemed like a nice enough guy—a safe enough guy—but they all seemed that way at first. It was best to just stay her course and not lose focus of her goal.

Eloise continued across the lobby, then drew to a halt in front of the hotel lounge and restaurant. "I forgot the carryout bag in the car."

"Are you hungry? I can share it if you want." One corner of his mouth rose into a smirk, and it suddenly occurred to her that he hadn't actually given her the food, just handed it to her as he'd gotten into the SUV.

"Um, no. Of course not. I mean, yes, I'm hungry. I'm always hungry lately, but I couldn't take your food from you."

"That's okay. I always know where I can get more." His words were polite, but his devious grin turned into a relieved smile.

One of the restaurant staff must've noticed them standing near the host stand and asked, "A table for two?"

"Oh, no thank you," Eloise said. "We're on our way upstairs."

The maître d' lifted one brow. "Maybe room service, then? We have a lovely charcuterie board that's the perfect size for couples. It pairs well with our chocolate-dipped strawberries, which is one of our most popular and romantic dessert selections. Might I suggest a bottle of champagne as well?"

Mortification raced through Eloise, but before she could correct him and explain that she didn't mean they were going upstairs for a romantic evening, Dante discreetly pointed at her midsection and said, "No champagne, but the room service sounds good. Do you have a menu?"

"Of course." The maître d's red face must've surely reflected Eloise's own embarrassed blush. He handed her a menu and added, "My apologies, ma'am, I didn't really notice because of the coat, you see."

"It seems to be a common response tonight," she mumbled as her eyes landed on the typed list of appetizers. She'd worn the heavier coat because November in Montana could be bone-chilling. And because it was the only one she owned that still fit her. It wasn't like she was trying to hide anything.

Dante was also reading the menu over her shoulder, standing close enough that she could smell his cologne. His voice was low and deep when he asked, "What looks good to you?"

"Not the charcuterie board," she said in a rush. Or any of the other romantic options the maître d' had erroneously suggested. She fought the urge to make eye contact with Dante. "Do you have any suggestions?"

"I've never actually eaten here, but my guess is that you can't go wrong with the burger. Although, don't tell my sister I recommended that. She's always on me to try new things that don't come with a side a fries. Don't get me wrong, I'll eat anything put in front of me.

But I'm a simple man who doesn't like to make things complicated."

Eloise couldn't resist and finally looked up from the menu to find Dante staring at her. Were his words a warning or an invitation? Her pulse picked up speed and suddenly she was extremely warm in her oversized coat.

She shrugged out of the thing, if only to remind him—and herself—that she was still pregnant under there. Then she ordered the most complicated sandwich she could find on the menu, making several substitutions and adding a side of extra pickles. Okay, the pickles were a legit craving and not just for show, so she asked for two sides. "And he'll have the burger made as simply as possible with no complications. Room 528."

"Can I get my burger wrapped to go?" Dante asked the maître d' as he pulled out his wallet. Then he looked at Eloise. "I wouldn't want anything keeping you from that hot steamy bubble bath you were talking about earlier."

The maître d's brows shot up again and he quickly added, "Our chocolate ganache layer cake is really quite sinful and—"

"No need for being sinful," Eloise interrupted rather loudly, causing several diners to turn their way. She immediately lowered her voice. "I mean, I'm not in the mood for anything too rich. How about the chocolate-covered strawberries instead? And a side of ice cream if you have any. Maybe a crème brûlée and, um, you know what, just send up one of each of the desserts."

Her cheeks were completely on fire at this point so Eloise didn't wait to have him read back her order. She turned on her heel and marched to the elevator bank, curling her fingernails tightly into her palms so she wouldn't be tempted to push the call button several times in an effort to speed the thing up.

"I'm just going to see my *friend* upstairs and then I'll come back down here for my burger, Jimmy," Dante said to the maître d, who'd thankfully acted as though it weren't completely out of the ordinary to see his son's teacher on his way up to a hotel room with a pregnant woman who'd just ordered every dessert ever made.

"No worries, Mr. Sanchez. Take all the time you need with your *friend*."

Dante wanted to explain that it wasn't what he thought. But Jimmy worked at a hotel restaurant and bar. He'd likely seen his share of guests claiming all sorts of things when they were really there for different purposes.

Instead, Dante added a hefty tip to the credit card receipt, then caught up with Eloise in front of the elevators. "You sure you're okay?"

"Yes. Perfectly fine. Just a hot flash." Eloise shifted the coat to her other arm and fanned her hand in front of her flushed face. "I think the hotel heater must be set to full blast."

Dante bit his lip, not wanting to point out that she had goose bumps on her bare arms. The elevator doors finally opened and the woman who'd stayed utterly silent the entire ride here suddenly couldn't stop talking.

"Or maybe it's my internal thermostat that's way off. My doctor warned that my hormones would totally wreak havoc on my moods and my emotions, and she was right. But no matter how well you think you can prepare for something mentally, it's a whole different experience when the physicality of it all hits you.

I mean, I can read a million articles about heartburn being a side effect in pregnancy, and my brain will read it literally as *heart burn*. So I'm thinking occasionally my heart is going to burn. Right?"

He could see his doubtful expression in the mirrored reflection of the elevator doors as he agreed with her. "Right."

"Wrong. It's not just my heart, it's my ribcage feeling as if its crackling over a rotisserie and my solar plexus pulsating with fire and my throat bubbling up with acid while I'm dumping out my entire purse looking for a roll of antacids and vowing that I'm never going to eat pork curry again. Yet, during that entire episode, when my brain is telling me to get to the nearest ice cream shop to cool down, my hormones will be telling me that chile rellenos would be amazing for dinner. I swear, my food cravings are so out of control that they listen to nobody. Including my clothes, which are now so snug, I can barely move without fear of a wardrobe malfunction in public."

She paused from her monologue just long enough to reach into her purse and Dante had a difficult time keeping his eyes off the way her dress dipped into a low V over her chest. Only a jerk would be hoping for a wardrobe malfunction at that exact second, so he forced himself to scan the hallway to see if anyone else was witnessing him outside her door.

"But I've been holding off for as long as I can on buying anything new because I don't want to become one of those people whose pregnancy totally defines them." She continued talking as she used her key and stepped inside her hotel room, leaving Dante little choice but to follow her.

"I mean, obviously, it defines me because I'm growing another human inside of my body. A human I'm ultimately going to be responsible for. But I'm also trying not to lose my own identity in the process. So as much as I want to do everything by the book, I also want to do it on my own terms because everyone's experience is going to be different. No matter how much I plan, I won't know what to expect until it happens. The only thing I can control at this point is my work schedule and staying as healthy as possible, both mentally and physically. Although, after tonight, I can assure you I'd much rather pop a few hundred micrograms of folic acid than confront my parents." She sighed. "If only there was a supplement I could take for dealing with all the family drama. Or shopping for new clothes. I'd love a pill for that. One of my clients recommended a protein shake, but it tasted like dish soap…"

He could barely keep up as she jumped from topic to topic, but he felt a strange contentment in listening to her share something as personal as her vitamin regimen. Probably because earlier in the evening, he'd had her pegged as one of those aloof, untouchable types. When she'd gotten into his car, he'd been apprehensive about what he was getting himself into. But then hearing her make so many accidental innuendos downstairs in the hotel lobby had him trying not to laugh. The confident way she carried herself at the party gave Dante the impression that she didn't get embarrassed easily. But then she'd gotten adorably flustered when she was ordering.

It was like the time he'd taken his class on a field trip to a museum and warned all the students not to touch anything, only to find out that the "dinosaur bones" were actually just replicas made out of a synthetic matérial and were meant to be handled. Once he was able to let down his guard, the kids were able to get a hands-on experience, and everyone learned more.

Sure, Eloise was a Taylor and probably had grown up with a life of privilege. Yet, there was also a vulnerability about her that Dante couldn't ignore. It would've been rude to abandon a woman who was clearly in need of a friend right now. Plus, he was completely intrigued and slightly entertained by her openness.

She slipped off her high heels as she walked into her room and threw her coat on the desk chair. She was about five foot five without the shoes and had a thin build. Her dress was slinky and clingy and, from behind, gave no indication that she was…

"And don't even get me started on the spontaneous crying for no reason. I've never in my life been a crier yet lately, every time I wake up, it's like a waterworks show. It's better than having morning sickness, though, since I love eating breakfast." She collapsed on the small sofa near the window and tucked her bare feet behind her. The room was beautifully appointed and probably cost a hefty sum per night, but it didn't have many seating options. Unless he moved her coat or squished beside her on the sofa, his only options were to sit on the edge of the enormous bed or remain standing.

"It was easy to satisfy my cravings when I was living in New York because the city has every type of food imaginable." Eloise was craning her slim neck up so she could look at him while she spoke. Apparently, they were back on the subject of food. "But it's been so long since I've been in Bronco, I didn't expect there to be so many offerings. Or for the first place I went to be so good. Where did Camilla learn to cook like that?"

"Our family is really big on Sunday dinners," Dante replied. When she blinked those long lashes up at him expectantly, he realized the monologue that had made her seem relatable was suddenly over and she was waiting for him to start participating in the conversation. Lowering himself to eye level, he sat on the very corner edge of the king-sized bed. "Growing up, both of my parents worked. We all had to learn to cook and take turns planning the menu, buying the ingredients, you know, doing the entire meal prep. I have two older brothers and two younger sisters, and we can be ultra-competitive at times. We are always trying to outdo each other with new recipes or new techniques."

"You said we *are*. As in you still take turns cooking every Sunday."

"We do. In fact, you probably would have met my brother Dylan tonight if he hadn't singed off his eyebrows a few weeks ago trying to make something he called flaming fajitas. He's avoiding social events until they grow back." Dante paused, enjoying the full-throated sound of her laughter. "Anyway, Camilla is obviously better at it than the rest of us, but I can hold my own if it involves five ingredients or less."

"Your family sounds like so much fun. We were never really encouraged to cook for ourselves." Eloise made it sound as though it weren't common knowledge that the Taylors were wealthy enough to employ an entire household staff, including a professional chef. "I'm pretty sure my dad would've had a fit if he'd ever seen my brothers cooking, not that he'd ever catch them since he doesn't dare venture into the kitchen himself."

"I'm getting the impression that your dad is a bit old-fashioned." What Dante didn't say was that this impression wasn't a new one. He was already pretty much convinced ol' Thaddeus was equally as chauvinistic as he was pompous.

"Let's just say that it isn't exactly easy being a female in the Taylor family. In my dad's mind, men rule the roost and work in the family business, and the women are expected to look pretty and not do anything that would interfere with the *natural order of things*." Eloise used her fingers to make air quotes over the last part. "Which probably explains why my two sisters and I prefer living out of town."

"Do you get along with your brothers?" Dante could've sworn he'd seen one of them, possibly two, congratulating her tonight. He was sure someone had mentioned them by name, but it was hard to keep track of all of Jordan's cousins and where Eloise fell in the family tree.

"For the most part. The three of them are not as uptight as our father, though I'd be lying if I didn't admit that I'm a little resentful that they got to work for Taylor Beef right out of college and that I—" A knock interrupted her. "That must be room service."

Eloise sprung off the sofa and made it to the door in record time, inviting the server to push the linen-draped cart into the room. There was an array of plates covered with silver domes, and on top sat a lone carryout box. Dante groaned inwardly, recalling his earlier request to get his burger to go. Jimmy must've doubted that Dante would be coming back downstairs to claim it.

"Don't I need to sign something?" Eloise asked the server when he turned to exit the room.

"Ah, no, ma'am." The server looked between Eloise, who was standing on the plush carpet in her bare feet, and Dante, who was still sitting on the foot of the bed. "The bill was already paid downstairs."

When the server left, Eloise turned to Dante, a chocolate-covered strawberry already in her fingers. "You didn't have to pay for all of this. The desserts alone were probably over a hundred dollars."

One hundred and forty-five, to be exact. Instead of responding, though, Dante stood up. He knew better than to discuss money with someone who likely didn't blink twice at ordering an entire menu without looking at the price.

"Consider it an early baby shower gift."

The strawberry paused halfway to her mouth and for a split second, Dante thought he might have insulted her. If so, she quickly recovered and he had to avert his eyes so he wouldn't stare at her full red lips taking a lush bite of the fruit.

"Anyway," he said as he picked up his wrapped burger a little too quickly, "I'm sure your father will come around once the baby is born. My parents are dying to become grandparents. Luckily, I'm off the hook and they only pester my married siblings about it."

Eloise sighed and he wasn't sure if it was from the decadent dessert she'd just swallowed or from his attempt to be positive. "My mom promised to talk to him, but her efforts to smooth things over have never really worked in the past. So we'll see. Anyway, thanks again for the ride and for listening. And for all the dessert that you shouldn't have let me order."

He wanted to tell her that he couldn't have stopped her from ordering that dessert any more than he could have stopped her from getting into his car. The only thing he had the power to stop was himself and this growing desire to stay. As he forced himself to walk out the door, Dante settled for saying, "Take care of yourself."

Eloise hoped she wouldn't have to face handsome Dante Sanchez again. Or at least not until she had her life—and her emotions—back under control. She'd made a complete fool out of herself last night, nervously talking nonstop about food and pregnancy hormones. Who knows what else she'd let slip. She was usually much more disciplined about staying on topic and had probably scared him off.

But maybe that was a good thing, she reasoned now in the light of day.

When he'd left her room—and after she'd made her way through the chocolate cake—she actually had called downstairs to the front desk and requested an upgrade to the bigger suite. She told herself that it was because she wanted the spa-like tub, but really it was because she needed to forget the image of the sexy man sitting on her king-sized bed just a few feet away from her, and her unexplainable attraction to him. Granted, he had behaved like a perfect gentleman, never once giving her the impression that he was interested in actually utilizing the bed. At least not with a woman who was nearly eight months pregnant.

In fact, he'd made that clear with his parting comment about fortunately being single and not at risk of providing his parents with a grandchild.

"I used to think the same thing," she told herself in the hallway mirror as she waited for the hotel elevator to the lobby. "Until I ended up here."

When she'd initially taken the home pregnancy test, she'd been stunned, then overwhelmed. When Wade told her he had no intention of being a part of their child's life, she'd been angry, then overwhelmed. When her obstetrician had asked about her support system for when she became a mother, Eloise had been terrified, and then defiant. Defiance at least gave her a sense of control. And there was nothing more defiant than confronting her own parents and her own past.

As she walked to a nearby Italian restaurant for her first official lunch meeting in Bronco, Eloise took several deep breaths and did what she always did when there was work to be done. She blocked out all the personal stuff and put her business first.

"Welcome to Pastabilities." A fresh-faced young woman greeted her from the hostess stand. Eloise had been just as young and earnest and full of "pastabilities" herself when she was that age.

"Hi, my reservation isn't until noon, but I was hoping to be seated early." Eloise had done as much of the preliminary work on her pitch as she could this morning and didn't want to pace around her suite, thinking of her family or Dante Sanchez or any of the other things that had gone wrong since she'd arrived in town yesterday.

The hostess seated her, and Eloise powered up her laptop and reviewed her PowerPoint presentation one more time.

"Eloise?" Robin Abernathy asked when she arrived at the table fifteen minutes later. "You still look just like your sister Charlotte."

"And you're still way prettier than your brother Billy." Eloise stood up to hug the woman. She and Robin had attended elementary school together but hadn't stayed in contact when Eloise and her sister Allison had been shipped off to boarding school following an unfortunate incident between Charlotte and Billy. Eloise gestured to the empty chair. "I'm so glad you reached out."

"When I saw that it was your firm that did that genius campaign for the French cologne, the one with the ad during the Olympics, I knew you were the perfect person to entrust with my vision. I'm so glad you agreed to take me on as a client."

"Are you kidding? I've been looking at the reports and Rein Rejuvenation has some amazing products."

"Thanks. Let's hope other ranchers and horse owners outside of Montana agree with you."

When Robin had called a few weeks ago, she said she'd been toying with the idea of taking her horse therapeutics company international and was looking for a bigger, more experienced marketing firm to launch her product. Signing Robin as a client also gave Eloise the perfect reason to return to her hometown and launch a remote branch of her successful business. Once Eloise got the idea in her head to move back to Bronco, she hadn't been able to shake it. Yet, even when she arrived into town less than twenty-four hours ago, it was still just an idea. It wasn't until last night when Eloise decided her father wasn't going to run her out of town again. She was staying for good.

"They will. Let me show you what my team has come up with so far." Eloise angled the screen toward Robin and they spent the next twenty minutes discussing digital platforms and target audiences, pausing briefly to order appetizers and then lunch.

Eloise put away her laptop when their plates arrived. The scent of her brown butter and sage sauce was enticing and she was ready to focus her attention on the pasta dish.

"Did I mention that you look incredible?" Robin said around a forkful of antipasto salad. "I hope I look as good as you when I finally get pregnant."

"Thanks. I didn't realize you were trying."

"Well, I'm not. Yet. But I'm thirty now and I'm tired of waiting for Mr. Right."

Eloise reached for her glass of Pellegrino. "Is there really any such thing as Mr. Right?"

"Exactly." Robin pointed a piece of bread at Eloise. "I admire the fact that you're independent and business savvy and that you clearly don't need a man. It's been on my mind more and more to follow the same path."

Eloise decided not to mention that single motherhood wasn't exactly something she had planned. Instead, she took another bite.

"How is Charlotte?" Robin asked.

"She's great. I don't see her as often as I'd like. She's a marine biologist now."

Robin sighed. "I still can't believe she and Billy never got back together."

"They were both pretty young." Eloise shrugged. "I guess it just wasn't the right time."

Speaking of bad timing, Dante chose that exact moment to walk up to the bar, right across from their table. One of the raviolis Eloise had been trying to spear went flying and skidded to the floor near his feet. She suddenly wished she would've utilized her knife to make more manageable size bites.

How was it possible that the man looked even better than he had last night? Ugh. Her pregnancy hormones really needed to take the day off. Eloise was in marketing and advertising. She worked with male models all the time. None of them made her think things a soon-to-be mom shouldn't be thinking.

Please don't look this way, she thought right as he turned around and spotted her.

"Hey," he said casually but didn't quite approach the table. Maybe he wanted to get away from her before she launched into another nervous soliloquy about being pregnant. Or maybe he didn't want to interrupt her lunch, which would have been the more rational and polite thought going through his mind. He didn't avert his eyes, though. So maybe he was waiting for her reaction? Why was she making this so weird?

"Hi," Eloise finally said. "I was just having lunch with my friend Robin. Robin Abernathy, this is Dante Sanchez."

"Yeah, I know Robin." Dante smiled and Eloise's tummy did a backflip. Or maybe that was all the extra butter from her sauce. Or the baby kicking. "We were voted Most Athletic our senior year." He gave a short laugh. "I like to leave my yearbook out every once in a while to remind my brother Dylan that he was voted Most Likely To Be Late To Class."

Eloise resisted the urge to slap her palm to her forehead. Of course they already knew each other. Kids from the Heights and the Valley usually went to different elementary schools, but everyone eventually funneled through Bronco High. Except those who were shuttled off to boarding school, like her.

"Dylan graduated before us, though," Robin pointed out. "I think he was always late because that was the year they switched to the new bell schedule."

"No, that was the year he saved up to buy that lifted pickup truck that always broke down on the way to school."

Dante gave his former classmate the same disarming grin he'd given Eloise earlier, and she was stung by an unexpected pang of jealousy. Robin was single, too. And attractive. And not pregnant.

"Dante," the bartender called as he held up a takeout bag. "Your order is ready."

"Thanks, man." Dante walked over to retrieve his food and talk about last night's varsity football score, then stopped by their table on his way out. Eloise wanted to make a joke about how she always saw him leaving places with carryout food. If only to prove that she had some shared memories with him, too. Before she could come up with something clever, he said, "It was nice seeing you ladies. Enjoy your lunch."

As soon as he was out the door, Robin leaned forward and asked, "So what's the scoop with you and the handsome Mr. Sanchez?"

Oh, no. Did people already know that he'd driven her back to the hotel last night? What if someone had seen him going up to Eloise's room? Would that make things worse with her father? Would she really care?

Eloise swallowed a bit too much water and nearly choked. "What do you mean?"

"I was definitely sensing some vibes between the two of you right now."

"Really?" Eloise flushed with embarrassment. "Because I thought maybe there was something going on with *you* and Dante."

"As if. My sister Stacy works with him at the elementary school. All the single moms—and some of the married ones—are half in love with Mr. Sanchez. I mean, he's amazing with kids and, according to gossip in the break room, he's a super good listener." Just like he'd been last night when Eloise had gone on and on about her nails not breaking as much since she'd been on the prenatal vitamins. Apparently, she wasn't special.

"I seriously doubt there's any vibe between us," Eloise confessed. "Unless the man gets turned on by listening to me talk about my estrogen levels."

"I wouldn't be so sure." Robin dipped another piece of bread in olive oil. "I'll admit, the Sanchez brothers' smiles should come with a warning label. But I've never seen Dante staring at someone the way he was just staring at you."

Chapter Three

His brother must have smelled the pasta in the to-go bag because when Dante walked into the car dealership ten minutes later, Dylan gave a young couple the keys to test drive a minivan without him. The only things Dante's brother loved more than closing the deal on a sale were food and sports.

And apparently a big scoop.

"So what happened when you left the party last night with Eloise Taylor?" Dylan asked as soon as the couple drove off the lot.

"How do you know about that?"

"Do you seriously need to ask?" Dylan grabbed one of the containers and opened it to inspect the contents. "Nothing spreads faster than Bronco gossip."

"I simply drove the lady home."

"Not to the Triple T, you didn't." Dylan retrieved a plastic fork from the bag. "Mrs. Waters was out walking her dog late last night and saw the two of you heading into the Heights Hotel. She told Mom and everyone else in the salon all about it this morning."

"Eloise Taylor is pregnant, Dylan. What do you think could have possibly happened between us?" Although, it wasn't as if the possibilities hadn't crossed Dante's own mind a million times since he'd dropped her off.

"Was her husband waiting for her inside the Heights Hotel?" his brother challenged.

Dante decided the best reaction was no reaction. He focused his eyes on the remaining container of food and used his most casual tone. "I don't think she's married. At least not that I'm aware of."

"I know you, little brother." Dylan smirked. "And I know that spark in your eyes."

"I always look at my lasagna like this." As if to prove it, Dante took a huge mouthful of layered pasta and groaned his approval. It really was delicious.

"It's not just the food you've got your eye on. But go ahead and keep your secrets."

The brothers continued to eat as their conversation shifted to which point guard would get the most assists this season—another topic they couldn't agree on—and then Dylan met up with the couple who test drove the minivan, successfully making another sale. Dante was sorting through some paperwork in the office when his brother appeared in the doorway two hours later. "So just to be clear, you don't have anything going with Eloise Taylor?"

Dante pulled a sales contract out of the service invoice pile. "I already told you I didn't."

"Cool. Because she just walked onto the lot and I'm going to show her the convertible coupe."

"No, you are not," Dante said, his neat stacks of paper collapsing as he strode out the door. He could hear his brother's footsteps behind him, so he picked up his pace. Dylan, who was equally athletic despite what the high school yearbooks said, matched his speed and then went a little faster.

The brothers were shoving into each other and nearly winded by the time they got to Eloise, who was peering in the window of a top-of-the-line sports car.

"Hey, Eloise." Dante gave Dylan one last elbow jab. "Is there something I can help you with?"

"Dante?" Eloise jerked her head around, her long dark lashes fluttering with surprise. "I thought Robin said you were a teacher. You sell cars?"

In the past, plenty of women had shown up at his place of work with some made up excuse about why they just happened to be stopping by. So, he was almost disheartened to realize that she was legitimately surprised to see him. But he brightened at the knowledge that she and Robin had at least talked about him.

"No." Dylan stepped in front of him and handed her a business card. "*I* sell cars. This is my dealership. I let my little brother help me out on Saturdays."

"You're his brother?" Eloise looked at the card, then smiled politely. "Your eyebrows seem to be growing back quite nicely."

Dylan swiveled his face to him. "You told her about the fajita incident?"

Dante nearly choked with laughter. "I didn't tell her about Mom teaching you how to draw on those temporary ones."

"Did you tell her that you shaved your legs in tenth grade because you'd heard that it would limit wind resistance when you were running track?" Dylan turned back to face Eloise, adding, "He still has these weird little bald spots on his calves."

"I'm sure that's quite a sight to see." One corner of her lips rose in a stifled laugh.

"It's more of a sight that can't be *unseen.* Anyway, can I interest you in a car?"

"We," Dante corrected. "Can *we* interest you in a car?"

Another potential customer walked onto the lot and Dylan, thankfully, had to excuse himself since the other salesperson was on break.

"So can I show you something?" Dante asked her when his brother walked away. "Other than my very muscular and very manly calves?"

He thought he caught a faint blush on her cheeks, but it was also fairly windy out. Eloise scanned the rows of cars. "That depends. Do you guys do leases? I don't know if I'm ready to commit to anything long term."

Dante had a sinking sensation that Eloise wasn't only talking about cars when it came to commitments. Not that he'd ever been the relationship type himself. As much as he hated it when people asked him about his love life, he had the sudden urge to ask her what was going on with her and the father of her child.

Oh, who was he kidding? He'd been wanting to ask her that since last night.

Clearly, he was going to have to find another more subtle way to get answers. "We do leases for the new models. But we have financing options if you're interested in a pre-owned car."

"This one looks nice enough." Eloise stroked the shiny

red paint of the convertible coupe and Dante steeled himself against a shiver when he thought of those long fingers touching him the same way.

"Are you sure you don't want something a bit more..." He tapped at the rear window. "Practical?"

She pushed back her shoulders and lifted her nose higher. "I assure you that I can afford the best. With my own money and not my father's, thank you very much."

Wow. Note to self: the Taylor family wealth was clearly a sensitive subject with Eloise.

Dante shook his head. "I wasn't pointing to the sticker price. I was pointing to the back seat. You might want to consider something with a little more room for a car seat."

"Sorry," she said on an exhaled breath, losing some of her bluster. "That was a bit defensive of me. I might've mentioned this already, because I embarrassingly mentioned way more than I should've last night. But I still haven't wrapped my head around what's going to happen after the baby gets here. I'm usually a list maker, too, and I try to anticipate things and plan for everything. Yet, when it comes to having a child, it's like my brain switches to autopilot mode and I've somehow convinced myself that I'll figure things out when I need to. My assistant thinks I'm too focused on work to worry about anything else, but my sister suggested it could be nature's way of keeping me from being an over-controlling parent."

"That makes sense." Dante nodded. He had no doubt that someone raised by Thaddeus and Imogen Taylor would want to approach parenting from a more...relaxed...angle. "I'm sure you've got this, though. Watching you walk into The Library last night with that kind of confidence and dignity, even though you knew how your parents were going to react, I could tell that you're the type of woman who can handle anything life throws your way."

"You know what?" Eloise squinted against the sun peeking through the clouds. "You may very well be the first man in Bronco to say those words to me."

No way could that be true. She had several male relatives, and they couldn't all be as stubborn and old-fashioned as her father. "You haven't been in town very long. I'm sure Jordan would say the same thing if he were here."

"Fair enough. Other than the curious questions and initial well-wishes at the restaurant, I've avoided getting into too many deep conversations about my current condition. My brother Ryan texted and wants to meet up for dinner, so we'll see how that goes. As of right now, though, you probably know more about my pregnancy than anyone else in town."

"Thank you, I think?" He decided to be flattered that she trusted him enough to reveal information that she clearly wasn't comfortable discussing with anyone else. "While I learned a lot last night, I certainly wouldn't consider myself an expert in the hot-flashes department."

She shoved a pair of designer sunglasses on her face, but not before he spotted another blush stealing up her cheeks. "You just know what types of cars are best for women?"

"No. But I do know what types of cars are good for families. When I was a kid, my mom's minivan was in the shop for a whole month, and she had to shuttle us around in a compact rental car. Just because something has five seat belts, doesn't mean it has room for all the baseball equipment and musical instruments and groceries you're going to need to haul around when you're a parent."

"Unlike your parents, though, I'll only be shuttling one child. And I don't think he or she is going to be playing either shortstop or the tuba any time soon. I'll worry about having room for all the gear when they're a teenager."

"Have you seen strollers nowadays?" Dante asked. "Those monsters are huge and complex. It takes a PhD in mechanical engineering just to open and collapse the things, let alone heft them into the car."

She tilted her head and grinned slyly. "How much experience do you have with strollers, Dante?"

"Not as much as that look suggests. But don't forget that I'm a teacher and my students often have younger brothers and sisters. We had a field trip to the pumpkin patch last week and one of the parents met us there with a toddler strapped into this contraption with off-road tires. Unfortunately, the trails were still muddy and I had to use a tow winch and a car jack to get the thing unstuck." He opened the door to the sports car and pushed a button inside to pop the miniscule trunk. "This thing can barely hold a yoga mat. Assuming you do yoga. There's no way you're getting a full-size stroller back here, muddy or otherwise. And forget about the diaper bag."

"So you're saying I need something bigger, huh? Why do I get the feeling that you're going to get some sort of bonus if I drive out of here in one of those?" She pointed to a van conversion with an industrial-sized roof rack.

"Nah, I don't work off commission. I handle the office stuff like bookkeeping and payroll. In fact, I rarely even go for test drives. But if I *were* going to go for a test drive," he said as he nodded toward a smaller crossover SUV, "it would be in one of those."

Eloise crossed her arms above her baby bump, looking somewhat doubtful. "So that's what you'd pick for yourself if you were a single dad and needed room for more than your yoga mat?"

He smiled at the way she'd framed the gotcha question. His brother Dylan always cautioned about typecasting female customers and assuming they wanted "girlie" or "mom" cars. Apparently, she'd been expecting him to do just that and was preemptively warning him against it. But she'd also just implied that she was single. A single mom.

"First of all, I'm terrible at yoga. Although I've been told I look good in the drawstring pants. Second of all, not only did I pick it for myself, just last night I drove a beautiful woman home in a similar model." Dante waited for realization to dawn across her face and was rewarded with her full lips forming a perfect and adorable little *O*. He winked, adding, "And I'm not even a dad."

"Sorry. I had a lot of other things going through my brain when the valet driver pulled up last night. But I remember the passenger seat was comfortable and it smelled amaz…" she trailed off and then cleared her throat. "So…does it come in red?"

* * *

Ten minutes later, Eloise was behind the wheel of a sporty crossover with plenty of room in both the back seat and cargo area.

Dante was in the passenger seat this time and, despite her growing attraction to the man, he was once again acting like a perfect gentleman and treating her totally and absolutely…normal. At least according to Robin Abernathy, his flirtatious smile was in fact normal for him—and all the other local ladies who'd been on the receiving end of it.

She'd enjoyed his banter with his brother earlier because it reinforced Eloise's initial impression that Dante had a great sense of humor. But maybe that was just an act they performed to lull a customer into a false sense of comfort. Kind of like a good cop/bad cop routine.

Eloise didn't know which sensation was stronger: the butterflies in her stomach from sitting so close to him or the growing disillusionment that there was no chance a guy like him could be interested in someone like her. Or at least someone in her condition. Doubt filled her as she tried not to dwell on Robin's words that Dante's vibe was somehow different with Eloise than it was with every other woman in town.

He pointed at the stoplight ahead. "Make a left up here if you want to head out to the highway."

"You might recall that I actually grew up in Bronco and know my way around the town." There went her defensive instincts again.

"You grew up in Bronco *Heights*, not here in the Valley. Despite all the attempts at gentrification recently, there's still a pretty big difference." His response was equally defensive this time.

And extremely valid. It was a lot more than roads that separated their town, and it was only fair for her to acknowledge the socioeconomic differences.

"True. But even back then I wasn't oblivious to the fact that some of my friends from dance class went to a different school than me. Or that their houses weren't exactly like mine." She wanted to look at him but needed to keep her eyes on the road. "Later on, I came home during school breaks and I was in Bronco for almost six weeks after I graduated college. You know, I'm pretty sure I would've remembered seeing you around town back then."

"I was still living in Bozeman getting my teaching credentials when you returned from college."

"And how do you know exactly when it was that I graduated college?" This time, she did risk a peek in his direction and caught him tugging at the collar of his shirt.

"I might've heard some things at the party last night and did the math."

"Oh," she said, before realizing how disappointed she sounded. Apparently, he hadn't actually asked about her. He just couldn't avoid the rumors. "What did you hear?"

"Something about you working for Taylor Beef for a few days before having a big blowout with your father."

"Did people make it seem like it was my fault?" She hated the fact that she even cared what the gossips thought.

"Not that I could tell. But then again, I haven't met many people lining up to take your dad's side in an argument. No offense."

"None taken. I love him, but he frustrates the hell out of me. He can be extremely stuck-up and controlling and terribly old-fashioned. But I'm hoping that maybe he can be eased into the current century. For example, you know how Taylor Beef is one of the largest beef suppliers in the country?"

"I'm pretty sure everyone who has ever been inside an American supermarket knows that, Eloise." Dante's sarcasm came out as flirtatious. Or maybe it was just the way her first name had so easily rolled off his tongue.

She suppressed a shiver by gripping the steering wheel tighter. "Well, last night I found out that my uncle Cornelius has finally come to terms with the fact that my cousin Daphne wasn't thumbing her nose at the family business when she announced that she was a vegetarian some years ago and wanted to run an animal sanctuary. I'm hoping my dad can do the same with me. Or at least not stomp out of the room in protest when I show up. You know what I mean?"

"Sure," Dante said simply. A bit too simply.

"Why did you say it like that? Like you're not convinced."

"I'm not the one you need to convince, Eloise." There he went using her name again in that intimate way of his. She'd never felt a need to explain herself to anyone, probably because she'd grown up with parents who wouldn't listen anyway. Yet there was something about this man that had her saying anything that came to her mind.

Feeling overly heated, she reached for the climate-control buttons and switched the air-conditioning to full blast. Dante tried to help her adjust the airflow and his fingers lightly grazed hers, making her internal temperature go even higher.

She slapped her hand back on the wheel, not wanting

to think about how much his light touch had affected her. "So you don't think my dad will come around?"

"I don't really know Thaddeus. I barely know Cornelius and only because he's Camilla's father-in-law. What I can tell you is that Cornelius might have begrudgingly accepted his children's choices in spouses and careers, but it wasn't like the guy has suddenly turned into a big teddy bear since you've been gone. In fact, the reason I was at that party last night was…"

He trailed off and suddenly Eloise was dying to know why Dante had in fact been at the Taylor party. She'd seen him mingling with her cousin Brandon and his wife, Cassidy, along with Jordan's assistant Mac and some of the other guests. But almost every time she made eye contact with him, he'd been sitting at the bar.

Eloise slowed the car for a pair of older cowboys herding several heads of cattle across the road from one pasture to another. Dante rolled down the window to wave because, of course, he knew everyone in town and outside of town.

When she was able to continue on the two lane highway, Dante had already moved on to a different subject. "Earlier, you made a comment about your baby and referred to it as he or she. Does that mean you're not going to be finding out ahead of time what you're having?"

"No. I wasn't sure that I wanted to know before the baby gets here. It's one of those things I'm trying not to overthink." Eloise shrugged. "I guess I figured that if I knew the gender, it might change the way I feel."

"Why? Do you have a preference for a boy or a girl?"

"Well, I'm not exactly happy with several of the men in my life right now." She sped up to see the range on the car. "Although, I know that when the baby gets here, I'll love a boy as much as a girl. No matter what, I'm certainly going to raise my child a lot differently than I was raised."

See? Why did she even feel the need to say something so personal to him?

"How were you raised?" His tone was curious without a single trace of judgment.

"Over-protected, yet under-protected at the same time. I'm not sure if that makes any sense. There was always this state of underlying fear growing up. My fear that I wouldn't live up to my parents' expectations of perfection and their fear that I'd do something to embarrass the family name."

"Did you?"

"I wasn't home often enough to embarrass them." She lovingly stroked her belly. "Not until now. And not intentionally."

"Then hopefully you can explain your situation and talk things out with your dad before you leave." Dante's suggestion made it seem as if it would be that easy. Or that she'd even want to make amends.

"Leave for where?"

"I thought you lived in New York City."

"I did live there. Up until two days ago. Now I live here."

Dante turned to look at the long dirt road they'd just passed. "Here? At the Broken Road Ranch?"

"No. Not here. And if I'm being honest, I don't exactly know where we are. I talked a big game earlier about growing up in Bronco and knowing my way around town, but…uh… I'm not recognizing anything out this far."

"That's because the city council rerouted the old

bridge at Hardy's Creek and put this road in as a by-pass. There's a turnout half a mile ahead where you can flip around."

When she safely executed a U-turn and they were heading back toward town, Dante asked, "So then you're living at the Heights Hotel?"

"I'm not living there exactly. I'll probably use the suite for another month or so. After the baby is born, I'll look for more permanent housing." What she didn't say was that she'd initially only planned to stay the weekend and scope out the possibility of relocating her business and her life to Bronco. It wasn't until she'd seen her parents' reaction that she'd decided she wasn't going to leave town in shame this time.

"You mean you plan to stay in Bronco indefinitely?" His tone was one of surprise. Well, he could join the club. She'd surprised herself with that decision, too.

"Why else would I need a new car? I can't keep waiting for rideshares or jumping in some hot guy's car and having him drive me home."

She immediately clenched her jaw, wishing she hadn't just admitted that right in front of him. Women who were seven weeks away from labor shouldn't be calling anyone hot. Should they?

Keep your mouth closed and your eyes on the road, she warned herself. *Don't you dare glance in his direction*. Ugh. She looked right at him. Judging from his satisfied smirk, he'd apparently caught the slip as well.

"It looks like we might get rain tomorrow," she attempted lamely.

"It's fall in Montana. We need to be prepared for any kind of weather," he replied. She could still feel the weight of his stare. And his grin. "If you're worried about road conditions, you'll be glad to know that this car is equipped with all-wheel drive."

"Yeah, the tire traction was obviously the first thing on my list when I was back on the lot looking at that midlife-crisis convertible." Eloise couldn't take it anymore and she whipped her head in his direction. "Why do you keep staring at me?"

"Because I'm trying to figure you out."

"There's nothing to figure out."

"Ha!" Dante didn't bother to hide the full-throated laugh.

"Fine." Eloise sat up straighter in the driver's seat. "I know you want to ask. So you might as well just put it out there. It's not like I haven't heard the question before."

"What if I'm a gentleman who was taught to mind my own business?" he asked, reminding her of her earlier assessment that he was in fact acting overly polite and normal toward her.

If so, she might as well shock his chivalrous senses and forego the polite chitchat.

"Yes, Dante, I do know the father of my child and no, he and I are no longer together."

He held up his palms. "For the record, I wasn't wondering about the first part. Only the second part."

She tried not to read too much into his admission. In the rare event that Dante might even be slightly interested in her, it was probably best to get everything out in the open.

"So, yes, I'm single. But I am done, done, done with men. I spent the last decade in one relationship after the next, subconsciously trying to prove to my parents that they shouldn't have tried to shelter me. I've dated men who didn't want to get serious, men who wanted to get too serious too fast and men who just wanted a piece of the Taylor wealth." She sighed. "The only thing I ended up proving was that my parents were still just as old-fashioned as they had been all those years ago."

If Dante was uncomfortable talking about her dating history, he certainly wasn't showing it. In fact, he kept the conversation going. "Your brothers went to high school with my brothers. I don't remember them being overly sheltered."

"Did I mention the double standard in my family?" She slowed for the intersection where she'd insisted on not turning at Dante's suggestion. When she finally had the opportunity to face him, she saw that he was pivoted in his seat, his attention focused solely on her. "You probably don't remember this because it happened when we were kids, but my sister Charlotte also attended Bronco High. She and Billy Abernathy had a—" Eloise paused suddenly, not wanting to divulge all the skeletons in her family's closet. At least not her sister's private business. "Well, they were going to get married right after high school and my sister got cold feet. The whole event caused more scandal than my parents wanted to deal with. Nobody told me and Allison anything before shipping us off to an all-girls boarding school. I guess they didn't want us getting married young either. Now they're probably just wishing I'd secured a husband at any age rather than having their thirty-year-old single daughter showing up in town in my current condition."

"Why?"

"Why am I in this condition?" Eloise asked as though it should be obvious.

"No. Why show up in town? Don't get me wrong, I'm glad you did." Dante's smile made her throat constrict and her pulse speed up. "But why now?"

"I've asked myself that a million times in the past twenty-four hours." She let out a deep breath. "Mostly it's because I want my kid to know their family. Just because I've been avoiding my parents all these years, doesn't mean I should deprive my child of the opportunity to grow up with their cousins here in Bronco. There's no way my son or daughter is going to experience the same loneliness I felt as a girl suddenly being shipped away to boarding school—away from everyone and everything I knew. But there's also a part of me that wants my parents to have to face the consequences of their actions. Why should I be the one who had to leave town? The one who was practically banished under the pretense of being protected? I like New York, but there's just something about being here in Bronco that feels right. Something that's always pulled me back here."

"So you've come home to put down more roots?"

"I don't know about all that. It just seemed like a good place for now. I loved growing up here before I left for school. I wanted to raise my child in a place like this. A small town where everyone knows each other, and a stranded lady can hop into a car with someone who knows her cousin and feel perfectly safe."

"Now I'm just someone who knows your cousin? Earlier I believe your words were, *a hot guy.*" This time she didn't need to look at him to hear the smugness in his voice.

"It doesn't matter how hot you were…are…were when we met." She tried to tell her heart to stop racing and her brain to start working. "I shouldn't have put you in an awkward position last night of having to drive me back to the hotel. So I'm sorry for that even though I'm glad that it was your car I hopped into last night."

"I'm glad it was my car, too," Dante said. "And please don't be sorry. For what it's worth, Bronco is a great place to raise a kid and I hear their schools aren't half bad either. I might be biased, but I think you've got pretty good taste so far."

Eloise's thumbs tapped nervously against the steering wheel, but couldn't fidget away this heightened awareness settling between them. She had one more block to go. One more block to make sure she didn't fully succumb to his flirtatious banter.

When they returned to the dealership, Dylan's brother was in the lot washing one of the trucks.

"Did Uncle Stanley stop by again?" Dante asked his brother.

"He did." Dylan had a nice enough smile, but it didn't make Eloise's heart race the way Dante's did when he grinned at her and explained, "Our uncle is eighty-six years old and met his girlfriend at Doug's bar when she did a psychic reading for him. Winona's in her nineties and refers to Uncle Stanley her 'younger man,' which only makes him more determined to prove he's still in his prime."

Dante groaned. "So you let him take the truck out again?"

Dylan blasted a stubborn clump of mud from the lifted wheel well. "It wasn't like I could tell him no. He had Winona with him this time and they're so damn cute together. I hope that when I'm their age, I have a cool nephew or niece who'll indulge me the same way."

"You better hope Felix or one of our sisters gives you that niece or nephew," Dante said, implying that he wouldn't be the sibling to do so. Eloise tried not to read too much into his comment, but it was hard not to. "The insurance company better not find out you let him go for a test drive any time he gets an urge to take his girlfriend off-roading."

"You're such a rule follower." Dylan made it sound like an accusation.

Dante rolled his eyes. "Try spending Monday through Friday with twenty-five kids and then tell me you don't appreciate a little law and order."

"At least you get to give them back to their parents at the end of the day," Dylan said, then turned his attention to Eloise. "How was the test drive? Did Mr. Sanchez here let you go over the speed limit at all?"

"It was good," Eloise murmured, but she was still stuck on the brothers' comments about kids. She'd never really spent any time around children—besides when she was a child. Parenthood surely couldn't be that chaotic, could it? This was why she didn't want to dwell too much on the things she couldn't control. Even if she was wholly unprepared to become a mom, at least she could make it seem like she knew what she was doing and drive something mom-ish. When she realized that both Dylan and Dante were still looking at her expectantly, she spoke louder. "I think this car will serve my purposes for now."

"You might want to do a bit more research first," Dante suggested. "There's other dealerships about an hour from here and you might want to try out some other models."

"Whoa, whoa, whoa, little brother." Dylan held up one palm. His other was still holding the hose nozzle. "We make more money when we actually sell the cars here on *our* lot instead of convincing the customers that they should buy from our competitors."

"I don't want Miss Taylor to make any impulsive decisions." Dante took a step closer to Eloise, who wished she wouldn't have admitted earlier that she'd already made one impulsive decision recently. "It's better if she knows all her options and considers everything first."

"This is why I keep you in the office and away from the customers." Dylan turned off the hose. "You're a terrible salesman."

"And this is why I only help you out one day a week. My third graders are more rational than you."

"Gentlemen," Eloise interrupted. "It's a car, not a tattoo. If I don't like it, I can bring it back."

"Actually, you can't," they both said at the same time.

"I mean you can under certain circumstances," Dante said. "But cars lose their value as soon as they drive off the lot."

"That's okay." Eloise pulled out her wallet. If she didn't purchase the family-friendly SUV now, it'd be one more thing she'd have to research later. She needed a car now and didn't want to overthink things. "I'll still take it."

"No." Dante shook his head. "This is where you act undecided and then we negotiate a lower price."

"I doubt Eloise needs you to be acting like an overprotective boyfriend," Dylan said half correctly. Dante was being mildly protective, but surely he wasn't casting himself in the boyfriend role. Or was he?

Not that it mattered. Eloise was about to show these Sanchez men that her MBA from Columbia was well earned and she could out-negotiate them any day of the week.

Chapter Four

"So I'm going to need some information for the lease paperwork," Dante told Eloise after she skillfully—and impressively—got his brother to agree to a monthly payment less than two-thirds of the original asking price. "How long of a term do you want for the lease? We can do twelve months, twenty-four months and thirty-six months."

"Let's go with the shortest term. For now."

"The bank is going to want information about your income. Are you comfortable providing that?"

"Why wouldn't I be?" Eloise asked.

Because it was Dante's experience that wealthy people like the Taylors didn't appreciate divulging too much information about their finances or their net worth unless it benefited them to flaunt it. Although judging by the expensive-looking accessories and jewelry he'd seen her wearing, Eloise allowed her designer shoes and handbags to subtly disclose her wealth for her.

Even though he'd be doing his job, if Dante asked her the questions outright, it might come across as an interrogation. This attraction, or whatever it was between them, had him spinning with curiosity and he didn't trust himself not to ask a bunch of follow-up questions. So he gave her several forms to complete on her own, then offered to grab her a snack and a bottle of water from the break room.

At least that way she was voluntarily disclosing the information. Sort of. Like when she'd confirmed that she was single. But she'd also said she was done with men. So it was possible her break-up was still too fresh, which meant she might still care about the other guy or be willing to give him a second chance once he realizes what he'd lost. Squelching the thought to the back of his mind, Dante reminded himself that Eloise's ex was none of his business.

She passed him the forms when he returned, trading him for the bag of Flamin' Hot Cheetos he'd selected from the vending machine.

"Um, those were for me. I got you the granola bar because you mentioned heartburn last night..." He trailed off when he saw her eyes narrow. "But you can have the chips. Or both snacks if you want."

He scanned the forms as she daintily chomped away at the snacks. Nope, there was no way he was going to get out of this without asking a few follow-up questions. Dante just couldn't help himself. "You put that you work at Taylor Marketing. Is that part of Taylor Beef?"

"No. I *own* Taylor Marketing. And it most definitely is not part of the family business."

"Wait. Is that the company who did the ad campaign for that cologne last year? Teacher Appreciation Week was right after all those commercials aired during the Olympics, and I got several bottles of that stuff as gifts."

"Your students buy you cologne?"

He winced before admitting, "Actually, it came from a couple of different moms. And the district superintendent. And a lady who volunteers at the rec center. And my widowed neighbor."

"Sounds like there's a lot of women in Bronco who think of you as *l'homme avec un appetit seduisant.*"

"Maybe they should've used the translation app on their phones because I'd hardly consider myself a man with a seductive appetite." Dante attempted his most modest expression, but Eloise bit the inside of her cheek as though she were trying to keep from laughing. "Anyway, I remember thinking the ads were brilliant. Jordan told me it was his cousin who'd come up with it, but at the time, I didn't realize you were the cousin. How long have you owned your firm?"

"Four years." Eloise took another puffed cheese snack. "I actually *did* work at Taylor Beef, though. I lasted a whole week. I tried to convince my father that with my degree, I had a lot to offer the company. Instead, he gave me a fluff job with no real responsibility. He liked to point out that the only reason he'd sent me to college in the first place was to find a suitable husband and that I'd never need to worry about earning a paycheck because I already had a trust fund." She must've seen Dante's expression because she immediately clarified. "Those were his words, not mine. The last thing I wanted to do was end up in a loveless marriage like my mom—just another pretty woman who'd given up everything for a man that didn't value her. So I enrolled in an MBA program with the determination to start a business that could rival my father's. Then I purposely named it Taylor Marketing. After all, my father didn't earn that last name. He was born into it, just like I was. I figured he had no bigger claim to it than I do. And if I'm being honest, I love owning a *Taylor* business that he can never control."

Dante tilted his head as he studied her. Not only had she single-handedly stood up to her father, but she was also creative and successful in her own right. He was finally figuring out what made Eloise Taylor tick and he admired her determination to go after what she wanted. "Do you at least like your job?"

"Oh, my gosh, I love it. Sorry for making it sound like my whole life's purpose these past few years is to get back at my father. That was only part of the reason I wanted to start my own business and I guess everything from last night brought all those feelings to the surface again. I promise that I really like what I do, especially because I've tailored my company in a way that empowers other females. Plus, my job allows for a lot of flexibility. I can work where I want, when I want and with whom I want."

"And right now you want to work in Bronco?"

"Exactly."

"Then I'm definitely glad you're here," he said, realizing that he actually meant it.

Eloise knew better than to stare dreamily at those sleepy bedroom eyes or that sexy, confident grin. But Dante Sanchez had this way of listening so attentively as she'd embarrassingly gone on and on about her entire family dynamic and her dating history, it lulled her into thinking they had some sort of connection already. Like they were the best of friends sharing secrets.

In reality, there was no way he was actually interested in any of her drama. Robin had mentioned that he had a reputation as a good listener and that must be the case. Women didn't go around giving expensive bottles of cologne to just anyone. And he'd received multiple bottles. From multiple women. Clearly, she wasn't the only lady who felt some sort of connection to him.

In fact, Eloise should really be thanking whoever had bought him the cologne. Or cursing them. As she sat across the desk from him, signing paperwork, she had to restrain herself from burying her nose into the nape of his neck and inhaling deeply.

"Congratulations on your new car," Dante finally said as he stood up and handed her the keys. "Where are you driving it to first?"

"Probably to dinner. I'm starving. I've only had those Cheetos and that granola bar since lunch."

She winced as soon as the words left her mouth, hoping that he didn't think she was fishing for an invitation to go out and eat together. Gathering her purse and copies of her paperwork, she wanted to get out of the office before he could politely decline her non-offer.

"Well, if you haven't been to LuLu's since you've been home, you should probably check it out. Dylan and I go there a lot on Saturday nights for the all-you-can-eat baby back ribs."

Was he trying to tell her where he was going to be for dinner? Or was he trying to tell her that she looked like the type of gal who could eat plate after plate of ribs? Or was he just being neighborly and suggesting a restaurant she should enjoy? Alone.

Once again, she silently scolded herself for trying to analyze everything the man said or did.

"I'll have to check it out some time," Eloise said, her tone noncommittal.

When they stepped outside, she suddenly wished she'd brought a coat. After lunch, Robin had taken her to the Bonnie B Ranch to get a feel for the business operation and see where she manufactured her products. When Robin dropped her back at the hotel, Eloise had seen an advertisement for Bronco Motors and come straight here, without bothering to even go up to her room for a coat.

Dante must've noticed her slight shiver because he looked up at the sky and said, "The temperature is supposed to drop again tonight. At this rate, we might get snow before Thanksgiving. I have a jacket inside if you want me to grab it."

A spiral of excitement shot through Eloise at the thought of borrowing something of his. Not only would it most likely smell like him, it would also give her a reason to see him again. But she silenced her inner teenager and replied, "I'm okay. The salesperson was sure to point out that my new car has heated seats."

"Your salesperson is a smart man, but no heated seats are that good. Your sweater is so thin I can see your—" He glanced away before she could see where he was looking. "Just wait here. I'll be right back."

Eloise turned to tell him not to bother and saw her reflection in the glass doors. She had to fight the urge not to wrap her arms around herself and immediately regretted her decision not to buy more maternity clothes.

The butter soft cashmere sweater was so snug it proudly displayed her nipples' response to the cold.

At least she hoped Dante assumed it was due to the cold and not her excitement any time he was within a few inches of her.

He returned with a fleece-lined coat and, as though she were one of his students, held it open so she could slip her arms into it. It was warm and soft and smelled just like Dante. She would've been tempted to never return it for that reason alone. Fortunately for him, though, the shoulders were too wide for her and the sleeves were way too long.

"Let me help you with that." His voice was a bit huskier as he brushed her fingers aside and rolled up the cuffs for her.

Dante's face was inches from hers and Eloise's wrists had never felt so alive and sensitive. She didn't want to think about how his touch would affect the rest of her body, but his hands had already moved to the open edges of the zipper. Eloise bit her lower lip and said the first thing she could think of to throw cold water on the situation. "So, is this a Mr. Sanchez thing? You probably zip up hundreds of coats a day when you're at school."

His brown eyes turned several shades darker and, still gripping the jacket lapels, he pulled Eloise closer. "Not like this, I don't."

When his mouth landed on hers, all the heat and the sparks and the unanswered questions between them blasted through her at once and all she could do was return the blast by meeting his kiss just as fervently. Dante angled his head and Eloise clutched his shoulders as she opened her lips to allow him better access.

His tongue was just as skilled as she'd expected and

she moaned when she felt his thumbs graze along her jawline, his fingers delving into her hair as he held her face. She had no idea how long they were fused together. All she knew was that she didn't want it to end.

Yet the sound of a car horn honking in the distance caused Dante to pull back. His eyes were still glazed over with passion, but after several seconds of the cool air blowing between them, that look of desire turned to a look of guilt.

Eloise squeezed her own eyes closed, as though that could keep her from hearing the words she knew he was about to say.

"I'm so sorry," he immediately said.

"Please don't say that you regret kissing me," she all but dared him. "Excuse it or justify it if you need to. But let's not add regret to the list."

"I *should* regret the kiss," Dante replied. "But I don't. I regret the fact that it was so reckless of me. And so unprofessional. My brother would kill me for acting like this with a customer. My mother would kill me for—"

He exhaled loudly, but didn't finish his sentence.

Eloise's heart sank a little, yet she refused to look away or be ashamed.

Not that she could blame his mom for disliking the fact that her son was making out with some pregnant woman he'd just met. Still. Eloise couldn't let it go. She wanted to hear him say it out loud. She was so tired of men hiding their feelings or using someone else as an excuse for their actions. "Why would your mom kill you, Dante?"

Dante didn't answer, but he also didn't look away. They were standing close enough that she could feel his chest rise and fall with each deep breath. Finally, he took a step back and ran a hand through his short, dark hair. "All I was trying to say was that I shouldn't have done that."

"Was it really that bad?" she asked.

She expected a denial of some sort. After all, Dante was unfailingly polite. What she didn't expect to hear was the sound of him chuckling. And not a nervous chuckle, either. Here she was preparing herself for rejection and the guy was apparently finding humor in what was, to her, a mortifying situation.

"Of course, it wasn't bad." He shook his head, a small smile still on his lips. "It was good. Too good. That's the problem."

Eloise blinked in confusion. "Why is it a problem?"

"Because we're standing out here in the middle of the lot where anyone driving by can see us. I've been wanting to kiss you since I stepped into your hotel room last night, Eloise. And if I wasn't all kinds of thrown off by my attraction toward you and trying so hard to play it cool, I would have done it back in the office. Or even when we were test-driving the car. Where we had a little bit of privacy."

Whoa. That wasn't what she'd been expecting to hear, either. If he'd been wanting to kiss her all this time, then why was he apologizing?

"Wait. Are you ashamed to be seen kissing me?"

As if to answer her, Dante pulled her back into his arms again and kissed her even deeper and longer than the first time. This time when he pulled back, there was absolutely zero remorse or guilt on his face. His expression could only be described as self-satisfied.

"Judging by the way you responded, I'm going to assume that you're not ashamed to be kissing me, either."

Dante glanced at a passing car on the street. "Although, I'm not the one who came back to town determined to prove a point to my parents who probably wouldn't want to see their daughter hanging out with some local guy."

It wasn't that she was ashamed to be kissing him. But maybe she should be laying a little low instead of fueling all the gossip and speculation more than she already had. "Obviously, I have other priorities right now, but I'm still a woman, Dante. It's not like I'm looking for a serious relationship or anything, but that doesn't mean that we can't be…uh…friendly with each other."

"Be *friendly*? Or be *friends*?" Dante tucked a strand of her hair behind her ear and she held her breath. "Because I've gotta tell you, I don't make out with my friends."

"Yeah, so maybe it's a little too late for the whole friend thing between us. But do we need to put a label on whatever this is?"

Dante's smile grew wider than Eloise thought possible. "I'm good with not having labels."

Eloise couldn't help but match his flirtatious grin as she resumed walking to her new car. "Are you good with writing down my number?"

Dante opened the car door for her. "I already memorized it when you wrote on your lease application."

Chapter Five

The following night, Dante walked into his parents' house wondering how long it would take before one of his family members would bring up Eloise.

As soon as he was in the front door, Dylan said, "It took you long enough. Sofia said Boone was finishing up with some ranch issue on Dalton's Grange and then stopping off at the store for reinforcements but would be here soon. Everyone else is in the kitchen already."

"I thought it was Felix and Shari's turn to cook. Why do they need our help?"

"Because their plan was to do individual pizzas, but the new double oven Camilla ordered for Mom and Dad is on backorder. So instead of doing individuals, we're doing partner pizzas."

Dante followed his brother into the kitchen, which was already on the small side when he was growing up. With all the new additions to the family, it was downright crammed with people. His parents didn't need another oven. They needed a whole remodel in here to fit everyone.

"You can get started on rolling this out," Felix handed Dante a soft white ball of dough. "Then you and Dylan can move on to the topping station over at that counter."

"Does anyone else want to be my pizza partner?" Dante asked the entire room. "Dylan always wants extra cheese and it'll ooze onto my side."

"Everybody already has a partner, Dante," their mother said. Felix and Shari were leading by example. His oldest brother had met the librarian at Doug's bar and, after several drinks, had to sneak her out of their parents' home the following morning. Camilla was working with Jordan, Sofia was making one for her and her husband Boone, and his parents were obviously a pair.

Whoa. He'd never really felt like an outsider in his family home, but suddenly he was keenly aware that everyone was coupled off but him and Dylan. From now on, they would always wind up as default partners. They already shared an apartment. Once his siblings started having kids, it would only be a matter of time before someone started referring to them as the "spinster uncles."

"Where's Uncle Stanley?" Dante asked. "I could be *his* partner."

"He's on his way, but he's bringing Winona with him so they'll make a pizza together." His dad sprinkled some flour on a wooden breadboard before Dante could drop his dough. "I'm not sure what's taking them so long. Dylan, you better not have let Uncle Stanley take that truck out again. His doctor is threatening to take away his license."

"Does anyone know the score of the football game?" Dylan asked, changing the subject. "I'm going to go check the TV really quickly."

As soon as his brother left the room, Sofia said, "You know, Dante, if you wanted a different partner for couples' pizza, you could've invited Eloise Taylor."

Five minutes.

It had only taken five minutes for someone to bring her up.

"I barely know the woman." Dante tried for a casual shrug. "Why would I subject her to all of you guys and all your questions?"

"You apparently know her well enough to be kissing her in the dealership parking lot," his mom said, causing a chorus of *oohs* and *aahs*. "Mrs. Waters told me about it. Again."

"Mrs. Waters and Peaches seem to be covering a lot of ground on their walks," Dante muttered. The tension in his muscles caused him to use more force on the pizza dough than was necessary.

"Oh, she didn't see you when she was out walking her dog. That was someone else. Mrs. Waters just sent me a screenshot of the post she saw on one of those neighborhood groups she follows on social media."

"Somebody posted about it?" Dante nearly shouted. When everyone stopped what they were doing to look at him, he ducked his head and pretended to be focused on his work.

"Take it easy on that dough, son," Aaron Sanchez said, and Dante loosened his grip. "Besides, the picture was too blurry to prove it was actually you two. In fact, with the Bronco Motors sign in the background, it could have just as easily looked like Dylan was the one kissing Eloise."

Dante wanted to rub his temples to ease the pounding ache forming there, but his hands were covered in flour. "Why in the world would Dylan be kissing her?"

"Why would *you* be?" Camilla asked.

"Because she's—" Dante caught himself. "That's really none of your business."

"Wait." Jordan narrowed his eyes. "You're not denying that you kissed my cousin?"

"Like you're one to talk." Dante wadded up his dough into a ball to start over again. "You kiss my sister all the time."

"Yeah, but is your sister almost eight months pregnant?"

"Camilla is pregnant?" Uncle Stanley asked as he entered the kitchen with Winona and Dylan right behind him.

"No," Felix replied as he handed their uncle some pizza dough. "Jordan's cousin is."

"Which cousin?" Uncle Stanley asked.

"The one Dante was making out with at my car dealership." Dylan's grin turned into a grimace as soon as he saw the hard blob in Dante's hands.

"How wonderful that Dante will be the first Sanchez to have a baby," Winona Cobbs said. His uncle's girlfriend had a long history of making strange proclamations that oddly enough came true. She also had a tendency to make her questions seem more like statements that couldn't be answered. Dante liked her just fine—you couldn't possibly not like Winona Cobbs. But right now he didn't need her fortune-telling.

"No. Eloise was already pregnant before Dante met

her. And just for the record," Felix added as he raised his hand, "I'm the oldest so I get dibs on having the first baby."

Shari tugged her fiancé's arm back down. "It doesn't work like that."

"Who's having a baby?" Boone, Dante's brother-in-law, appeared with a can of olives, a case of beer, and two bottles of red wine. Dante wished it were something stronger.

"Nobody," the three younger women said in unison, while Denise Sanchez muttered, "I wish someone would."

Several groans sounded around the kitchen.

"What?" Their mom pointed a slice of pepperoni at the entire room. "Is it wrong for me to want a grandchild?"

Camilla rolled her eyes. "Can we please focus on Dante dating Jordan's cousin?"

Jordan shuddered. "I'd rather not focus on that."

"We're not dating," Dante protested. "We just kissed."

Dylan popped a piece of bell pepper into his mouth. "Remember when you went out with Corinne Hawkins a month ago? You said that wasn't a date, either."

"In my defense," Dante brushed the flour off his hands. "Corinne was new in town, and I was under the impression that we were just going to dinner as friends. If it had been an actual date, she wouldn't have talked about Mike Burris the whole time. I even told her that I could see things from her ex-boyfriend's point of view because I have the same commitment issues he does."

"At least one of you has gotten over those commitment issues since Mike and Corinne are back together and totally in love." Felix passed Dante a fresh ball of dough. "Mrs. Waters brought Peaches into the clinic and showed my vet tech the social media post about their engagement."

"See?" Dante said to nobody in particular. "This is the reason why I don't date women from Bronco. I don't want everyone knowing my business."

"So then why did you go up to Eloise's hotel room on a Friday night and then kiss her in public yesterday?" his dad asked.

"I don't know why," Dante muttered. But he knew why. Because he hadn't been able to stop himself.

"It's the pull," Winona said, but since she wasn't looking in his direction, the psychic could just as easily have been commenting on Stanley's dough-stretching technique.

"Just be careful," Camilla said. "Eloise has a lot going on in her life and it wouldn't be fair to lead someone on when you're just looking for a good time."

Ouch. That stung. Dante's reputation around town as a confirmed bachelor was not only well-earned, it was also convenient. However, he wasn't some sort of player. Especially not when it came to women who, as his sister said, had a lot going on in their life. He'd always been very careful not to lead anyone on or make promises he couldn't keep.

Before he could defend himself, though, the oven timer went off and chaos ensued as last-minute toppings were added and pizzas were switched out. Dylan got a little heavy handed with the cheese and Dante had to scoop some off when he wasn't looking. Luckily, big family dinners were a time to get caught up on everyone else's busy lives and each sibling had their turn getting questioned and teased. Nobody brought up Eloise's name again.

For some reason, though, that made Dante think about her even more. He'd been waiting to call her because he hadn't wanted to appear too eager and scare her off. But now he was wondering if he should be reaching out and reassuring her that he wasn't some player and that the kiss they'd shared yesterday wasn't a one-off. At the very least he should warn her about that post on the social media neighborhood page.

When he got back to his apartment, he decided to send her a quick text.

Hey. It's Dante. I just left my parents' house and everyone asked about you. So if my family knows we were seen together, then I'm sure your family knows as well.

As soon as he pushed send, he began questioning whether his message sounded too ominous. He added a follow-up text with only the emoji of the winking face. He didn't get a response right away, so he pulled out his laptop and worked on the flyers announcing the new after-school rec league his brother-in-law had so generously contributed to.

It was an hour later when she finally replied.

Thanks for the warning. I just got back from dinner with my brother. If Ryan knew anything, he was too subtle to bring it up.

My family isn't as subtle, Dante replied.

They don't have to be because you see them every week. Besides, Ryan had other pressing questions to ask me.

Dante was immediately humbled. Ryan Taylor was a couple of years ahead of him in high school and they'd never run in the same circles. In fact, up until Jordan and Camilla's wedding, there really wasn't much reason for the Taylors and the Sanchezes to socialize at all, let alone talk about each other. Obviously, Ryan's priority topics of conversation would be Eloise's pregnancy, her return to Bronco and even her career. They probably had a lot more important things to catch up on than whom his sister was kissing at the car dealership.

But he did like my car, Eloise added when Dante didn't reply right away.

It's a nice car. Did you try the BBQ place I mentioned when you drove it off the lot?

See, he could do subtle and ease into familiar territory. Now she would be thinking about what else had happened that day.

Not yet. I got a call from one of my clients and ended up ordering takeout and working in my hotel room all night.

Dante's thumbs were flying over the keyboard before he'd even finished his thought. You want to go there with me on Wednesday night?

Three dots appeared on the screen and then disappeared, as though she had been writing and then changed her mind. His heart dropped. Five minutes later, his phone pinged with a notification.

It was a calendar invite from Eloise for Wednesday at six o'clock. The location was the address for LuLu's.

He smiled as he accepted the invite. So this was how ultra-successful career women scheduled dates, huh? Or maybe the formal calendar invite was her way of telling him it *wasn't* a date. Either way, Dante would be there. And he'd try to keep his expectations in check.

"The hotel concierge said the pulled pork sandwiches here are amazing," Eloise told Dante when she saw him on Wednesday in front of LuLu's. After their kiss on Saturday, she'd scolded herself any time her mind even considered the possibility of dating Dante Sanchez. She shouldn't have returned the kiss, let alone suggested he call her. She definitely shouldn't have shrieked out loud when she'd read his text on Sunday night inviting her to dinner.

That's why she was going to take things nice and easy tonight and not so much as hug him hello or sit too close to him.

"They are, but the desserts are even better." He was wearing black jeans and a button-up shirt that was trendy and modern, yet still had a Western vibe. Unlike many of the other men in town, he had on hiking boots instead of cowboy boots. Although, being from Bronco, she was sure he owned at least one pair.

The door opened and a family with two children exited the restaurant. One of the boys—the one with barbeque sauce smeared across his cheek—said, "Oh hi, Mr. Sanchez. I didn't know you were going to be here."

"Hi, Mason." Dante extended his knuckles and did a fist bump with the kid. "I've been known to occasionally go places when I'm not at school. Did you leave any ribs for me?"

The boy giggled, showing a large gap where one of

his teeth was growing in. "I ate so many, we have a big pile of bones to take home to Bert."

"I'm sure Bert will like them much better than he liked your pencil case." Dante turned to Eloise and said, "Mason here is one of my students. His new puppy enjoys chewing things."

"Are you Mr. Sanchez's girlfriend?" Mason asked Eloise in the most direct way.

His mom immediately made a shushing sound and patted Mason on the head. "Remember, we don't ask people personal questions."

The younger boy, who must be Mason's little brother, pointed at her stomach. "Is that a baby in your tummy?"

"We especially don't ask *super* personal questions," the dad said before hefting the smaller child onto his shoulders in a smooth flip move. The boy squealed with excitement and Mason began jumping up and down, asking to be next.

"Sorry," the mother mouthed to Eloise before asking her kids, "Okay, who's ready to go home and feed Bert some bones?"

"Me!" the children yelped in unison. Then Mason added, "See you tomorrow, Mr. Sanchez."

Dante told the parents goodbye and Eloise managed a polite wave.

"I would've introduced you to Mason's parents, but I'm not sure who you already know in town."

"Or who knows me," she replied.

"Oh, I assure you, most of them probably know you by now. Or at least know who you are. On Monday morning, the copy machine in the teacher's lounge was the most popular spot on campus."

He was smiling in that charming way of his, but this

wasn't the first time he'd mentioned people seeing them together and the resulting gossip. She was already at the center of her family's drama. It didn't bother her what anyone thought, but Dante might not feel the same way.

Eloise took a deep breath and then let it out with a sigh. "Are you sure you want to eat together? I don't want to cause any problems for you at work. Or with your family."

"I appreciate that. But as soon as Mason's mom gets to the car, she will have probably already texted at least one parent group chat to tell them she saw us here." He nodded his chin at a restaurant patron seated inside near one of the windows. Eloise had also noted the older man who kept glancing in their direction. "If we left now, it would look like we had something to hide. Besides, I've been dreaming about LuLu's banana pudding all day."

"In that case, we might as well get some dinner since we're already providing this evening's entertainment."

Dante held open the door and Eloise followed the smoky, tangy aroma inside. Her hope for getting a secluded table in back was immediately dashed when she saw the wide-open layout. Then the host led them right to the middle of the restaurant, as though they were sitting center stage. The wooden picnic bench tables gave Eloise a moment of pause as she tried to figure out the most graceful way to lower her pregnant body onto the seat.

"It may not be the fanciest place," Dante said as he moved the roll of paper towels and the stainless steel bucket of peanuts to the side of the table. "But they have the coldest beer in town."

"Do I look like the fancy type, Dante?" she asked as she picked up one of the laminated menus.

"As a matter of fact, you do." When her eyes shot up to his, he casually shrugged. "It's not a bad thing. You just dress like you're used to finer things."

She peeked at her black leggings and her white top, which were probably the most casual items in her closet, but still an expensive brand. It just so happened that they were both stretchy and went really well with her red suede coat.

"Well, it's not like I'm trying to look fancy on purpose. I don't even really like shopping all that much. It's just that I do a lot of work with clients in the fashion industry and to be successful in marketing, I have to dress with my company's image in mind." Her eyes landed on her designer handbag as though she were seeing it for the first time. "But I guess some of my accessories could be a little more understated."

A server came to take their drink order and Eloise asked for a lemonade.

"I'll have the same," Dante said.

Eloise lifted an eyebrow after the server left. "I thought you wanted a beer?"

"No, I was just pointing out that they served cold ones."

"Dante, I saw you drinking beers the night of the party. Right before we met. Just because I'm not drinking alcohol, doesn't mean that you shouldn't."

"I assure you that this is what I'd normally drink when I'm out on a school night," Dante said, which made sense when she considered how he'd already run into one of his students. "Although, I'm flattered that you were studying me so intently on Friday you memorized what I was drinking."

Despite the fact that she could tell him exactly how

many buttons were on his shirt the night they met—it was seven, while tonight there were only six—she replied, "I wasn't studying you *that* intently."

He grinned mischievously as he shelled a peanut. Having recently experienced those same lips on hers, his grin was more intoxicating than any alcoholic drink would have been. Thankfully, she was resolved not to get too drunk on his smile. Or on anything else.

Between the time they ordered and the time their food arrived, two people she didn't know stopped by to say hello to Dante and one of the ranch foremen from the Triple T tipped his hat as he walked by, saying, "Evening, Miz Taylor."

"These really are good ribs," Eloise said as she tried not to get sauce all over her face. She'd been tempted to order a salad with smoked chicken, or anything else she could eat with a fork and knife. Yet, when Dante made that comment about her looking like the fancy type, Eloise needed to prove that she wouldn't shy away from eating something messy with her fingers.

What she hadn't expected, though, was how Dante would look with his own messy hands. After each rib, he would lick the sauce methodically off each finger and Eloise would have to focus all her attention on the neon beer sign behind the bar so she didn't stare at him with the same longing she'd felt after driving away from the dealership on Saturday.

"Did I mention the banana pudding?" Dante asked.

"Several times." Eloise slathered a piece of warm cornbread with honey butter. "I can't believe I've never heard of this place. It looks like it's been here forever."

"The building has. It used to be the old blacksmith and livery. Then it was a warehouse for a while."

"Do you know who owns it now?"

"Sure. I'll introduce you." Dante waved over a plus-sized middle-aged woman in a tight pair of jeans and an even tighter pink T-shirt that said When Pigs Fly. "LuLu, I want you to meet my friend, Eloise Taylor. Eloise, LuLu is the owner and the creator of the most incredible dessert I've ever tasted."

"Dante, that sweet talk may work on all the other gals in town. But I'm still not giving you a pint of my sauce just so you can pass it off as your own at your next Sunday dinner." LuLu's accent had a slight twang, suggesting she was originally from one of the southern states. She turned to shake Eloise's hand. "Nice to meet you, Eloise. I'm guessing you're related to the rest of the Taylors from these parts?"

"I am." Eloise smiled. "It's been a while since I've been back to Bronco, though."

"I just moved here a few years ago myself."

Eloise recognized the tingle of interest she got whenever she met a female business owner. "What made you decide to open a restaurant in Montana, LuLu?"

"Well, it wasn't some lifelong dream of mine or anything. My ex-husband inherited this property from some long lost relative he never even knew. I had no idea he had it until we were going through our divorce and had to list our assets. When we sold the house and divided up the rest, he got the big-screen TV and the fishing boat and I got all this." LuLu's thick arms jiggled slightly as she gestured at the interior of the building. "I was gonna try to turn the place into one of those antique malls, but when I got here, I found out Bronco already had one. I saw the big smoker out back that looked just like the one my granddaddy used to have down in

Arkansas. My mama sent me some of his recipes and next thing you know, I'm in business. Now, boys like this one and his salesman brother are always coming in trying to buy my sauce."

"Dylan was in here asking about your sauce?" Dante asked. "My dad told him he wasn't allowed to use the grill after the fajitas incident."

LuLu giggled. "The reminds me, I need to stop by your mama's salon and get my eyebrows done. She did a great job on his."

Eloise, though, had already switched into professional mode. "Do you sell the sauce?"

"I might give it some thought in a few years." LuLu shrugged. "I already have my hands full with running the restaurant. I wouldn't really know how to go about it."

"I know how to go about it." Eloise pulled a business card from her purse and handed it to the woman. "There's a bottle manufacturer in Missoula who gives me a great rate on these little glass jars. I also have a graphic designer on retainer who could come up with a fun label to match that little pig on your shirt."

"Taylor Marketing? Y'all are the ones who did those cologne commercials, right?" LuLu's face immediately went from excitement to concern. She set the business card down on the table. "Thanks, but I'm barely keeping my head above water as it is right now. There's no way I could ever afford to hire someone like you."

"LuLu," Eloise said as she pushed the card toward her again, "you'd be the one doing *me* a favor. I'm trying to build up my portfolio here in Bronco and, to be honest, a lot of people in this town who do business with my dad and uncles are going to be hesitant about becoming my clients. I'd be willing to work on this for free since it would also be helping my business launch here in Montana. I'd only charge the occasional banana pudding as compensation. Please just consider it."

LuLu slowly lifted the card and put it in her apron pocket. "I guess if it'll make your daddy mad, I might be willing to think about it. Now let me go see about fixin' you two up with some dessert."

The owner left and Dante took a long drink of his lemonade as he studied Eloise across the table.

"Do I have sauce on my face still?" Eloise struggled to tear open the tiny package holding a wet wipe.

"No, your face is perfect." Dante took the package from her, the brush of his fingers sending a wave of heat all the way down to her toes.

"Then why are you looking at me like that?" She glanced at his hand, which had dropped the wipe altogether and was now cradling hers.

"You know why." He was pretty much holding her hand in a very public restaurant and seemed to be in no hurry to pull away before someone saw them.

"No, I don't."

"Let's not pretend that any business owner in Bronco isn't going to jump at the chance to be one of your clients. Your dad and his brothers hold some power in this town, but not like they used to. And I don't have a marketing degree, but I'm pretty sure you don't need a portfolio for every city. You offered to work for LuLu for free because you've got a soft heart, Eloise Taylor."

"I offered to work for free because LuLu has a good product and I can help her sell it." Eloise forgot about the wipe and reached for the paper towel roll. She still wasn't convinced she didn't have sauce on her face.

"And because I like supporting women like her who start something from nothing. And maybe a little bit because I have a soft heart. But mostly it's for the banana pudding."

Chapter Six

Dante wanted to kiss her again.

He was walking Eloise to her car after dinner and all he could think about was feeling her lips against his. It wasn't like they hadn't already made out in public. But as much as he wanted to kiss her, he also wanted to keep the gossip from getting too far ahead of itself. It was one thing for people to talk about them seeing each other. Dante didn't need half the town speculating about their nonexistent wedding date.

Whoa. Where had that thought come from?

Eloise had already admitted she was still wrapping her head around what things would be like when the baby arrived, which was likely only six weeks away. There was no way she was even possibly ready to consider a future relationship way down the road. Not that he was. He needed to slow everything way down.

"So what's the rest of your week looking like?" Dante

asked. Because apparently his way of slowing things down was already strategizing for the next time he'd be able to see her.

She pulled out her phone and tapped at her calendar app. "I have online meetings all day tomorrow. Then dinner with my cousin Daphne and her husband, Evan. I'm going to try to squeeze in a Pilates class on Friday morning and follow that up with more meetings in the afternoon. Saturday, I need to FaceTime with my assistant and have her ship me some winter clothes. I was hoping to hold off until I move to a place with a bigger closet, but I can only borrow so many coats before I have to start returning them. Speaking of which, I have your jacket in the car."

"I don't need it back any time soon. Besides, I'm sure it looks better on you."

"I'm sure it doesn't. But it zips up, which is a lot more than I can say for this one." She tucked her phone into the pocket of the red suede jacket that made her ordinary black leggings and white V-neck T-shirt somehow look even more expensive and trendy.

"Before you put your calendar away, what do you have going on this Sunday?"

"I'm flying to Jackson Hole for a photo shoot with one of my snowboarding equipment clients."

Dante recalled that when Jordan and Camilla started dating, Jordan had flown his sister across the state in his company's private helicopter. Of course, it would be no big deal for someone like Eloise to charter a jet to whisk her away for a quick day trip. He heard the playful sarcasm in his own voice when he asked, "You have multiple clients with snowboarding companies?"

"Just three," Eloise replied, with a knowing wiggle

of her eyebrows. Man, he liked a woman who could out-banter him. "Although, one of them primarily makes snow apparel, and is barely starting to branch out into a line for boots and boards. I'm free on Monday morning, though."

"That won't do me much good since I have… Wait." An idea popped into Dante's head, and without thinking it through, he asked before her schedule became full. "We're doing a career day at school on Monday. The high school does their annual fair next month, but we started this program at the elementary level to bring in speakers in the hopes of exposing the kids to different job opportunities. Monday's theme is supposed to be women in STEM. But then one of the fifth grade grandmothers, who is a divorce lawyer, insisted on speaking and someone else invited their aunt who's in the military. So now the theme is more about promoting women in the workplace. Even my sister Sofia will be there to talk about fashion design. But what we don't have is a volunteer to come speak to the students about business and marketing."

Eloise blinked several times. "You want me to come to your school?"

"Yes."

"On Monday?"

"Yes?" He'd thought he'd said all of that when he'd floated the idea to her, but judging by the uncertainty in her expression, he wasn't so sure. When she didn't respond right away, he added, "It would only be for about five minutes. Just a short speech about what you do and some of the best things about your job. Maybe take a couple of questions afterward."

"I'm familiar with the concept of a career day, Dante.

What I meant was are you sure it's a good idea for me to come to your school and talk to the kids when I'm like this—" she gestured to her stomach, then tapped at her empty ring finger "—without one of these?"

Wow. Dante had seriously underestimated the lasting impact of Thaddeus Taylor's reaction to his unwed daughter's pregnancy. If the man were here right this second... Nope. Dante wasn't going to go there. He always taught his students that violence was never the answer.

Instead, he said, "Eloise, we aren't living in the Victorian era. Do you know how many of our students are from single-family households? It's just not that big of a deal to kids today. They care more about your favorite YouTube creator and which TikTok dances you know than whether or not you're married. Nobody is going to ask about anything that personal."

"Is it true that Mr. Sanchez is your boyfriend?" a girl in a butterfly sweatshirt asked, and several students giggled.

Eloise, in her opinion, had just made a more interesting presentation than Kim Kona, the divorce lawyer grandmother who'd gone way over her allotted time talking about shared pension plans and the importance of financial audits before the mediation stage. So when twenty hands flew up in the air after Eloise spoke, she thought she might have even wowed the kids more than the firefighter who'd gone first.

Apparently, though, this library full of elementary-aged kids cared more about the third-grade teacher's dating status. She shot Dante an I-told-you-so look, but he was pinching the bridge of his nose, which likely prevented him from seeing her. Dante's sister Sofia, who'd already presented, was standing beside him, trying to smother a grin.

"No, Mr. Sanchez is not my boyfriend," Eloise said a bit too loudly. But she wanted to get her point across. "We're just friends."

Another girl raised her hand. This one was wearing colorful patterned pants, a solid black turtleneck and an artistically funky side ponytail. Hoping for a creative question, Eloise called on her next.

"But if Mr. Sanchez *wanted* you to be his girlfriend, then you would you be, right?"

"Just because a man wants you to be his girlfriend doesn't mean you have to accept," the divorce attorney chimed in loudly from the side of the room where all the guests were watching. Some of the other speakers nodded, but a few eye rolls suggested that they already knew what was coming next. "Ms. Taylor might not want a boyfriend at all, and that's okay. I hate to ruin the fairy tale for some of you girls, but not all the men in this world are exactly Prince Charmings."

"I think what Ms. Kona is trying to say," Dante said as he expertly sidestepped backpacks and chairs to make his way to the front, "is that Miss Taylor is very successful at her *career*, which is what we're talking about today. Not whether or not someone wants or chooses to have a boyfriend."

Eloise was impressed by Dante's attempt at redirection, but she feared it was a little too late. She'd once been a curious and inquisitive child like the ones seated before her. And she would've been asking the same things. It was why she'd hesitated about coming today.

"Then why were you kissing her if she didn't want to

be your girlfriend, Mr. Sanchez?" This question from an older girl wearing a T-shirt bearing the handsome face of a popular K-Pop artist.

"I wasn't..." Dante paused as though he were trying to find a way out of this without outright denying it. "We weren't..."

This time, it was a boy who stood up. "My brother said a kid on his wrestling team was riding by on his bike and saw you guys kissing. With your mouths and everything."

There were several *ewwws*, but a lot more *awwws*. Sofia wasn't even bothering to hide her amusement at her brother's obvious discomfort. Eloise knew she should be equally embarrassed, but she was too busy enjoying the tinge of pink on Dante's tan cheeks and the funny way he was rocking back on his heels as though he would've sprinted out of the room if he weren't required to be here.

Dante clapped his hands three times, which seemed to get everyone's attention. "Let's get back on track here. Does anyone have any questions for Miss Taylor that are about her career and not about who she kisses? Yes, Antonia, what's your career-related question for Ms. Taylor?"

"When you made the commercials for that cologne, did you get to kiss *that* man?"

Dante tried to interject again, but Eloise didn't want these kids thinking she needed him to answer for her. "No, I didn't. He was a model my company hired."

"My mom says Mr. Sanchez looks like a model." It was hard to tell which student had just said those words because several children—and even Kim Kona—were now nodding in agreement. Numerous conversations broke out at once as the kids began talking amongst themselves.

Luckily, though, the lunch bell rang and Dante was able to get the students' attention long enough to remind them to give a round of applause for their guest speakers before they left.

"I am so sorry about that," Dante murmured to Eloise as the children filtered out of the library. "I'm even more sorry that I can't walk you out because I have cafeteria duty today. But I can take you out to dinner after basketball practice."

"Do you think that's a good idea after the interrogation we just got?"

"You said it yourself." Dante smirked without a trace of his earlier embarrassment before lowering his voice even more. "We're *just friends*."

He sure rebounded quickly from being put on the spot like that. "In that case, I feel like you might owe me at least a couple of dinners, *friend*."

"Perfect," Dante said right before a loud commotion sounded in the hallway. As he walked quickly toward the noise, he called out over his shoulder, "Put me down for tonight at six and Wednesday at seven. And also this weekend, if you're free."

Several of the speakers and a handful of parent volunteers had already made their exits when the kids were leaving, so not everybody heard him ask her out. Not that he was really asking.

Still.

He was pretty much making it sound like they were seeing each other on a regular basis. Although, even his bold and somewhat public declaration didn't stop a few moms from calling his name as they followed him to the cafeteria.

Eloise unplugged her laptop from the projector and began packing up her briefcase.

"That was smart of you to make a kid-friendly PowerPoint presentation," Kim Kona told Eloise. "I try to keep up with all this new technology, but half the time my granddaughter is the one teaching me. If I would've known I'd be going after the aerospace engineer who passed out miniature rocket ships, I would've done something with a little more pizzazz."

"I'm sure the students loved all the presentations," Stacy Abernathy, who was also a teacher at the school, said diplomatically as she straightened chairs.

"They especially loved that question and answer session at the end," Sofia Sanchez-Dalton added as she collected her own tote bag and a giant sketch pad from the librarian's desk. "I haven't seen my brother's face that red in a long time."

Eloise had met the woman briefly before the event started, but they hadn't had an opportunity to talk. Now she was dying to ask Dante's sister all sorts of questions.

Unfortunately, Kim Kona chose that exact moment to hand Eloise a business card. "Before I take off, I wanted to give you this. Now, I don't want to assume anything about your situation like other people in this town have. But you should know that I handle all types of family law, including paternity cases if you ever need anything."

Eloise bristled at the comment, but the woman was already out the door before she could tell her that she had no need of her services.

"Do you get that a lot?" Sofia asked quietly, concern clearly etched on her face.

"People telling me they don't want to assume anything and then immediately assume everything?" Eloise smiled with a stiff upper lip. "All the time. Although, if I'm being fair, I kind of did the same thing to LuLu the other night when I offered to market her BBQ sauce. I'm sure Kim intended it as one woman looking out for another, but it was also a reminder that people in town have been speculating about me."

"Then I won't assume anything about where you got that dress. I saw it during Fashion Week and wanted it for the boutique I work at, but I was told it was a one of a kind. We were able to get our hands on a few pieces from that designer's fall line, but they sold out as soon as they arrived."

"Thanks. They gave it to me after my company did some PR work for them. It's one of my favorites. I was trying to hold off as long as I could before buying maternity clothes, but I don't know how much more stretch I can get out of this one."

"I hear you. I'm not pregnant yet, but I'm already thinking about designing some functional pieces for myself for when that time comes. Don't get me wrong, maternity clothes have come a long way since our moms were wearing them. Just not all the way."

"Where's the shop you work at?" Eloise asked, an idea already forming in her mind.

"In the Heights. It's called BH Couture. Let me know if you want to stop by and I can pull a few pieces for you that might work."

"Would three o'clock be too soon for you?" Eloise retrieved her phone from her purse and almost giggled when she saw that Dante had already sent her a calendar request for dinner tonight and on Wednesday. The man was certainly learning that she was a schedule-driven woman. As long as he saw her as more than just a pregnant woman, then she might have a chance. Hopefully, his sister would be able to help with some of that.

"How about three thirty?" Sofia countered. "We just got in a pair of boots that will have everyone in town looking in your direction."

Eloise didn't need everyone looking at her. Just one man.

"Sorry, I couldn't see you out after the career event," Dante said when he gave Eloise a side hug later that evening. The last time he'd met her at a restaurant, he'd only touched her hand briefly across the table. Then today at school, he'd had to settle for a professional handshake. He'd been determined to figure out a friendly but still physical way to greet her.

It must've been a good choice because she'd leaned into the casual hug, giving him the opportunity to inhale the fresh scent of her shampoo.

"That's okay. After everyone left, Robin's sister Stacy told me that she traded lunch duty with you last Monday because you knew those moms would be there and you wanted a reason to be busy."

"I never told Stacy that was why I wanted to trade."

"She said that as well. That you'd be too polite to admit it."

"More like I want to pretend that they don't think of me any differently than they would any other teacher at the school. The problem is that they never ask the band teacher, what he thinks of their new workout pants. Or the school psychologist, if he wants to go to Doug's on Friday night for happy hour."

"You're a popular man, Dante Sanchez."

"I don't know why. It's certainly not because I want to be." Since he'd gone in for the side hug, it was natural to slip his arm around her waist and lead her to the entrance. "Hey, this isn't the same dress you were wearing earlier today."

"Maybe the ladies like you because you're so good at remembering their fashion choices."

"Nope. I couldn't tell you what any other woman at the career event was wearing today except for Staff Sergeant Ramirez, and only because the camouflage made her stand out. Ironically."

Eloise looked up at his face, her brown eyes framed by thick lashes. "Then how do you remember what I had on?"

"Because I was staring at you for three straight minutes while you talked, wondering how soft the fabric would feel against my fingers if I were to do this." He made a circular motion with his palm on her lower back and felt her shiver, but also lean in closer. Her response made his blood pump faster. "But this fabric is even silkier and a lot shorter."

"Thanks," Eloise said, her voice raspy. "I bought it this afternoon from the shop where your sister works. She suggested the boots, too. I hope it's not too much for a Monday night."

Hell. The first thing he'd noticed when she walked up was her bare toned legs encased in knee-high suede boots. Dante said under his breath, "It's only too much if you're trying to kill me."

"What's that?" Eloise asked, but the hostess was already welcoming them to DJ's Deluxe and asking if it would just be the two of them tonight.

Dante had to let go of her so that they could weave their way to their table, and he found himself already longing to touch her again. This was bad. He was never like this with other women, never drawn to them this way. Or worried that they weren't going to be drawn to him.

"This place looks great," Eloise said when they were seated with their menus. "Wasn't it the old grain storage warehouse?"

"It was. Camilla worked here when she and Jordan first started dating. They have great steaks, but for some reason I always end up getting the burger."

"You did warn me that you were a simple burger guy."

"That was back when my life seemed simpler."

"Are you saying that your life is suddenly more complex than it was a little over a week ago? What changed?"

"I met you."

"I'm not sure how I should take that."

"I didn't mean to say that you were complex. I was just thinking that things have gotten a lot more…" Dante paused to think of the right word. "…interesting lately."

"Yeah, I'm still not convinced whether that's supposed to be a compliment or a complaint."

"It's definitely a compliment." He flashed her a grin.

The server, who'd worked with Camilla and was familiar with Dante's penchant for burgers, appeared just then. Eloise requested the chicken and when it was Dante's turn to order, he said, "I'm going to have the rib eye, please."

"Oh," Fay said crossing off something on her pad.

"I wasn't expecting that. I guess we're changing things up tonight."

"Just keeping things interesting," Dante told her.

When she left, Eloise tilted her head. "So just to clarify… I made things more interesting. And now this rib eye is going to make things more interesting?"

"Yes." Dante nodded. "But in two completely different ways."

"In that case, I hope I can hold your interest longer than the steak does." Eloise lifted her water glass to toast him.

"I have no doubt you will." He sent her a reassuring wink.

"Any other competition I should be worried about?"

"You mean like other women?"

"Or, you know, anything else that's making your life more interesting at the moment?"

"No other women, but my after-school rec league started today and that's going to require a lot of my time. We're doing basketball this season. Once Little League starts in the spring, I'll lose around half of my players. I might try to do a girls' softball team if there's enough interest."

"Remember when we were at LuLu's and you told me I had a soft heart?" Eloise asked.

"That was only a few days ago. Of course, I remember."

"Well, you have a soft heart, too, Dante Sanchez."

"Or maybe I'm just super competitive and really love sports, but have resigned myself to the fact that I'll never make the pros. So I try to relive my glory days by coaching."

"It could be that. But mostly because you have a soft heart."

He'd been thinking about hearts way too often lately and the possibility of his getting broken. Dante took a deep drink of his iced tea and looked around to see if the basket of bread was coming. "Speaking of hearts, have your parents showed any signs of softening up theirs where you and the baby are concerned?"

Eloise sighed. "I'm supposed to see my mom tomorrow. I have a feeling she didn't tell my dad, though."

"What makes you think that?" Dante asked.

"Because she wants to meet me at the hotel and not at the ranch. She said she doesn't want me driving too much in my condition, but the Triple T is only about ten minutes away. It's also full of employees who would likely tell my dad if I showed up there."

"What about your other siblings besides Ryan?" Dante waited for Fay to put their salads on the table before continuing. "Have they reached out at all?"

"My sisters have been super supportive, obviously, since they know what it's like being on the outs with my parents. Seth and Daniel are way older, so we've never been big on hanging out and bonding. Since the party, Seth has sent a few texts, asking me if I need anything, and Daniel sent me a funny animal video. To be fair, though, it's not like I've ever gone out of my way to connect with them, either. I know I made a big scene initially at the party, but it was never my intention to force my way back into the family fold and demand everyone upend their lives for me. I was hoping to gradually ease into things. You know, put myself on their radar and see if there was any interest in improving our relationship from the ground up. I'm hoping they'll come around eventually."

"It sounds like a grassroots marketing campaign."

"I figure that approach works well in my business when I'm trying to appeal to a target audience. And the Taylors are definitely a target group." Eloise looked pointedly at Dante's empty plate. "Did that actually have salad on it when it arrived at the table a couple of minutes ago?"

"I skipped lunch because I was on duty and only had time for a protein bar before basketball practice."

"Good evening, Dante." Dr. Burris, a distinguished-looking older gentleman greeted him, then turned to Eloise. "Is this the Miss Taylor I've been hearing so much about?"

"Yes?" Eloise said cautiously, as though every time she met someone new lately she had to determine if they were going to be reporting back to her father.

Dante made quick introductions to assure her that this was one of the good guys. "Dr. Burris is the principal at Bronco High School. He's also the father of some of Bronco's most popular rodeo stars."

Eloise's polite smile became genuine as she extended her hand. "It's a pleasure to meet you, Dr. Burris."

"The pleasure is all mine. My wife, Jeanne, teaches with Dante and said lots of students couldn't stop talking about your presentation this afternoon, despite getting a few tough questions during the Q and A session. We still have a couple of booths available for our annual career fair at the high school next month. Is there any chance you'd be available?"

"Of course. Let me give you my contact information and you can send me the details."

Dante watched them exchange information and then politely waited until the principal left before he voiced his concern. "Eloise, do you mind me asking when your due date is?"

"Probably mid to late December." She picked up her fork and resumed eating.

"Probably? You don't have it in your calendar app?"

"Those are never exact and first babies usually come late. I didn't want to lock in a date and limit my availability until after the baby gets here."

She'd mentioned at the car dealership that she was possibly shying away from making definite plans regarding the baby because she didn't want to be overcontrolling like her parents. However, she had to at least be giving it a little thought.

Dante hoped his puzzled expression wasn't too obvious. "But what if the baby comes early? Don't you want to have a plan in place?"

"If that happens, which isn't very likely, then I'll clear my schedule and my assistant will coordinate with my clients so I can go on maternity leave. But in the meantime, I need to get as much done as possible. Why do you ask?"

"Because the career fair at the high school is December 9."

Eloise shrugged. "I'll keep that in mind. This salad is amazing. No wonder this place is so popular."

He noted the abrupt change in conversation and decided not to pry. At least not yet. Dante scanned the restaurant, which was only three-quarters full. "You should see this place on a Saturday. Luckily, it's a Monday and I didn't have to call in any favors to get a reservation."

"Why do I get the feeling you're owed plenty of favors in this town?"

"I wouldn't say *owed*." Dante chuckled. "Although, being the guy in charge of judging the science fair *and* the guy who gets to pick the all-star team for the youth soccer tournament means I've been offered all sorts of things I've had to decline. I don't want anyone thinking I'm giving preferential treatment."

"That's good to know. I'll make a mental note that you're above all manners of bribery."

Not all bribes, Dante thought as he recalled his brother-in-law's recent contribution to the school. "I try to be when it comes to the personal stuff. Even when it's court-side seats to the Chicago Bulls for Game 7 of the Conference Finals."

Fay delivered their entrées and Dante made a mental note to try to take his time with the rest of his meal. His rib eye was perfectly seared and the still-bubbling au gratin potatoes were practically begging to be inhaled. However, the quicker he ate, the sooner his date with Eloise would be over. Instead of diving into his plate, he reached for another piece of bread.

"That must've been a difficult decision," Eloise said.

"My plate is still sizzling, so I'm letting it cool down," Dante explained.

"No, I meant turning down the free tickets to the basketball game."

Dante held up his butter knife. "Not just any basketball game. Did I mention it was Game 7 of the Conference Finals?"

"Oh, are you a basketball fan?" Eloise lifted the corner of her lips in an adorable smile. "I'd never have guessed."

As they ate, they talked about sports in general and then about what they played in high school. He wasn't surprised to learn that she'd been captain of the varsity tennis team. But he was surprised to find out that she was only an alternate on the equestrian team.

"How many horses does your family own?" Dante finished the last of his asparagus, and only because he'd already eaten everything else in front of him, as well as the entire contents of the bread basket.

"Too many to count. But on the ranch, we only rode Western style. My school was on the East Coast and their team focused more on the dressage and hunt seat competitions."

"With your posture, I bet you look all prim and proper on a horse, no matter which style you ride."

"Too bad you won't be able to find out any time soon since there isn't a stable at the hotel." She rested her hands on her tummy, which didn't look too cumbersome for riding. "Or was that your way of slipping in another wisecrack about me being used to the finer things?"

"I still stand by that comment." Dante drank the rest of his iced tea. "There's nothing wrong with liking the finer things. Especially if it means I'll get to see you wearing those boots again."

"Is it me you want to see, Dante? Or just my boots?" Her eyes held a glint of challenge before she brought up their earlier conversation. "Because you should probably be warned that neither are very simple."

"How was the steak?" Fay asked when she came to take their plates.

"It was better than I expected." Dante didn't take his eyes off Eloise. If she was going to issue a flirtatious challenge, then she better be ready for him to respond in kind. "Sometimes when I try to change things up and make things more interesting, I end up wishing that I would've just stuck with my usual burger. But after tonight, I think the rib eye might be my new favorite thing."

"Uh-huh. Okay, then, I'll just go ahead and bring the dessert menu now," Fay said as she retreated hastily.

Eloise shook her head at Dante. "Even the server knows you weren't talking about the food."

"Was it that obvious?"

"That you were comparing me to meat again? Yes. But, I guess in a strange way, I am flattered. Just don't compare me to the side salad when we go to the Gemstone Diner on Wednesday."

Dante knew then that Eloise was already looking forward to their next date just as much as he was.

Chapter Seven

"I hear you've been spending quite a bit of time with Camilla Taylor's brother," Eloise's mom said as soon as the initial pleasantries about the weather and the hotel suite's color scheme were out of the way. Because, of course, Imogen Taylor would be more concerned about the latest gossip than how her future grandchild was doing.

"It's Camilla Sanchez-Taylor." Eloise had requested afternoon tea service be delivered to the room since her mother was making a brief stop following a luncheon she'd already scheduled. More like Imogen didn't want anyone seeing her dining with her pregnant daughter in public. "She hyphenated her maiden name when she married Jordan."

"One of my sorority sisters did that," her mother said off-handedly. "Kept her name and insisted on being a career woman even after she got married. Just like so many girls in your generation are doing nowadays."

Eloise's spirits lifted at her mom's seemingly progressive observation. Maybe this conversation was going to be more pleasant than she'd expected. "Did I meet her when you hosted one of your sorority reunions at the Triple T?"

"Of course not, dear. Her husband ended up running off with the nanny, which often happens when men don't get their needs met at home. Last I heard, her oldest son was back in rehab, which often happens to children of divorce."

"None of those things *often happen*, Mother." Eloise shook her head at her mother's flawed statistics. "Sometimes men have affairs and sometimes children have addiction issues no matter how perfect a wife or mother you are."

"Possibly. But why chance it? I can't help but think how differently her life would've been if she'd just done things more traditionally. Now she's a ball-busting divorce attorney who hates men and has to raise her grandchildren because her son can't stay away from the bourbon."

"Mom, there are so many things wrong with everything you just said, I don't even know where to start. How—" A thought struck her from out of the blue. "Wait. Are you talking about Kim Kona?"

"You know her?"

"I met her at a career event at the elementary school. She gave me her business card."

"Is that where you met Donovan?"

"Who?" Eloise lifted her brow in confusion.

"Camilla Taylor's— I mean Camilla *Sanchez*-Taylor's brother. I heard he was a teacher in the Valley."

"His name is Dante," Eloise said, wondering if her

mom had always pronounced *Valley* that way, as though she had to whisper it so nobody would hear. "And no, I met him that night of the party at The Library."

"Then if he's not the father," Imogen began as she glanced at her daughter's midsection, "do you plan to retain her?"

"Retain who?" So much for Eloise taking charge of this conversation and remaining poised under her mother's scrutiny. This was the second time Imogen had steered them right off course.

"Kim Kona. My attorney friend. She does have quite the reputation for getting favorable outcomes for her clients, especially in custody cases. If you need help with the fees, I have some money in my private account. Your father won't have to know."

"Now, all of a sudden, she's your attorney *friend*?" Eloise looked to the ceiling, hoping for divine intervention or even a moment of clarity. "Don't answer that. I think we're getting ahead of things, Mom. Let's start with some of the basics."

"The tea is going to get cold, dear. Why don't I serve?"

Imogen was very accomplished when it came to manners and hostess duties. But her real skill set lay in her ability to diplomatically deflect and divert unpleasantries while making everything appear smooth on the surface. Eloise knew that her mother would be reluctant to have too deep of a conversation and expected her to ask off-topic questions to sidetrack toward more neutral subjects. That's why Eloise had prepared a list of things she wanted to discuss, then planned for all the potential questions her mom might have and included those at the anticipated spots to limit the opportunity for distraction. "Great, you serve the tea while I talk. I have a lot I want to get out, so it'd be great if you could save all questions until the end."

"Of course, dear. I wouldn't dream of interrupting you." When Eloise picked up the list from the side table, her mother added, "Your nails look incredible, by the way. It must be the pregnancy hormones. After six kids, I thought my own nails would stay like that, but once you were born I had to start getting those paraffin manicures—"

"Mom, I need you to focus."

Imogen took a sip of tea, sighed delicately, then said, "All right. I'm focused now. Please continue."

"As you know, I'm eight months pregnant and I don't know whether it's going to be a boy or a girl. I'll be happy either way. No, you don't know the father of the baby and no, he will not be in the picture. I met him when I was living in New York City and even though we were being careful, sometimes these things happen. We'd talked about marriage early on in our relationship, but never about kids. When he found out I was pregnant, he couldn't run fast enough. Which, in hindsight, is really for the best since we weren't that compatible." Eloise dared to look up from her list just in time to see her mother's lips open as though she were about to ask a question. Rushing to continue, she said, "No, he does not want anything to do with the baby and yes, I already did seek legal counsel and have everything squared away in that department. His family also comes from money, so no, you don't need to worry about him showing up one day, insisting he has some right to the child or to the Taylor fortune. If he changes his mind in the future about wanting to meet his child, or if my child has questions about him when they grow up, then I'll decide the best course of action at that time.

"I appreciate your offer for financial assistance, but I'm more than capable of supporting myself. Although I do have questions about this private bank account of yours, which we can discuss later." Eloise stopped talking long enough to glance at her mom, who was nibbling on a cucumber sandwich as though they were discussing the latest dress styles. But at least Eloise could continue her prepared remarks without an emotional argument. "Thankfully my company is quite successful. I can work from anywhere and, for the foreseeable future, I plan to work from Bronco. I want to raise my baby here and I want them to know their family, or at least the ones who are willing to accept and love them unconditionally. I know this isn't what you and Dad envisioned, but I wouldn't have been satisfied with the life you'd chosen for me." She took a deep breath. "I'm happy, Mom, and I hope you can be happy for me, too."

When she finished, Eloise inhaled again deeply, then let out a long breath as she waited for her mom's response. When Imogen didn't say anything right away, Eloise asked, "Do you have any questions?"

"Of course, but you asked me to wait. So I'm waiting."

"Well, I'm done now." Eloise waved away the petit four her mother tried to pass her because she'd already eaten six of the things when she was anxiously pacing the room, waiting for her mom to arrive. "Go for it."

Imogen took another dainty sip of tea and then set down her cup. "Is Dante your boyfriend?"

"That's the same thing the kids asked when I did my career presentation at the school," Eloise muttered.

"It's a good question."

"It was also a good presentation, but nobody seemed to care about that. Don't you want to talk about all the other stuff I just said?"

"If you want to, we can. I'm glad you shared how this all came to pass and it answered many of my questions about how you got to this exact moment. However, there's nothing I can say that's going to change what's already done. My concern is what happens now. What does your future look like, Eloise?"

"It looks like I'm going to have a baby, Mom."

"Don't get smart with me, Eloise Magnolia Taylor. You might not have spent every night of your childhood under my roof, but I'm still your mother and I know you the way only a mother can know her daughter. You're smart and you're fearless and, like your sisters, you have this deep capacity to love. But you've also been headstrong and a bit on the reactionary side when it comes to rushing decisions that require more patience and forethought. So, what I want to know is whether you have thought all of this through. I mean really, *really* thought about it down the road. What's it going to look like to run an international marketing company from a small town like Bronco? What's your travel schedule going to look like when your clients from across the globe don't want to fly here for meetings?"

"We have online meetings, Mom."

Her mother continued as though she hadn't heard. "Who is going to be by your side through all of this? Single parenthood is lonely, Eloise. How is it going to feel when your baby wakes up in the middle of the night for the fifth time and you're the only one who knows their favorite song to get them back to sleep? How are you going to comfort them when it's the father-daughter dance at school and your child is in tears because they can't go? Who is going to be there to tell you to stop pacing the floor when your sixteen-year-old gets their driver's license and doesn't make curfew and you're sick with worry? Parenthood is full of joys and sorrows. Who is going to be there to share them with you?"

They were all the same questions Eloise had asked herself when she'd first found out about the pregnancy. She didn't have the answers then any more than she did now. So she'd conditioned herself to only focus on what she could control, what she *should* control. And that was loving her baby no matter what.

"I don't know, Mom. But who shared them with you? Let's not pretend that Dad participated in either the mental or physical burden of raising us. You were a stay-at-home mom with household staff and all the money you needed. Yet, I know there were nights when Dad stayed an extra day at a beef convention, or couldn't be bothered to show up for a music recital and you cried yourself to sleep. Like you, I'll have the money to pay for all the help I need, which is an advantage, but not a substitute. Unlike you, though, I would rather be all alone than be in a marriage that makes me feel lonely."

Imogen winced, then blinked several times. Her hands trembled, causing the teacup and saucer to rattle as she sat it down.

"Mom, I'm sorry if that sounded harsh. I know your relationship with Dad is your business. But just like you think *I* deserve the best, I think *you* deserve the same."

"Your father is a complicated man and I've made

my peace with that because that's the life I chose. Is our marriage perfect? No. But we've all had to make sacrifices."

"You, maybe. But what has Dad ever sacrificed?"

A sad expression crossed her mom's face as she stared across the suite at nothing in particular. "All parents make sacrifices, dear. All of them. The goal is to never let your children see what you had to give up. And in that, your father has been very successful."

Whoa. A wave of emotions vibrated through Eloise, and she sat there stunned.

This conversation was going way deeper than what she'd expected and there was nothing written on her notepad covering any of this. Her family didn't talk about their feelings and for a second, Eloise had to fight through her trained instinct to change the subject to something more pleasant. Just when she was about to roll up her sleeves and find out more, her mom snapped right back into familiar territory.

"So back to my original question. What's going on between you and Dante Sanchez?"

And just like that, the deep conversation was over. Eloise shrugged. "I don't know what's going on between us, Mom. I think we like each other, but we're not quite friends and we're not quite dating. Maybe, if the timing were different, things would be more definable. But for now, it's not one of my top priorities."

What she didn't reveal to her mother was that so far, Dante had only kissed her that one day. They'd held hands, he'd put his arm around her, they'd even hugged hello and goodbye. But despite the obvious flirtation and heated looks, there had yet to be a repeat of their kisses.

If Eloise could barely plan for what would happen

after the baby arrived, how could she expect Dante to plan for anything more serious than the occasional dinner?

Imogen scanned the surroundings. "Is one of your top priorities finding suitable housing?"

"Eventually. But this suite has everything I need for now."

"Your bedroom at the ranch also has everything you need. Plus, a heated spa if your pregnancy is anything like mine and your lower back muscles need it. I can have Lina arrange for a couple of the ranch hands to move some office furniture into the den for you to use for your business and—"

Eloise interrupted her mom. "Does Dad know you're extending this olive branch?"

"He will, once we get you all settled in and he returns from his trip to the stockyards in Fort Worth."

"So you haven't run it by him?" Not that Eloise was even willing to consider moving back home. She just wanted to know if anyone at the Triple T was allowed to bring up her name in her father's presence.

"It's my house, too, Eloise," Imogen said almost defiantly, which caused Eloise to startle. "Doesn't it matter that I want you there? This is my first grandchild and I plan to spoil them to pieces. I already picked out my new grandma name. How does *Imo-Gram* sound? Like Imogen, but with gram at the end."

Eloise's brows slammed together at the unexpected revelation. "Yeah, I caught that. The name may need some work. We'll see how the baby does pronouncing it. But back to me staying on the ranch, Mom. I appreciate the offer, but I can't live someplace where I'm going to be constantly judged by my choices. And Dad is a harsh critic."

"At least come for Thanksgiving and see how it goes," her mother suggested, refusing to give up. "Your brothers will be there, obviously, and I've invited your sisters as well. Charlotte said she'd consider it. I'm still waiting to hear back from Allison. But if they know you'll be there, then I'm sure they'll come."

Eloise had her doubts. But if Charlotte and Allison were willing to put their grievances aside, then Eloise had no choice but to do the same. After all, this was the whole reason why she'd moved back to Bronco. To raise her child amongst family. Hopefully, she'd made the right decision.

"Are you going to go?" Dante asked when Eloise told him about her mom's invitation to Thanksgiving. They'd already gone to eat at the Gemstone Diner on Wednesday and were back at The Library, Camilla's restaurant, for dinner on Saturday. Or, as Eloise referred to it when he'd called to invite her, the *Scene of the Crime*.

"I don't know. I talked to my sister Charlotte to confirm that my mom actually had invited her, and she said she's going to try to make it."

Try to make it? Dante didn't love the idea of Eloise taking on Thaddeus without someone else in her corner to back her up. Since he couldn't invite himself to a holiday dinner at her parents' home, he'd have to trust that one of her siblings would have her back. Not that Eloise didn't already know what she was up against and wasn't perfectly capable of defending herself. It was just that he felt this overwhelming urge to protect her.

He kept his opinion to himself, though, because at

the end of the day, Eloise had to make her own decisions. The best he could do was help her weigh the pros and cons. "There's definitely safety in numbers."

Eloise nodded. "That's exactly what I was thinking. Having tea with my mom was the start of something... I don't know how to explain it. It was like a shifting of sorts. At first, I was anxious about how she was going to act and, don't get me wrong, she'll always be the way she is. But at least she was showing some self-awareness and, I guess, a sense of understanding where I was coming from. It wasn't a total breakthrough, but it felt as though we managed to put a few little cracks in the emotional wall between us. I know she wants to be a part of my life and especially a part of the baby's life. I'm just not sure she's strong enough to convince my father to be quite as accepting."

"Fortunately, she has a daughter who's strong enough to convince even the most stubborn of men to rethink things."

"You mean you're actually considering adding riding to your recreation league?" Eloise reached for a tortilla chip and dipped it into the creamy white queso. In between dates, she'd been texting him ideas for expanding the after school program to other sports. He loved it that she was interested in something he was so passionate about, but he also had to wonder where she found the time. Especially, when she always seemed to be too busy to focus on anything baby-related.

"I'm not considering it exactly." Dante reached across the table to wipe a spot of cheese sauce from the corner of her mouth. "But I'm keeping it on my radar, so to speak. The very far outer reaches of my radar."

"Oh, come on, it's a good idea. Just because we live

in a ranching town, doesn't mean all the kids have access to horses."

"I know, but who's going to be their riding coach?" Dante asked. "I know you're probably sitting there thinking that I'm some sort of athletically gifted superstar, but I've only really excelled at football, basketball, baseball, soccer, track and a little bit of competitive swimming."

"Is this your way of telling me you're not athletically gifted? Because it sounds like you're trying to do the exact opposite, listing your whole résumé like that."

"All I'm saying is that I don't know the first thing about horses. Other than I see them in town sometimes and at the rodeo."

"You don't have to be the coach for everything, Dante."

"I know, but it's my program." Man, that sounded as though he were being territorial, and he winced before quickly correcting himself. "I promise I'm not being a control freak. It's just that some of these kids have been let down in the past and I don't want to overcommit and then disappoint them."

"It'll still be your program, just with some extra volunteers."

He exhaled a bit too forcefully and it came out like a resigned groan. Normally, he would've jumped wholeheartedly into expanding the league, despite it still being in the beginning stages. But their schedules were already so full, he only got to see Eloise two or three times a week. When the baby arrived, things between them would surely change. Instead of being selfish with his time, maybe he should be focusing his energy on what he was going to do after Eloise became a full-time mom. "Fine. It'll be a closer blip on my radar. I'll talk to some people. Gary, the bartender over there, said he'd help."

"What about my snowboarding idea?" Eloise asked.

"The nearest skiing area is two hours away. Who's going to pay for the busses and lift tickets?"

"We find some donors. I'll work on that."

It was none of his business, he told himself even as the words slipped out of his mouth. "Don't you think you already have enough you're working on?"

Eloise paused, her smile fading slightly. "What does that mean?"

"It means have you met with a real estate agent yet to look at houses?"

"I will. After the holidays. I need to get as much work done as I can before I go on maternity leave."

"I'd be happy to go with you to look at places."

Something changed in Eloise's expression. "Don't you think that might send the wrong kind of signal?"

"What do you mean?"

"If people see us out shopping for a new house, they might get the impression that we're moving in together. Or at least challenging that noncommittal bachelor reputation you've worked so hard to earn."

Her last sentence stung. Maybe Dante had earned that reputation fair and square in the past, but it wasn't as though people weren't already thinking he'd forfeited the title. Hell, they were currently sitting at a table for two in one of the most romantic restaurants in town. On a Saturday night. They were practically begging people to assume they were already a couple. Too bad *his* reputation wasn't the only one on the line.

Dante folded his hands on the table as he studied her. "It might also give them the impression that you're back in Bronco to stay."

"I *am* back in Bronco to stay."

"Eloise, you're still living in a hotel. You could just pack up your car and leave at a moment's notice." Or with no notice at all, Dante realized, making his gut harden. There really was nothing keeping her here. Least of all her family. He might not be ready to have everyone in town think of them as a happy little couple with a baby on the way, but he wasn't quite ready to lose her friendship, either.

"I could." Eloise nodded in agreement, which only made Dante's stomach clench more. "But my mom made a comment to me the other day about how I've always been reactionary, and it wasn't until she left that it sunk in. I *am* quick to react, which can be a good thing in an emergency or in my career when I need to do damage control for a client. But it can also make me impulsive and prone to rush into something I'm not ready for. Most of the big decisions I've made in my life have been in response to a situation that could've been resolved if only I'd been more determined to stick with it and make things work. I'm not saying that I regret any of those decisions, especially leaving Taylor Beef to go back to school and start my own company. The jury is still out on whether I should've relocated my business to Bronco on a whim like I did, yet my pride is telling me it's too late change my mind now. But with the baby coming, I can't risk making any more impulsive decisions that will affect their future, too. I don't want to rush into buying a house and then have it turn out to be one I hate."

"You do know that this is the exact opposite philosophy you used when you were at the car dealership and I suggested you look at other options."

"I know." Eloise sagged against the chair. "That

might've been one of my reactionary times because I wasn't expecting to see you there and when you showed up, you were so handsome with that smile and all your charm, and I didn't think I could trust myself not to hop in your car again for another ride home. Besides, I really did need a vehicle and, in my defense, I didn't go with my first choice."

Dante knew better than to press the issue, even though he thought it was odd that she wasn't feeling that common pregnancy urge to nest. After all, what did he know about expecting a baby? Instead, he tilted his head. "You think I'm handsome?"

"Everyone thinks you're handsome, Dante."

"But you said I was so handsome you couldn't trust yourself around me." His grin was so wide his cheeks almost hurt.

"Those weren't my exact words." Eloise rolled her eyes playfully. "But I will admit that I find you attractive and I like spending time with you."

"If you want to spend more time together, you could always come with me to our Thanksgiving." It was the first time Dante had ever invited a woman to his family's home. Or at least a woman he was seeing in a "friendly" way.

He didn't realize he was holding his breath, waiting for her response, until Jordan chose that exact moment to stop at their table.

"Camilla mentioned you two had a reservation tonight," his brother-in-law said. "I don't want to interrupt but wanted to say hi."

More like he wanted to check in on his cousin and make sure Dante wasn't putting the moves on her. Although, on cold rainy nights like this one, Jordan did usually come to help Camilla close the restaurant so he could drive her home safely. His sudden appearance was likely a bit of both reasons.

Dante stood to shake Jordan's hand, then his brother-in-law bent to give Eloise a peck on the cheek before asking, "What were you guys talking about?"

"Thanksgiving with the Sanchezes," Eloise answered a bit too honestly.

"Oh, cool. You should come," Jordan told his cousin, which Dante took as him approving of their relationship—not that they needed anyone's approval. "I've been to Thanksgiving at Uncle Thad and Aunt Imogen's house before and trust me, you'll definitely have more fun with the Sanchezes."

Jordan then looked at Dante. "By the way, your sister said you're in charge of pies this year because you eat more dessert than anyone else."

Dante threw up his arms in defeat. He was horrible at baking. "If that's the standard, then Dylan should be in charge of appetizers."

Camilla joined her husband, sliding her arm around his waist. "Nobody wants Dylan to do the appetizers. Remember that time he tried to shape mini turkey drumsticks out of processed cheese and brown food coloring? They looked exactly how you'd expect them to look and tasted even worse."

"Dante invited Eloise to Thanksgiving," Jordan told his wife.

Camilla's jaw dropped, but she quickly recovered. "To Thanksgiving at my parents' house?"

"Technically it's *our* parents' house," Dante corrected. "Am I not allowed to invite a guest for dinner?"

"Of course you are," Camilla said, then turned to

Eloise, who was doing that polite-smile thing that she tended to do in uncomfortable situations. "Of course he is, and my parents would love to have you, Eloise. Everyone's been dying to meet you and since Dante talks about you so much, it's almost as though you've been coming to family dinners all along."

"I don't talk about you in a crazy obsessed way, El," Dante interjected before his sister could embarrass him further. "Just in a casual way because my family is so nosy and asks way too many questions."

"They do ask a lot of questions," Jordan confirmed to his cousin, not exactly selling the Sanchezes as a sane option for a holiday meal. "But only on your first couple of visits."

"As appealing as you guys are making it sound," Eloise finally said, "I told my mom I'd consider having Thanksgiving out at the Triple T and my sisters might be flying in for the occasion."

"Well, if you change your mind, we would love to have you," Camilla said to Eloise, then faced Dante. "I'm leaving for the night, but I already told your server to charge you for every dessert you order this time. No more freebies."

"Siblings aren't embarrassing at all," Dante said when Camilla and Jordan left. "If you decide you don't want to hang out with yours on Thanksgiving, I'll gladly share mine."

Later that night, Dylan's face was somber when Dante brought home a to-go bag full of food from their sister's restaurant.

"What's wrong?" Dante asked.

"Camilla texted and said you were at the Library with Eloise. Again."

"What does that mean? *Again?*" And they'd only left forty-five minutes ago. Was his family tracking his whereabouts in some sort of group chat he wasn't included in?

Dylan paused the TV during the middle of a college basketball recap, a sure sign that he wanted to have a serious conversation. "I'm just trying to figure out what the endgame is here."

Dante tried to shrug casually. "Why does there need to be an endgame?"

"Because there's always an endgame, whether you plan for it or not. You guys can't keep this up long-term. She's having a baby, man."

"Yeah, I know."

"Then don't you think it's pretty reckless of you to be leading her on like this?"

"Who says I'm leading her on?" Dante asked, his tone defensive. "Maybe *she's* the one leading *me* on."

It wasn't the first time Dante had doubted whether Eloise would be interested in something serious with him. Or that she wouldn't want to see him as often after the baby arrived.

"Maybe she is." Dylan relaxed against the sofa cushions. "I've never seen you like this around any other woman before, so I guess it's possible. Just remember, though, if the clock runs out on whatever is going on between you two, you're not the one who has something to lose."

Dante's heart squeezed in his chest. He thought about how he'd walked her to the door of her hotel room tonight, their hugs lasting longer and longer every time they said goodbye. He also thought about how he'd had to put one foot in front of the other to not carry her to that king-sized bed and stay the night. Then he thought about how he would feel if he showed up at the hotel one day to pick her up and found out she'd already checked out. Now that would definitely feel like a loss.

"You're great with kids, Dante. But you get to send your students home to their actual parents at the end of the day. Guys like us have never been the type who can commit to something long-term. You can barely take care of a houseplant. And now with your new rec league, you don't have much time to help out at the dealership."

"Is that what this is about? You miss hanging out and my free labor at your dealership?"

"No." Dylan answered finally. "But you should probably know that I hired someone to work in the office full time and another salesperson."

A different sort of worry pricked at Dante's skin. "Please tell me you didn't do what I think you did."

"It's a good opportunity, Dante. I couldn't turn down the deal."

"The Broken Road Ranch?" When his brother nodded, Dante shook his head. "You actually accepted it in exchange for a new truck?"

"You know I've always wanted my own tract of land." Sure, his brother had always talked about buying property, something big enough to start his own ranch. But he'd also talked about getting drafted to play for the Bulls. It was supposed to be a pipe dream, not something he was actually considering. Dylan was great at selling cars, but he didn't know the first thing about cattle.

"I knew you wanted to buy some undeveloped land, yes. But do you really see yourself making a go of this? Taking over another man's ranch?"

"Do you really see yourself playing daddy to another man's child?" Dylan asked, then immediately apologized. "Sorry. That was a bad word choice."

"A really bad word choice," Dante agreed, even though he'd be lying if he said he hadn't considered the same thing. "Eloise's ex is no longer in the picture, and she's had to put up with a lot of speculation about that."

"It has nothing to do with Eloise as a person. I actually like the two of you together. Look, I can always sell the ranch, Dante. But once you take on parenthood, it's forever. There's no such thing as summer break anymore. I just want to make sure you've thought all of this through."

"I haven't exactly thought any of this through." Dante shoved his hand through his hair, immediately understanding Eloise's habit of being both impulsive with certain situations while completely avoiding others. "Even if I do want something long-term with her—which I'm not saying I do—but if I did, she might not feel the same way. We're trying to keep things casual for now."

"Trying?" Dylan asked. "Has it been a struggle?"

"It's starting to become one."

"Maybe you should invite her for Thanksgiving and see how she does with the rest of our family. If we don't scare her off and have her running out before dessert, then at least you'll know where you stand."

"I did invite her, but I think she's going to spend Thanksgiving with her own family."

"Whew. Five bucks says she doesn't make it through appetizers with that bunch."

"You still owe me five dollars from the score of last week's football game."

"It went into overtime. We said nothing about the overtime." And just like that, Dante and his brother were back to being themselves.

Or at least Dylan was. Dante was still thinking about Eloise and whether or not they could ever have a future together.

Chapter Eight

"Eloise?" Dante asked on Tuesday afternoon when he saw her with her head down in the parking lot of the small medical complex in Bronco Heights. "What are you doing here?"

She glanced up from her phone screen, surprise clearly etched on her face. "I have an appointment with Dr. Kimball. What are you doing here?"

"One of my students hurt his arm trying to climb to the top of the handball court during recess. The hospital referred them to an ortho specialist in this office so he could get a cast. It's been a long day for the patient and his folks, so I was delivering smoothies."

She smiled as she shook her head at him. "Now that's a dedicated teacher, right there. If I would've known you were making deliveries, I would've placed an order for a strawberry-banana with a protein boost."

"I don't mind sticking around and waiting until you're

done. We can go to Java and Juice and grab one together. Or even get some dinner."

"Dinner actually sounds amazing since I worked through lunch. Come to think of it, that should help with my weigh-in. My mom reminded me that she never gained more than eighteen pounds with each of her pregnancies. I know she's going to ask, so I want to be sure my number is lower than hers."

He let his eyes scan down her still toned body that only showed a small bump not even the size of a basketball yet. "I don't know what you looked like before, but if it helps, tell your mom that I think you're the hottest looking pregnant woman I ever saw."

"I'm not going to tell her that, Dante." She shoved his bicep when he wiggled his eyebrows at her. "I wasn't fishing for compliments, either. My point was that I don't know how long I'll be in there and I don't want to keep you."

"You said your appointment is with Dr. Kimball?" Dante asked, and Eloise nodded. "Then you'll likely be out of there in ten minutes or so."

"Really? My obstetrician in New York usually takes at least thirty to forty-five minutes, and that's not including the time in her waiting room."

"Oh, I doubt there'll be many patients in his waiting room."

"What are you talking about? My mom said he's one of the best doctors in town. In fact, he delivered all of her children."

"Yeah, he delivered me and my siblings, too. Thirty plus years ago. Forty plus years for some of *your* siblings. He probably should've retired a decade ago."

Eloise gave him a stern look. "Don't be an ageist, Dante."

"I'm being a realist. A teacher at my school just had a baby and could give you a recommendation. Better yet, Jace Abernathy's fiancée, Tamara, is a maternity nurse at Bronco Valley. She can tell you which doctors are the best."

"I think you're being a little overprotective." She gestured toward the state-of-the-art medical complex that was new to the wealthier neighborhood in the Heights and housed several specialties. "Clearly the man has enough patients that he can afford an office here."

"I'm sure he's had plenty of patients over the years. Which was why he was able to purchase the building himself and then rent out the space. But that doesn't mean he's still at the top of his game when it comes to all the latest advances in medicine."

"How advanced does he need to be? Women have been having babies since the beginning of time. I've already had all the ultrasounds and the tests and the bloodwork and I'm still doing video calls with my original obstetrician, who said she will follow up after Dr. Kimball does his exam. Besides, when it comes time to actually deliver the baby, I'll be at the hospital with all the modern technology and a floor full of labor nurses."

"Then I'll pop inside with you. To make sure for myself that his board certification didn't expire a few decades ago."

Eloise glanced around the parking lot surreptitiously and lowered her voice. "You can't come with me to my doctor's appointment, Dante."

"Why not? People always bring their husbands to these kinds of appointments. Jace even delivered his own baby. Although, technically he didn't know it was his baby at the time since he responded to an emergency call and then later adopted Frankie."

"Yes, but you're not my husband. Nor are you medically trained to deliver a baby."

"Fine. Then I'll wait out here and you can tell me all about how I was right and you were wrong once you see how Dr. Kimball accidentally crashes his walker into the exam table."

An older woman exited the building, spotted Eloise and Dante, and waved. Dante recognized her as Mrs. Epson, one of Imogen Taylor's cronies and quite the busybody in both the Heights and the Valley—at least when she came to his mom's salon. Eloise mumbled something that sounded like a curse word.

"Is that Eloise Taylor?" Mrs. Epson said, adjusting the dark wraparound sunglasses people were given after eye surgery. "I'd heard you were back in town and in the family way. Is this your husband?"

"Hi, Mrs. Epson. It's me, Dante Sanchez. My mom is your hairdresser."

"Right! Denise's boy. Are you the veterinarian?"

"No, that's my brother Felix."

"Then you must be the one who owns the car dealership."

"Nope. That's my other brother Dylan. I'm the teacher."

"Of course you are." Mrs. Epson nudged Eloise with an elbow. "I would've done a lot better in school if *my* teachers looked like him."

Eloise smiled politely. Mrs. Epson glanced down at her midsection. "Oh, are you here for an appointment with Dr. Kimball? He delivered all my babies, except my youngest, Roger."

"Roger's one of my *Dad's* buddies. In his *senior* bowling league." Dante gave Eloise a pointed look. "They call themselves the Silver Strikers. Get it? Because most of them have gray—"

"I get it, Dante," Eloise said, her smile tighter than usual. "It sounds like Dr. Kimball must be very experienced to be delivering babies for as long as he has."

"And he went to Harvard at the same time Ted Kennedy was there," Mrs. Epson told Eloise in that casual way people name drop. "Anyway, it was nice seeing you two lovebirds. I'll be sure to tell your folks you looked well."

Eloise didn't correct the woman, so Dante stayed quiet until Mrs. Epson shuffled off to her car. Then he said, "You know she's going to tell everyone we were at your appointment together, right?"

"I know." Eloise was cute when she groaned. "You might as well come inside with me, then. But I'm warning you, you better not look at the scale. I don't want you to have to lie to my mom for me."

Dante didn't know what he was expecting from an obstetrics appointment, but it certainly wasn't to get stuck in the waiting room. Not that he expected more than that. He wasn't Eloise's actual partner. But he'd at least been hoping to hear the baby's heartbeat. Instead, he got to hear an earful of gossip from Dr. Kimball's wife, who was also his receptionist and kept confusing Dante with his brothers. Although, she did tell him that Dr. Kimball would be retiring at the end of the month and was selling his practice to a new (and hopefully younger) doctor who was moving to Bronco.

When Eloise came out of the exam room, she was

smiling, so that was a relief. "He says the baby and I are in tip-top shape."

"That's good," Dante admitted, keeping his own skepticism at bay. After all, he didn't want to stress Eloise out. If she thought the doctor was competent, then she probably knew best. "So dinner?"

"Would you mind if we didn't go out tonight?"

Dante's heart sank, but he tried not to let her see his disappointment. "No worries. It's not like we had it scheduled in your little calendar app."

"Oh, no, I still want to get dinner. I meant do you mind if we get takeout and eat it at your place or mine?"

His spirits lifted and his smile grew wide. "That sounds perfect. Except Dylan is going to be home tonight, so unless you want to share an extra cheese pizza with him while he yells at a bunch of basketball players on TV, then I'd suggest we not go to my apartment."

"How did you know that I was craving pizza?"

"Because I think Bronco Brick Oven is the only restaurant in town we haven't been to yet."

And that was how, an hour later, Dante ended up sitting side by side next to Eloise on the small sofa in her hotel suite. Before they dug into their food, Dante saw a yellow legal pad on the end table next to him. It was completely filled with notes that were none of his business. But one word jumped out at him and he knew he wouldn't be able to keep looking away.

Dante jerked his thumb at the side table. "Hey. I'm not trying to be nosy, but I couldn't help but notice my name on this notepad that you probably don't want me reading."

"It's nothing," Eloise yelped as she dove across his torso and scooped it off the table, indicating that it definitely was something. When he lifted a brow in doubt, she sighed, then shoved the pad at him. "Fine. Go ahead and read it. I made a list of things I wanted to tell my mom when she was here because she's notorious for getting me off topic and asking random questions to distract me. I added in some answers for things she might ask and then I pretty much read through it verbatim while she listened. I do the same thing when I have meetings with clients who waffle back and forth and struggle to make decisions. It helps keep everyone focused."

Dante wanted to hand the list back to her. To insist that whatever prepared notes she'd written were a private matter between her and her mom. But he couldn't drag his eyes away. When he read the part about how the father of her baby was officially out of the picture, how they'd already signed legal paperwork with an attorney, something inside his chest began vibrating and he sat up straighter. Ever since Dylan had brought it up the other night, Dante had to admit that he'd been subconsciously wondering if he might be in competition with some man he'd never met. It was one thing to hear Eloise casually mention that she was no longer with her ex. It was quite another to realize how final it was.

How Dante might have a chance for something more with her.

The sudden thought reverberated in his head and he tried not to jump to any conclusions. Instead, he pointed at the bottom line. "But why is my name circled here at the end? With all those exclamation points?"

"I actually wrote that after my mom left. It was the one question I should've anticipated but didn't because when I had dinner with my brother Ryan, he didn't bring up your name. It was more of a note to myself not to make that mistake. Again."

"Good idea. You might want to add a slide with a picture of me to your PowerPoint presentation for the next career day at school, as well." His joke brought another tinge of pink to her cheeks. He loved it when she got flustered so he continued. "I can even help you come up with an informational brochure to pass out when people ask you about me. Like the pharmaceutical ones I was stuck reading in Dr. Kimball's waiting room. Except mine wouldn't be as boring."

Eloise rolled her eyes, then used the remote to turn on the TV. As if that would get him to stop thinking about how people were starting to see them as a couple. "I don't know what you want to watch, but I'm pretty sure it involves a ball and lots of sweaty people running around."

"You know, I do watch things other than sports."

"Do you?" She set down the remote, leaving it on a channel that was known for its holiday-themed movies about people leaving the big city and finding love in a small town.

Dante recognized her silent challenge and, even though his fingers itched to turn on ESPN, he responded, "Is this the one where his family's bakery is closing and she's the only one who can save it?"

"I think it's the one where she runs a tree farm and he's an executive from the lumber company."

They were both wrong when the movie started and they saw the actors in front of an old castle turned into a bed-and-breakfast. But neither one reached for the remote as they filled up on breadsticks and slices of sausage-and-mushroom pizza and watched the happily-ever-after play out on the screen. Eloise had her feet up on the coffee table and when the cologne commercial came on, she quickly pulled down her legs and pivoted so she could stare at his profile.

"Don't say it," he warned her.

She smothered her giggle, but apparently couldn't contain herself. "It just that you really do look like him."

"If you're going to make comments like that," Dante said as he wedged a throw pillow between them, "then I suggest you stay over there on your side of the sofa."

She pushed the pillow out of the way and inched closer, a dare in her eyes. "You're not the boss of where I sit."

"Oh, I'm not, am I?" He wrapped one arm behind her back and one arm under her knees and hauled her in one motion across his lap.

She threw back her head and laughed and he pulled her closer.

"Now who's the boss of where you sit?" he asked, trying to maintain a stern expression.

"How do you know that this wasn't my plan all along?" She wrapped her arms around his neck. "That you fell right into my trap?"

"How could this be your plan since I've been thinking about it since the day I did this." He leaned in to kiss her, no longer able or willing to hold off.

He couldn't have worse luck, because right then her phone rang on the coffee table, interrupting him. "Should you get that?"

"Maybe. Let me see who it is." Eloise sagged against him, lowering her arms. He got the impression she was just as disappointed as he was. But she also didn't ignore the call, which was what he would've done. "It's my sister. I should take this."

"Hey, Charlotte. What's up?" Eloise answered as she stood up. "Well, I have company, but I can talk."

Dante shifted on the sofa enough to adjust his jeans. He might need a few more moments before he could stand up.

"Yes, my company is a man," Eloise said to her sister, but winked in his direction. "And if you're calling to tell me you're coming to Bronco for Thanksgiving, then maybe you can meet him."

Pride rushed through him at the thought that Eloise was willing to introduce him to her family. Or at least one sibling. Maybe things were getting serious between them.

"Uh-oh," Eloise said next, frowning. "Tell me what happened."

It certainly wasn't any of Dante's business what was going down on the opposite end of the line, but if Eloise and her sister were anything like Camilla and Sofia, they would likely be on the phone for a while.

He stood, then grabbed his jacket off one of the side chairs.

"Hold on a sec, Char." Eloise covered the mouthpiece and whispered to Dante, "Are you leaving?"

He whispered back, "Yeah. You need to catch up with your sister. I'll see myself out."

She mouthed *Sorry*, then said, "Thanks for dinner. I get to pay next time."

"Maybe." Dante smiled, then, because he'd been thinking about it this long, he leaned forward and gave her a quick kiss on her lips. "We'll talk later."

He turned back for one last glance when he got to the

door and saw her touching her lower lip. Good. Hopefully, she would want more the next time they saw each other.

Because he didn't know how much longer he could go without kissing her again.

Chapter Nine

Eloise sat in her parked car for several minutes as she stared up at the massive log, river rock, and glass structure where she'd grown up. Or at least where she'd lived until being shipped off to boarding school. It wasn't as though her childhood was all bad, she told herself. She'd had plenty of good memories riding horses, swimming in the lake with her cousins and practicing for her ballet recital in the children's game room.

Cornelius, as the oldest Taylor brother had taken over the main house, while the remaining three brothers each chose their own corners of the ranch to build equally impressive homes. The Triple T was so large that the wives of the four patriarchs could often go weeks without running into each other.

When Thaddeus had hired the architect to design their home, Eloise's mother had wisely requested a separate area for her children to play, hang out or do homework.

As a child, Eloise had found it a wonderful reprieve from the demands of school and etiquette lessons and her disapproving father. Now that she was an adult, though, she realized that the room hadn't been built for the kids. It had been built for their father, who had always preferred the company of adults and hadn't wanted his offspring interrupting him.

Remembering how her dad had barely tolerated his own children, she couldn't help but compare him to someone like Dante, who'd not only chosen a profession that allowed him to work with kids, he also volunteered to spend more time with them after school.

Her phone pinged and a message from Charlotte popped on the screen. Are you going to sit out there all afternoon?

Eloise took a deep breath and steeled her spine before exiting the car. As she approached the imposing front doors, she paused, wondering if she should knock or just let herself in. How could a place feel like home while simultaneously making her feel like a guest? Luckily, her sister Allison opened the door before Eloise had to decide.

"Thank God you're here," Allison said before pulling Eloise into a tight hug. "Dad and Charlotte are already ignoring each other, Daniel and Seth won't stop looking at their phones, Ryan keeps slipping into the kitchen to see how much longer dinner is going to be and Mom is too busy trying to engage everyone in polite small talk that she can't even see how much underlying tension there is." She stepped back and swept Eloise with an assessing look. "Wow, are you sure you're pregnant? You look exactly the same."

"The obstetrician confirmed it again this week," Eloise joked before shrugging off her newer—and looser—coat and showing off her baby bump. "Have Mom or Dad brought it up yet?"

"To me? No. But I'm not sure they've even noticed I'm here. And I got into town yesterday." Allison was the shy sibling, the quiet one who often got overlooked in a house with five other children. There'd never been enough attention to go around, so Allison had buried herself in books and become somewhat of a loner. Of all the siblings, she was probably closest to Eloise. At least she had been until they were sent away to different boarding schools after Charlotte and her parents had a falling out.

"I'm glad you're here." Eloise took her sister's hand and squeezed it. "Seeing you and Charlotte is the only reason I came today."

"Is that Eloise?" Their mother met them in the entryway. "Allison, bring your sister into the living room to say hello to everyone."

Eloise always got a kick out of the fact that Imogen and Thaddeus referred to the spacious and well-decorated area as a *living* room. It was so formal and grand they only used it for the occasional large gathering. There were zero signs that any actual living took place inside of it. Not even a family photo.

"Look, everyone, Eloise is here."

"I think they can see that, Mom," Allison muttered, but nobody showed any sign of hearing her sister's sarcasm.

Charlotte was the first to greet her, her tight hug reminding Eloise of a drowning man holding onto a life preserver. "It took you forever," she whispered into Eloise's ear. "I've only been here an hour and I can't imagine staying the night. Can I catch a ride back to the hotel with you when you leave and get a room?"

"All the rooms are booked for the holiday weekend," Allison said. "I already checked."

Eloise squeezed her sisters' hands in a show of support. She felt bad they had to stay at the Taylor ranch and hadn't thought to book ahead. Hopefully, they'd at least had the foresight to rent a car. If not, they better hope someone like Dante was nearby and could give them a ride if they suddenly needed to get away from their parents.

Next, Daniel and Seth greeted her with less enthusiastic hugs—after all, they'd seen her more recently at the Taylor party at The Library—and a brotherly peck on the cheek. Ryan entered the room at that moment and gave her a more affectionate squeeze. "Perfect timing," he said. "Lina just finished in the kitchen and is setting the food out on the table now. Mom, I hope you don't mind, but I told her she could leave in a few minutes."

"Of course you did," their father said from his seat in one of the plush upholstered armchairs that dominated the room. "Because you're not the one paying her salary."

Thaddeus hadn't stood to greet Eloise, let alone give her a hug, but that was okay. She would rather they not pretend that he was the pillar of politeness. She was only surprised he hadn't shot her a snide look or made a condescending comment toward her, much like this one he aimed at Ryan.

"If I were paying her salary," Ryan said as he took a drink of what appeared to be whiskey, "I would've given her a raise a long time ago for having to put up with everything she does around here."

Whoa. Where did that come from? Eloise wasn't used to any of her siblings, let alone good-natured Ryan, firing right back at their dad. Eloise looked for Allison to confirm that she'd heard the same thing, but her sister was at the bar, pouring herself a glass of wine.

"El, would you like a drink?" Allison called over her shoulder.

The last person to call her El had been Dante, which made her wish he was here with her now.

"I'm having a lovely Pinot Noir, dear." Her mom claimed her wineglass from the coffee table. "But I could open a bottle of something else if you'd prefer."

"She can't have wine in her condition, Imogen," Thad said boldly, making Eloise wish she could, just to prove him wrong. Then her father glanced down at her stomach and added, "Unless you're trying to break *all* the rules. You seem to enjoy being careless."

Eloise squared her shoulders. This was the battle she'd been expecting and she was ready, but before she could open her mouth, Daniel said, "Give it a rest, Dad."

Eloise blinked in surprise. Here was another brother challenging her father. And he'd barely looked up from his phone screen as he did it.

"You once called me careless, too, Dad. As I recall," Charlotte added as she tapped her chin, "it didn't work out well for you."

"More like it didn't work out well for *you*," their father snapped back. "You could've done worse than marry into the Abernathy family."

"I'm very happy with my choices, Father. Especially because they were *my* choices and not the ones you tried to force on me."

"Shall we go into the dining room now?" Imogen

asked brightly. Their mother grabbed the opened bottle of wine as she led the way, accustomed to having guests follow behind her.

"What is going on with everyone?" Eloise whispered to Allison as they made their way to another formal room, where the long dining table was set with their mother's most expensive china plates and crystal goblets.

"I don't know, but it's weird to see anyone standing up to Dad, let alone most of his children."

"It's not that weird," Charlotte said from behind them. "It happens when sharks get a scent of blood in the water. They start circling around, waiting for the right time to make their attack."

"What are you girls talking about?" Imogen asked from the foot of the table, which was already laden with the matching platters and bowls of food, courtesy of Lina. When she was a child, Eloise had always thought the food appeared on the table as if by magic.

"Nothing," Eloise replied. She looked at her siblings and noticed the men were all standing at their chairs, well trained not to sit until the ladies took their seats.

She remembered Dante and Dylan both elbowing each other that day at the car dealership and wondered if the Sanchez brothers were ever this formal around *their* parents.

"Is this another new dining set, Mom?" Ryan asked, one hand on the back of his chair, the other holding a place card with his name written in calligraphy. Because, of course, their mother had gone all out for Thanksgiving dinner. "What was wrong with the last one?"

Ryan had mentioned that he lived on the ranch in

his own cabin, which wasn't actually a cabin but a two-thousand-square foot custom-built home. The fact that he was only now noticing the new table told Eloise that he wasn't attending many family dinners at the main house, either.

"You know your mother," Dad said. "She gets bored every few years and has to completely redecorate everything."

"Hey, Dad, have you ever asked yourself why Mom would be so bored?" Seth's smile was polite, but his tone was condescending. "Or if there was anything you could do at home to make her life more fulfilling?"

Their father narrowed his eyes, the wrinkles along his temples and brow making him appear older than his sixty-six years. "Are you suggesting that I'm not—"

"My life is very fulfilling. I simply like to decorate." Imogen had another gulp of wine, then took her seat. "Sit down, girls. Thad, would you like to say grace?"

Eloise was too in shock to bow her head or close her eyes as her father recited his standard blessing. She couldn't remember a time when Imogen had ever interrupted her husband before. Even when she was purposely trying to change the subject.

Soon the plates were passed, and the food was served and their mom was able to lead everyone through several polite comments about the weather. But then someone brought up interior decorating again.

"You know, Mom, one of the staff lounges at Taylor headquarters is being remodeled." Ryan paused to look at Eloise. "They're adding a nursing room for employees returning from maternity leave."

"Seems like a waste of space if you ask me," their dad replied as he helped himself to one of the turkey legs.

"Did someone ask you?" Charlotte asked a bit too sweetly.

"No, but if they *had*, I would tell them that—"

Seth interrupted by taking the bowl of mashed potatoes out of their father's hands mid-scoop. "The nursing room isn't really meant for you, Dad."

Their father frowned and snatched the bowl back. Imogen took another drink of wine. Eloise's eyes darted back and forth as though she were watching a tennis match. Maybe she *didn't* wish Dante were here with her after all. She could only imagine what he'd think of this mess.

Ryan continued. "Anyway, Mom, I was thinking that you could help pick out some furniture and wall art. Possibly give your opinion about a soothing color scheme. I figure you had six babies and might know what would be most comfortable for a nursing mother."

"How would she know?" Thad asked. "She bottle-fed you kids."

Several voices erupted at once and Eloise stopped watching and stared directly at the green beans on her plate, trying to tune out this argument before someone put her on the spot as the only pregnant woman who'd actually be dealing with newborn feedings soon. Even Allison appeared to be humming softly to herself to drown out the noise.

Unfortunately, Eloise still caught some of the argument. Something about their father not wanting their mom to breastfeed…something about the cost of formula…something about breast pumps…something about postpartum depression, which actually *did* make Eloise look up, but by then Imogen was asking everyone their opinion on Lina's new recipe for corn bread dressing.

"It tastes like her old recipe to me," Ryan said, his plate now empty and ready for a second serving. "Like I was saying, Mom. Let me know if you'd be interested in doing some interior decorating at the office. You'll be compensated, obviously."

"Not obviously," Thaddeus argued. "Your mother doesn't need to be paid like she's an employee."

"Why not? You get paid when you show up to the office," Daniel said.

"I'm sure he also gets paid when he *doesn't* show up," Allison suggested, having rejoined the conversation.

"I'm not an employee, though. I'm an owner." Their father's nostrils flared noticeably. "And she's my wife."

"Call me crazy," Charlotte said as she shrugged, "but if someone is doing a job or performing a service, like interior decorating, then they should be paid."

"I don't need to be paid," their mother said, then took a deep breath. "I'll stop by the office on Monday, Ryan, and you can show me the space so I can get some ideas."

"See?" Thaddeus nodded, seemingly oblivious to the fact that his wife had just outmaneuvered him. "Unlike some of the women in this family, your mother is perfectly content not having to do menial labor."

Allison raised her hand. "I don't do menial labor. Not that anyone's asked me about my job."

"If you ask me, the women in this family are the lucky ones." Seth rattled the ice in his cocktail glass as he looked at Allison. "I don't even know what you do for work, Ally, but it's got to be better than working in the family business. Having everyone thinking the only reason you're there is because of your last name. I wish I could've gone off like you three did and picked my own path."

Eloise, Charlotte and Allison all stared dumbfounded at their second oldest brother. She couldn't speak for her sisters, but Eloise had always been resentful that she'd been sent away. She'd also been too ashamed to bring it up to her brothers for fear of coming across as jealous. It was a bit shocking to realize the men in her family might have been feeling just as much resentment that they had been expected to stay put and follow in their father's footsteps.

Their mother broke the awkward silence. "Daniel, would you like more brussels sprouts?"

"No thank you. I didn't even want the ones I just ate."

"Which path would you have picked, Seth?" Eloise asked. It felt almost foreign to hear her own voice because she'd been so silent, watching her family implode in slow motion.

"I don't know. But I would've liked to at least have some choice in my career."

"You make it sound like I never gave you a choice." Their father wiped his mouth on his napkin. "Like I've been holding you hostage."

"Physically, no. Emotionally? Let's just say that you threatened to stop paying for my tuition and my health insurance if I so much as considered switching majors in college."

"You father loves you, dear. He would never cut you off."

Eloise sputtered at their mother's words, then started coughing. Allison passed her a glass of water and said, "In case you haven't noticed, Mom, Dad's cut off three out of six of his children so far. So, Seth's odds were fifty-fifty."

Their dad muttered a curse word and Imogen told her husband not to swear at the dinner table. Instead, he scowled. "I didn't cut you girls off. You were welcome to come home at any time. You still are."

"And live by your rules?" Charlotte shook her head. "I'm good."

"I always wanted to be a teacher," Daniel said to nobody in particular. "Like Dante Sanchez. I think I'd be pretty good at it."

Their mom scooped the brussels sprouts onto his plate anyway. "If you think about it, Daniel, you are a teacher of sorts."

"I'm the director of training and employee development at Taylor Beef, Mom. It's not quite as rewarding as shaping and challenging young minds. I heard Dante's really popular with his students."

Eloise's ears perked up at the opportunity to discuss something in her life—or at least some*one* in her life—but she wasn't quick enough.

"So now you hate your job, too?" their dad accused.

"I thought we were talking about different career paths and I'm just saying my current job is not the one I would've chosen for myself."

"You're a Taylor!" Thad pounded a fist on the table, causing the expensive dishes to rattle. "Our only paths are the ones bestowed upon us at birth."

"Did he just say bestowed?" Allison asked the room at large. "Like we're living in some sort of medieval dynasty."

"I think that was stamped on my birth certificate at the hospital when I was born," Ryan said with a wink.

"They must only do that for the male bloodline, though. Us girls are only good for marriages that keep us barefoot and in the kitchen."

"Don't be absurd, Charlotte." Imogen took another sip of wine. Had her mom always drunk this much at dinner? "We don't run around the house in our bare feet."

"I do." Allison raised her hand again. "But that's the beauty of living alone. I can do whatever I want."

"It's still unseemly for a lady, dear."

"Ladies are doing all sorts of unseemly things, nowadays, Mom. In fact, did you know that banks even allow women to open their own checking accounts?" Allison asked flippantly. "I'm pretty sure that was frowned upon when you got married."

"Why would your mother need her own checking account?" Their dad's face was now turning red. "This is the second time tonight that someone is suggesting I don't provide for my own wife."

"Technically, it's the third," Seth corrected.

"You provide for me very well, dear," Imogen said, before flashing a warning look at Eloise as though she were worried her daughter would mention the secret bank account. "Charlotte, did you try the potatoes? I had Lina use the soy milk like you requested."

Out of all the things said since Eloise arrived, this was the thing that got the vein in Thaddeus Taylor's forehead pulsing. He threw down his fork in disgust. "Our family has raised cattle for several generations now. What's wrong with regular cow milk?"

"Since when do you only do soy milk?" Eloise whispered behind her napkin.

"Since this morning when I wanted to get Dad all riled up," Charlotte whispered back.

"No wonder none of my daughters can settle down and get married." Their dad dropped his hands to his sides and looked up to the ornate gold leaf ceiling in defeat. His expression would've been comical if Thaddeus were the type of man to ever actually admit defeat. "You're all so picky, no man would want to deal with that."

"Or maybe the men we date just wouldn't want to deal with an overbearing and controlling father-in-law," Allison suggested with a sweet smile.

"To be fair, Dad, none of your children are married," Ryan pointed out. "So you shouldn't be holding the girls to a double standard."

"Speaking of marriage," Imogen said as she clapped her hands together, "I was talking to Mimi John the other day and one of her daughters is single and quite beautiful. Perhaps one of you boys would want to take her out?"

"Not me," Daniel said immediately. "For obvious reasons."

"What obvious reasons are those?" Thaddeus challenged.

"Because I'm gay, Dad. I only date men."

Thaddeus blinked. "Since when?"

Charlotte sighed. "He came out when he was twenty, Dad. Now that was a Thanksgiving dinner to remember."

Their father's expression softened as he tilted his head and studied his oldest son. "I thought that was just a college phase and you outgrew it."

Several voices around the table groaned in frustration, including Eloise's.

"I'm forty-two years old, and I've never brought a

woman home to meet you." Daniel's tone held a trace of animosity, and Eloise felt a pang of guilt for expecting more support from her siblings when she hadn't exactly been here to support them, either. "It clearly isn't something one simply outgrows."

Their father opened and closed his mouth several times, apparently at a rare loss for words. But his silence only lasted a few moments. "In my defense, it's not like you've brought any men home, either. Only your friend Greg from Accounting… Ohhh. Right. Then maybe Ryan or Seth might like the Johns' daughter. Their family is from good stock."

"We're not farm animals, Dad," Charlotte said through gritted teeth.

"Speaking of animals, Charlotte, tell us about being a marine biologist." Their mother really couldn't stand any sort of reminder of the past. "All that deep sea diving has been great for your figure. I hope you're using a quality sunscreen with a high SPF when you're out on the boats. My facialist recommended a brand that really helps with the premature aging of the skin."

"Sunscreen also helps with skin cancer, which I would think would be a bigger concern." Allison was the daughter who'd been most resistant to their mother's beauty recommendations.

"Does sunscreen attract sharks, though?" Daniel asked. "I heard sharks can smell scents from miles away."

"I think I'd rather suffer the premature aging over a shark attack," Seth added.

"That's because you're a man, Seth. Unlike me and Allison and Eloise, you weren't raised to value your appearance over everything else."

"I think Mom and Dad gave up on my appearance a while ago," Allison muttered.

"Enough," their father growled from the head of the table. "You kids can make your passive-aggressive comments about how your mother and I raised you all you want. But you will *not* do it at my dinner table."

The silence was almost deafening, with the exception of Ryan still scraping his fork across his plate to get the last bits of gravy. Eloise had no idea how he could eat at a time like this. She felt as though she were in some sort of parallel universe and everything she thought she'd known about her family had completely shifted off its axis.

Yep, she'd definitely made the right decision not to invite Dante to witness...whatever this was. But if there was ever a time she needed to look across a table and see his reassuring grin and his steady gaze, right this second would be it.

Finally, Seth asked, "Are you saying we should save our parenting critique until after dinner, then?"

"No. You should keep it to yourselves. It's not like you were abused or mistreated or lacked for anything monetarily. When you have your own children," her father said as he slowly pointed at each of her siblings, his finger landing on Eloise not so coincidentally, "then you can come talk to me about my failures as a parent. Until then, I suggest all of you hold off any criticism until you prove that you can do a better job than your mom and I did."

Everyone, even Ryan, stared at their father while nobody said a word. Her siblings were likely processing their own feelings and experiences with Thaddeus Taylor, but one thing they all probably shared was the knowledge that this was possibly the closest their father had ever come to admitting that he wasn't perfect.

"Speaking of having children of their own, Eloise, do you have any names picked out for the baby?"

Really? Her mother was going to just gloss over their father's revealing statement and choose this exact moment to draw attention to Eloise? Great.

Her throat went dry and she took a sip of water. "No, Mom. Not yet."

"You're due around Christmas, right?" Imogen asked. "I always wanted a Christmas baby."

"I gave you plenty of babies, Imogen," their father muttered. It was as though the volcano within him had already erupted and now he was just sputtering puffs of hot air.

"I know, dear. And it's so wonderful to have them all home with us for the holiday. I was just being fanciful. I've always been partial to themes, and if it's a Christmas baby, we could do the nursery in a winter wonderland motif with gold and silver and lots of fluffy white blankets. Maybe even give the baby a name honoring the season, like Noelle or Christopher."

"If Eloise wants the baby to have an honorable name," her dad replied slowly, and Eloise sat up straighter, ready to face his coming blow, "she should consider Harold after my dad or Delores after my grandmother."

Eloise slumped forward, her forehead landing in her hands. She'd been expecting him to say something about the illustrious Taylor name or even make a snide comment about the baby's father's name. Instead, he was sitting here talking about Harold and Delores?

"Dear, we don't put our elbows on the table," her mother tsked, and Eloise instinctively put her arms down.

"I thought you didn't like your Grandma Delores, Dad?" Daniel said.

"Who said I didn't like her?"

"You, Uncle Cornelius, Uncle Victor, Uncle Lester. Every year at the annual Taylor holiday party, you guys always complain about her."

"No, that was my Grandma Doris. On my mom's side. She was meaner than a one-eyed snake. My dad's mom, though, was a saint of a woman. Used to hand-knit us these beautiful matching sweaters every Christmas and bake us our own tiny fruitcakes without nuts, because Les once broke his tooth on an almond cookie."

"Wait." Allison tapped her finger on her crystal goblet. Eloise had never wanted a glass of wine more than she did right then. "Isn't Grandma Delores the one who Grandpa had committed to a mental health facility?"

"I believe it was called a sanatorium, dear," their mom said, downing enough Pinot for both herself and Eloise. "Lots of women used to go to those for some rest and relaxation."

"It certainly sounds more appealing than living on this ranch with the Taylor men," Charlotte murmured under her breath.

"Not all the Taylor men," Ryan said. "Will someone pass the rolls, please?"

Eloise's head was spinning, and she couldn't resist the need to get out of this dining room and go…anywhere but here.

She'd arrived this afternoon not knowing what to expect. She'd done the notepad thing again, where she was ready with a list of things she wanted to say along with answers to any potential questions. What she hadn't anticipated, though, was that she wasn't the only one who'd also chosen Thanksgiving to say whatever they'd been holding back.

She looked at the arched doorway leading back to the living room. Why did it seem farther away than ever? She'd expected to feel cornered tonight, to have all eyes on her and to have to fight off the judgmental attitudes and condescending remarks as though the walls were closing in on her. Instead, it was the opposite sensation of feeling trapped. The walls were all being knocked down and the doors thrown wide open and she hadn't been prepared for the tornado of dysfunction that she'd sheltered herself from for so long.

While she'd been gone, the entire Taylor family dynamic had shifted. They weren't little kids anymore trying to appease their domineering father, despite her mother's continued attempts to keep the peace. As frustrating as it was to watch Imogen enable her husband's tyrannical behavior all these years, it was also Eloise's normal. Her mom's impassioned speech two weeks ago in the hotel suite and whatever was going on today was most definitely *not* her normal.

Had Eloise been misreading the situation all these years? Or had she just been away at school and then off pursuing her career that she'd never considered what was going on at the ranch when she wasn't there? It was all too much, and, like a child, she lifted her hand and said, "May I be excused?"

Catching the slip and determined to prove that she wasn't actually asking permission, Eloise scooted her chair away from the table and headed to the powder room down the hall. She grabbed her purse on the way and pulled out her cell phone.

There was a text notification and when she opened it, she saw that Dante had sent her a picture of a pumpkin pie. The crust was browner on one side and the filling looked off-center. In the message he wrote, See? It didn't turn out that bad. Once I put the whipped cream on, it'll even things out. Crap. I just realized I forgot to buy whipped cream. I'm sure it'll still taste great. Stop by for dessert if you want to try some.

Immediately, Eloise's heart felt lighter than it had the past hour. *This* was her normal. Well, maybe not quite her normal, but it was her right now. She wanted to kiss the man for making her feel more like herself again. In fact, she did just that. Eloise pressed her lips to the phone screen where Dante's contact picture was and then almost dropped her phone in the sink when she realized she'd accidentally kissed the call button.

"Hello?" Dante answered on the second ring. The noise in the background was loud and chaotic and... happy.

"Hey," she said. "I hope I'm not interrupting your dinner."

"No, we haven't even started eating yet. It's a long story, but my parents' oven is having a hard time keeping up with this many people. Camilla was hoping to surprise them with a new double oven, but it's on backorder. We're trying to pace ourselves with some appetizers, but Dylan is hogging the whole tray."

"I heard that," a voice that sounded like Dylan's yelled in the background. "Is that Eloise? Ask her if she can bring some chips and dip when she comes. I don't think I can wait another hour for dinner."

Eloise smiled, almost touched that Dante's brother all but expected her to join their family.

"Here, give me the phone," a woman said, and Eloise heard some muffled sounds that almost reminded her of a wrestling match. "Hi, Eloise, it's Sofia. We do *not* need you to bring chips and dip. We have plenty, we're just hiding them from Dylan so he doesn't ruin his appetite. However, if you guys have an extra can or two of whipped cream, you might want to bring them. Dante's pies look like they could use an extra layer of… something."

More wrestling sounded and Dante was back on the line. "Hey, it's me again. I'm sorry my family is being super obnoxious."

"Don't apologize. It already sounds way better than how my family is acting right now."

She expected him to ask her what was going on. Instead, her phone pinged and all he said was, "Come over."

"Come over where?" she asked, but the line had already disconnected. When she looked down at her screen, she saw the alert was a dropped map pin showing his parents' address.

Was he seriously expecting her to just show up?

Was she seriously considering it?

When she walked out of the restroom, she heard the front door slam—a big no-no in the Taylor household—and realized that if one of her siblings had already stormed off, she certainly wasn't about to stay here and be the last. Eloise crept down the hall to the kitchen, which had also been renovated since her last visit. She found a pint of heavy cream inside the fridge and two bottles of Sauvignon Blanc in the wine cellar, then let herself out the back door.

Chapter Ten

Thanksgiving with the Sanchezes could not have been more different from any holiday Eloise had ever shared with the Taylors. The living room, for example, actually looked lived in. And the dining room table looked like it held too many memories to simply be discarded when the mood to redecorate struck every couple of years. In fact, there was an additional mismatched table added to the end and several folding chairs to provide enough seating. The noise level was high and the football game was on the TV, causing some playful arguments and a few light shoves, as everyone moved back and forth between the open spaces. The most different thing of all, though, was that the small kitchen was crowded with love.

"Here, Eloise," Dante's mom said as she pushed an electric hand mixer her way. "You can use this to whip the cream."

"Thanks, Mrs. Sanchez."

"Call me Denise." The friendly woman smiled as she passed her a bowl. "Aaron picked up the spray cans of whipped cream at the store last week, but apparently *one* of my children—I won't name names—borrowed them from my fridge because he'd promised his class they could play that pie-in-the-face game."

"I was going to replace it, Mom," Dante said. "But it was a busy week and it slipped my mind."

"Now that it's halftime," Denise said as she pushed a wire masher at her son, "you can do the potatoes."

"Why don't you tell Mom and Dad why you've been so busy lately?" Dylan challenged his brother, then winked at Eloise.

Dante shrugged. "I've been working on that after-school rec league."

"And making the rounds on Bronco's restaurant scene," Sofia chimed in from where she was stirring something over the stove. "Camilla said you guys have been to The Library twice already and to LuLu's at least three times."

"Actually, I'm helping LuLu with a marketing project so one of those times was just me on my own." Eloise struggled to shove the beaters into the electric mixer. Every time she thought they were locked in, they fell out. She held one up. "Am I doing this wrong?"

"Here," Dante said from behind her. He set down his own masher and reached his arms around either side of her. Her back pressed against the front of him and his chin was directly over her shoulder as he took his time with the small appliance.

Whew. This kitchen was certainly getting hot. And all the eyes in the room seemed to be focused in their direction.

"Sorry," Eloise said, hoping her cheeks weren't as red as they felt. "I'm not very handy when it comes to cooking."

"We'll teach you," Camilla said as she came in from what looked to be an enclosed back porch/laundry room conversion carrying a roasting pan with the biggest turkey Eloise had ever seen. "Mom, the electric oven is officially retiring after this year. There's nowhere to put it inside and we can't keep plugging it in out there with the clothesline full of Dad's referee jerseys and all of Dante's old hockey equipment."

"I don't think you mentioned hockey as one of your preferred sports," Eloise said over her shoulder to Dante since he was still standing so closely behind her.

"That's because *I* was the hockey star of the family," Felix announced as he came into the kitchen. Eloise had already met his fiancée, Shari, who jumped in to scoop the stuffing out of the perfectly roasted turkey. "That gear is actually mine. I loaned it to Dante, and he left it here. But Camilla's right, Mom. The family is growing and, at this rate, it's going to take more than a double oven to get all the food on the table. You're going to need a lot more counter space."

"I thought we were waiting until dinner to tell them," Dylan said, causing at least three people to shush him.

"Tell us what?" Denise and Aaron Sanchez asked in unison.

"We *were* waiting to tell them." Camilla threw a pot holder at Dylan. "But since we're all crammed in here together, we might as well make our big announcement."

"Camilla's pregnant?" A much older man asked the question as he squeezed into the kitchen. There was an equally older woman with him wearing a long flowy skirt and a bright purple sweater. Eloise hadn't met her, but recognized the woman as Winona Cobbs, the psychic who'd opened a shop in Bronco a couple years ago.

"No, Uncle Stanley," Camilla said kindly. "But I promise you'll be the first to know when I decide to have kids."

Jordan raised his hand. "Actually, *I'd* like to be the first to know. Because I'm ready to get started."

"Eww," the younger Sanchez men said at once and Eloise smothered a giggle.

"I didn't say right this second." Jordan returned Dylan's playful shove. "I just meant that I was ready for kids."

Eloise studied her cousin, who was so much different than she remembered him. So much more relaxed and lighthearted. Or maybe the Sanchez family had just been a good influence on him. She loved the way this entire family interacted. This was what Eloise wanted for her own child. And even for her own siblings and parents if they could ever get past all the resentment. At least her brothers and sisters had developed the ability to say whatever was on their minds. Now that Eloise had some distance from what had happened earlier at the Taylor house, she had to admit that some of their smart aleck comments had been fairly witty—and definitely deserved. Maybe there was some hope for them.

"You boys save that roughhousing for the court," Aaron Sanchez warned his son and son-in-law.

"The court?" Eloise repeated out the side of her mouth so only Dante could hear.

"It's a tradition to shoot some hoops in the backyard after family dinners," Dante whispered back.

"Can we get back to whatever this big announcement is?" Denise asked as she stood beside Sofia at the stove, stirring the gravy.

"Mom, Dad," Camilla started, causing everyone to stop what they were doing and share knowing grins at each other. "All of us kids have come together and decided that for Christmas this year, we're getting you a combined gift."

"It's not another cruise, is it?" Their dad's face seemed to have lost some of its color. "Because those seasick patches didn't do anything for me last time."

"No, it's not a cruise, Dad," Camila said.

"It's a new kitchen," Felix announced.

Chaos broke out in the room. Felix and Dylan began arguing about who should have been the one to make the announcement. Sofia and Shari began talking about cabinet colors. Camilla and Boone were discussing the commercial-grade appliances recently installed in the bunkhouse kitchen at Dalton's Grange, Boone's family's ranch. Mr. Sanchez was asking Jordan how much all of this was going to cost. Yet, it was Dante who immediately left Eloise and went directly to his mom. Denise was standing motionless, a wooden spoon dripping gravy on the linoleum floor.

Dante tuned off the stove burner and wrapped his smaller mother in an enormous hug. "Mom, why are you crying?"

"Because I don't want a new kitchen. I want this one. I have so many memories in here with all of you."

Everyone quieted as they realized that the matriarch of the family didn't seem to be as excited as they were.

"You'll still have those memories, Mom," Dante said. "Nothing will ever replace them."

"I hope we didn't upset you, Mom." Camilla came over next, followed by their other siblings.

"We just thought you'd like something bigger," Felix offered.

"I know. I know you kids all meant well." Denise used the corner of her apron to wipe a tear from her eye. "It's a very thoughtful and generous gift. It just caught me by surprise."

The oven timer went off and Aaron clapped his hands together. "Okay, everyone, it's showtime. Let's get all the food to the table and then we can talk about it more when we have something in our bellies."

If it was any more possible for thirteen people to cause a flurry of activity, the Sanchez family achieved it. Within five minutes, they were all sitting around the mismatched tables and Uncle Stanley was saying grace. It was adorable the way he mentioned everyone's name at the table individually—unlike her own father who'd rushed through a generic blessing—and then ended by stating his gratitude that the Lord had seen fit to bring the wonderful Winona into his life.

When all the plates had been passed around and elbows kept bumping into arms, Denise sighed and admitted that maybe they could use a little more room in the kitchen.

"But when all of you are gone during the week and it's just me and Dad, it'll feel so big and empty. Eloise, since this is your first time here with us—and I hope it won't be your last—I'd like to hear your thoughts." Denise's expression was difficult to read. Especially since Eloise didn't know her very well. "Do you think I should let my well-meaning children tear up my kitchen?"

She felt Dante's reassuring hand on her leg under

the table. See, this is what she had been missing at her own family's Thanksgiving meal. She'd been missing that secure feeling anytime he was nearby. She'd been missing him.

A slight nod of his head suggested that she share her opinion. Not that she really had a right to one. But since all the siblings seemed to be on one side of the argument with the parents on the other, maybe they were hoping she could be a mediator of sorts. Or at least cast the deciding vote. She took a fortifying breath.

"The first thing I noticed about this kitchen when I walked inside, Mrs. Sanchez—" Eloise immediately corrected herself when Dante's mom gave her a stern look "—I mean Denise, is that it was full of love."

"See?" Denise nodded. "You get it."

"I'm not much of a cook and I'm definitely no expert when it comes to making meals," Eloise continued quickly, not wanting the siblings to think she was taking sides. "But if you really want to know my opinion, it's not the room that provides that kind of love. I've lived in homes with huge elaborate kitchens that were only used for catered parties, and in tiny studio apartments with kitchenettes that could barely accommodate an electric teakettle and a cup of ramen. I've lived in magazine-cover kitchens and kitchens where my roommate left her dishes in the sink for two straight months. Yet, I've learned in the past hour that it doesn't matter a single bit what a kitchen looks like or what kind of meals come out of it if it's not filled with people and laughter. And this space is always going to be filled with so much love whether you remodel it or not."

Dante squeezed Eloise's knee and Denise used her

orange cloth napkin to wipe her eyes. Aaron raised his wineglass in a toast. "Well said!"

Glassware clinked and Eloise sat back in her chair in relief, feeling as though she'd just passed a pop quiz she hadn't studied for.

"That was perfect," Dante whispered, his warm lips brushing against her ear. "You're perfect."

Heat crept up the back of Eloise's neck and desire curled around her heart.

"This space is also going to be filled with lots of new grandbabies soon." Winona's bracelets jingled as she held up her drink again. "So, here's to the next generation giving you lots of new memories."

Everyone turned their face toward the psychic, except for Shari and Sofia who were shooting warning looks across the table at each other. Eloise made a mental note to find out if she wasn't the only one at this table expecting.

It was Uncle Stanley that finally broke the confused silence and said, "Eloise, I understand you're Jordan's cousin?"

"Yes. His father and my father are brothers."

"I bet your dad is excited to become a grandpa soon," Stanley said before Winona could shush him. The table remained silent.

As Eloise was debating how much to explain, Dante quickly interjected. "Thaddeus Taylor is a little old-fashioned, Uncle Stanley. He was hoping Eloise would be married first."

"That's not old-fashioned, Dante. That's just plain…" His uncle looked at Aaron. *"Como se dice arcaico?"*

"Archaic," Aaron said around a mouthful of turkey.

"Yes. Archaic. I've got at least two decades on the

man and even *I* know that babies sometimes come before the wedding. But if it's such a big deal, then why don't you two just get married already?"

Eloise held her breath, not wanting to hear Dante's answer. Or her own. She wasn't ready for either of them to be put on the spot like that.

"Because Felix doesn't want me or Dylan to upstage him before his big day." Dante brought his hand up from under the table and laid his arm across the back of Eloise's chair. Almost possessively. Then he looked down the table and asked his brother and Shari, "How's the wedding planning going, you guys?"

Before either could answer, Winona pointed an age-spotted finger at Eloise and Dante. "This magnetic attraction pulling you toward each other isn't going to wait for anyone anymore. In fact, if Thaddeus and Imogen hadn't sent you away in high school, Eloise, you and Dante would've had several kids by now instead of just this one."

Nobody corrected the psychic about Dante being the father of the baby. Not even Eloise. Partially because she was in shock by the *magnetic attraction* comment and partially because Winona Cobbs didn't seem like the type of woman who was ever proven incorrect.

Felix and Shari—and most everyone else—seemed to forget what they were going to say, as well.

Dylan, bless his heart, jumped in for the rescue. "Since we're on the subject of predicting the future, Ms. Cobbs, do you have any insight about my new ranch?"

"If you want a reading, son, you'll have to stop by my shop. Like all my other paying customers do."

"What new ranch?" Aaron narrowed his eyes.

"Yeah. So that was going to be my big announcement after dinner." Dylan placed his palms on either side of his empty plate. "But now that we already got the kitchen remodel announcement out of the way, I guess it's my turn. I bought a new ranch."

"More like he traded a brand new truck for an old very run-down ranch," Dante muttered.

Everyone suddenly found their voices again—all at the same time—and Eloise missed half of what was being said. She was too busy contemplating Winona Cobbs's words. Had the older woman suggested that Eloise and Dante were somehow fated to be together and it was only circumstances that had kept them apart until now?

No. It was one thing to hope for love, but it was a whole other level to believe in having only one soulmate. She wasn't one for fortune tellers or palm readers and had never considered consulting a psychic. It wasn't that she was a skeptic, but Eloise liked to think she was in control of her own destiny.

So then why was she suddenly feeling as though she had absolutely zero control when it came to her fate? Even the tight bun she'd twisted her hair into so that she'd appear polished and poised felt like it was about to topple over.

"Hey." Dante leaned close to her ear again, his arm still across the back of her chair. His hand lightly stroked her shoulder, and she couldn't help but lean into his comforting touch. "You look overwhelmed. Is my family too much for you?"

Eloise was definitely overwhelmed, but it wasn't because of the Sanchezes. It was because of everything else today that had led up to this exact moment. She shook her head, but he must've felt the tension in her shoulders.

"Why don't we take a walk after dinner?" Dante suggested. "Maybe get some fresh air?"

Eloise tapped her feet under the table as her pulse kept speeding up and slowing down. If she could go for a nice long run right now, that would clear her head. But a walk would be the next best thing.

"What about your pumpkin pie?" she whispered.

"It can wait." He tucked a strand of her hair behind her ear, and her heart stopped spinning out of control. When he looked at her like that, the whole world stopped spinning. "Everything can wait."

"Are you cold?" Dante asked Eloise as they started out on the sidewalk in front of his parents' house. She was dressed in one of her fancy dresses with the boots he loved exposing only her knees. The tailored cashmere coat was a new addition to her wardrobe, but he'd been in such a rush to get her away from all the noise, they hadn't brought gloves or scarves.

"No, but I feel guilty not helping your dad with the dishes."

"Please don't. That's his thing. After big meals, he sends everyone out so he can have his *quiet time*." Dante used air quotes, then took one of Eloise's hands in his own. Her fingers were long and slender and curled around his. "He says nobody ever loads the dishwasher right. I don't know how the man does it, but he will get every last plate and serving spoon in that thing like he's playing Tetris."

"I doubt my father would even know how to turn the dishwashers on."

"Dishwashers? Plural?" Dante asked.

"There's a backup one in the prep kitchen. It only gets used when my parents have big dinner parties and hire a catering staff."

It was another reminder of how different their backgrounds were. Dante's parents could barely fit another person in their modest kitchen, let alone another dishwasher and a team of caterers. But listening to Eloise talk about the types of kitchens she'd had in the past and the lack of love in them, there was no way Dante would trade the Sanchez family home for the Taylors'.

"Speaking of dinner parties, what happened earlier on the Triple T?" As he spoke, he wrapped Eloise's hand in his to warm her icy fingers.

"Well, it wasn't dinner, since my father insists on eating at three o'clock on holidays." Eloise switched sides with him as they walked and offered her other hand to be warmed. "And it definitely wasn't a party."

"That bad, huh? Did anyone at least stand up to him?"

"That's the wild thing. *Everyone* was standing up to him. In fact, they were all so busy calling him out for their own grievances, I barely had a chance to say a word. I was also too busy coming to the realization that all this time, my siblings and I had all been in the same boat. Or at least in our own boats fighting the same tide."

"Did you take your list with you?" Dante asked.

"I did. But I didn't even get the chance to use it."

"That's good, right? It means he didn't have a chance to say anything negative about the baby." Dante paused, unsure if mentioning his next thought might make him seem desperate for info about what the rest of her family knew about him. Then he decided he might as well put it out there. "Or about you dating me."

"Your name actually did come up," Eloise said.

Dante stopped walking. "It did? Did you give them the brochure like I suggested?"

"No. Nor will I ever have any made." Eloise tugged on his hand to get him to resume his pace. "My brother Daniel mentioned your job when he told everyone he'd always wanted to be a teacher. It led to this unexpected conversation about careers and apparently some deep-seated resentments that my brothers were all expected to work in the family business. I'd been so determined to prove myself to my parents, it never dawned on me that my siblings would've wanted to do what I did. Does that make me self-centered?"

This time, it was Eloise who stopped walking and stared off in the distance. Light snow flurries began falling from the sky, the glow of the streetlights making it look like bright confetti surrounding her.

Dante lifted her chin until their eyes met. "You are one of the least self-centered people I know, Eloise Taylor. I've seen you interact with the women and the girls in this town and how motivated you are to do for them what nobody ever did for you. I've watched some of your commercials online and looked at some of your marketing campaigns and the reason they're all so amazing is because you get people. You're empathetic and you know what sells because you know what people want. What you said to my mom back there about the kitchen remodel? Everyone was holding their breaths and Jordan was getting ready to kiss his deposit to the contractor goodbye. The last thing I expected was for my mom to change her mind. Yet, you knew how to speak from your heart and say the exact right thing at the right time. So maybe you had no idea what your siblings were going through, but how could you? Were any of you ever allowed to speak your minds or be yourselves?"

"Not really. Not before I moved out, at least." Her thick lashes blinked up at him and he dusted a small snowflake from the corner of her eyelid.

Man, she was stunning. But there was so much more to her than the woman who'd made him do a double take the first night she'd walked into that party at The Library. His chest filled with wonder at her ability to connect with people. And with him. "You are an amazing woman, Eloise, and you're going to be an amazing mother."

"Sometimes I'm not so sure. Back there with your family, I was watching all of you and I couldn't stop thinking *this is what I want for my child. This is how I want to raise them.* But what if I can't do it? What if I default to my own upbringing because it's all I know and I end up becoming more like my own parents? Like a cycle I can't get out of?"

Dante pulled her hand up to his neck, then wrapped his own arms around her waist, tugging her in for a hug. He wanted to comfort her, yet he was the one who was comforted by holding her this close. "Then we make sure you don't."

"*We*, Dante?" She put a finger to his lips when he opened his mouth to insist. "Please don't make promises you can't keep."

"I always keep my promises," he protested.

Eloise's finger lowered to his chin and then traced his jaw. "I'm sure you do. Which is why I'm asking you not to make any promises at all. It's enough to know that you're in my corner for now."

"I'll always want to be in your corner," he said. "But if you keep touching my face like that, I'm going to want to be in your bed as well."

Using her other hand, which was still wrapped around his neck, she pulled his head to hers and opened her mouth to his.

With the snow and the moonlight surrounding them, the kiss was the most romantic thing Dante had ever experienced. And he was a guy who didn't do romance. Kissing her, outside like this in the neighborhood where he'd grown up, his life finally felt as though he'd come full circle. He wanted to hold her to him and experience the joy of being in the place he loved most with the woman he—

Eloise was the first to pull back, the desire in her expression making him forget all rational thought.

"I want you in my bed, too, Dante," she said, her chest rising and falling under her coat. "I've tried not to, but all the smiles and the sexy looks and the dinners together have only made it worse. The other night when you were at the hotel, before my sister called, I was trying to think of a way of asking you to stay."

Dante groaned at the missed opportunity. "I really wish you would have. The only reason I've been trying to hold myself back is because I'm not sure we could with…in your condition."

"I assure you that we can," she said, then, to prove it, she kissed him again. This time deeper and more thoroughly, holding nothing back until he couldn't even think of where they were.

Dante was all but panting as he broke away and

trailed small kisses along her cheek. "Come back to my apartment with me. Tonight. Dylan said he was staying out on his ranch, so he won't be there."

"Really?" Eloise was also gasping in small breaths, equally as affected by their kissing. "There were so many people talking during that conversation, how were you even able to pay attention to all of that?"

"Lots of practice. And because I've been waiting for him to go out of town so I could invite you over to stay the night. People are less likely to see us there than at your hotel."

Eloise pulled back slightly, studying his face. "They might see me at your apartment, too."

"Then we'll deal with that if it happens."

"Do we need to go inside and say goodbye to your family first? Because they might guess what we were doing out here."

He almost told her that his family wouldn't have to guess. They probably had no doubt why Dante and Eloise had been gone this long. But despite her claims of not caring what her own family thought about her, Eloise was respectful enough to care what *his* family thought. Except he didn't want her thinking about anything but them being together.

"No. I'll text them and say something came up. Come on, I'll drive."

Chapter Eleven

Dante's apartment was surprisingly clean. That was Eloise's first thought when he held open the door for her. Her second thought was how far away was his bedroom? They'd already determined that they didn't need to stop for condoms, since they'd both been tested and she couldn't get any more pregnant than she already was. She'd kept herself from climbing over the console in his car when they'd started making out again after he'd parked. Now she knew she couldn't wait much longer.

Neither could he, apparently. Dante had his lips on hers as soon as he closed the front door. He was walking her backward while yanking off his jacket. Eloise immediately did the same. Her coat came off somewhere in the hallway, and the back of her dress was already unzipped as he steered her into his bedroom.

She knew how she must have appeared to him, her

body rounded with her pregnancy, her functional bra and underwear not the least bit alluring. However, Eloise didn't care. She wasn't thinking about anything but the ache between her legs and how soon she could feel Dante there.

A button popped off and she heard the fabric rip in her haste to peel his shirt from him. Her dress fell to the floor at the exact same time his belt unbuckled. Stepping out of the pooled material, she was finally able to take in the sight of his bare chest and his chiseled abs. And what a sight it was. Eloise almost asked for a moment just so she could stare at him and get her fill. Almost.

Dante's hands stilled on the fly of his jeans as he returned her stare. His eyes filled with heat. "Those knee high boots you keep wearing are going to be the death of me."

"You want me to keep them on?" Her voice sounded husky and foreign to her own ears, but it hardly mattered. As she slowly undid her bra and eased down her panties, the fire inside her made her skin feel as though it were glowing. There was something unapologetically bold about the way Dante watched her that heightened all of Eloise's senses. That made her feel as though she were the sexiest woman alive.

She didn't think about the fact that her own stomach wasn't as flat as his or that her breasts were fuller and heavier than they'd ever been. She didn't think at all. When Dante eased her onto the bed and spread her legs before him, when he lowered his head to the core of her heat and took her into his mouth, all Eloise could do was twist her fingers into the bedding and moan in appreciation as he brought her to new heights.

She was still shuddering from the waves of pleasure when he deftly lifted his head and slid his hands down to the zipper of her left boot and then her right. When he'd shucked them, he eased her legs together and lifted one of her hips until she was angled on her side. Dante settled his own body behind her, his mouth now on her nape and his fingers stroking the same area he'd just so thoroughly loved.

His shaft was hard against the back of her upper thighs, and she rocked her hips against his, needing to feel more of him.

"Are you sure it's okay?" he asked, his voice low and deep.

"Please," she gasped.

He groaned as he entered her from behind. "Eloise. I'm going to try to go slowly. But you feel so perfect and I've been thinking about doing this for so long."

She arched her neck, moaning as his thumb brushed against her sensitive nub while he slid his length out and then back in.

Her second orgasm was longer and harder than the first. When he shouted out her name with his own release, Eloise's only thought was that they should have done this much, much sooner.

The fact that she'd forgotten her purse and left her car parked in another neighborhood never crossed her mind before she drifted off to sleep in Dante's arms.

"El," Dante said as he stroked her bare hip under the tangled sheets the following morning. "I'm starting to have some regrets."

"Already?" She shifted, taking the covers with her. The hurt was evident on her face.

"No! Not those kinds of regrets. Hell, woman, I don't think I can ever regret the sight of you in those boots lying on my bed—" Her hand flew to his mouth before he could reminisce about his favorite part of last night's lovemaking. He nipped at her palm until she lowered it. "What I *should've* said was that I wish we would've been thinking ahead and brought the pie home with us last night."

He saw tears gathering in the corner of her eyes and his heart dropped. "Don't cry. I can drive over right now and pick it up. Hell, I'll even run to the store and get the ingredients to make you a new one."

"I'm not crying," she said, obviously crying. "I just sometimes get emotional with all the hormones. I'm pretty sure I mentioned it the night we met when I was going on and on about all the embarrassing side effects of my pregnancy. I do this every morning. It's like drinking a coffee but without the benefit of caffeine."

The pounding in his heart slowed. "So, it's not because I said I had regrets?"

"No." She wiped some of the dampness with the back of her hand.

"And it's not the pie?"

"It's definitely not the pie. Although, I wouldn't say no to some breakfast."

"Wait, you're not crying because *you're* having regrets, are you?"

"Stop accusing me of crying." Eloise sat up, tears clearly streaming down her cheeks "This is nothing compared to how I get when I see those videos of soldiers coming home from deployment to surprise their loved ones. It's just all the extra hormones from my pregnancy leaving my body at once so that I can get started with the rest of my day. It's probably totally normal, or at least normal for me."

"Are you sure?" He studied her, not completely convinced.

"I promise that it's not you or the pie. Or the fact that I'm going to have to do the walk of shame this morning to get my purse and my car at your parents' house." She fell back on the pillows and pulled the covers over her head, muffling the sound of her voice. "I can't believe I didn't think about at least taking my keys and my phone with me when we left."

Unexplainable hormones weren't Dante's specialty but give him a concrete task to perform and he could spring into action. "I'll run over and grab your purse. My parents usually go door-busting for Black Friday sales, so they're probably not even home. You want me to grab some food on my way back?"

She pulled the sheet off her head long enough to say, "Maybe a muffin from Bean & Biscotti if it's not out of the way? And a decaf latte, please." Then she immediately buried her face again.

Once Dante stood up to pull on his jeans, though, he noticed she'd lowered the bedding just enough to peek at him. He smiled and made sure she got a good view before giving her a kiss goodbye.

When he returned about thirty minutes later, he saw Eloise coming down the hallway toward the kitchen. Her hair was wrapped in a towel and she was wearing his T-shirt that said Montana State Rugby. She looked so at home in his place he almost asked her to move in with him right then and there.

Slow down, man. You can't invite her to shack up with you—and your brother—just because she looks hot in your old college gear. You've got to offer her more than that.

Instead of saying what he was thinking, he held up a cardboard drink holder in one hand and her purse in the other. "The day has been saved."

"My hero." She smiled, but her eyes were slightly puffy. He hoped it wasn't from more crying after he left. Dante knew how to deal with tears in the classroom but not tears in the bedroom. That alone should tell him that maybe he wasn't ready for anything serious like moving in together. No matter how right this felt.

She reached for the drink first and moaned as she took a long sip. When he set her purse on the counter, she asked, "Did your parents say anything to you about us not coming back last night?"

He knew this question would be coming and, on the drive home, he'd tried to think of how he was going to answer. He started with a simple but truthful response. "No. They weren't there."

"But...?" she asked.

"How did you know there was a *but*?"

"Because your pupils looked up to the left. You always do that when you're trying to come up with a diplomatic answer. My mom does the same thing."

"Are you comparing me to Imogen Taylor?"

"Only in that regard. And really, you're no comparison. She's had a lot more practice than you, so her tell is less noticeable."

Dante lifted one brow. "I'm not sure how that went from a possible insult to a potential compliment to a full-blown diss. But now I want to go look in the mirror and practice my poker face."

"You're not escaping that easily." Eloise raised up

on her tiptoes and gave him a peck on the cheek, preventing him from leaving the room or the conversation. "So what's the *but*?"

Dante exhaled deeply. "My parents left a sticky note on your purse."

"Where is it?" She scanned the bag.

"It fell off when I was trying to balance your muffin and the coffees." He pulled the crumpled note out of his pocket. "Are you sure you want to see it?"

"Yes." She extended her hand.

"Do you promise you won't cry again?"

"No," she said, using her fingers to make the give-it-here motion.

He passed it over, grimacing with one eye closed as he watched her read it.

"'Eloise, it was nice to finally meet you,'" she read aloud. "'It's Dante's turn to cook dinner on Sunday but don't feel like you have to help him. He's a big boy and can do it himself. Aaron and Denise.'"

She looked up to Dante. "Why is this a bad thing?"

"Because they're assuming you're coming to dinner on Sunday, and I wasn't sure if you'd want to go."

"Either way, I think it's very nice that they invited me."

He tilted his head. "You know that it means they think we're official now, right?"

"Official what?"

"Officially dating."

"Oh. But didn't you tell them we were just friends?"

Was she serious? Did she really think anyone was going to buy that anymore? Was *she* buying it? "Eloise, I've never brought a woman home for Sunday dinner, let alone for Thanksgiving. They know things with you are...special."

"Hmm," she said, not giving a real response as she set the note down and pulled her cell phone from her purse. She seemed to be scanning her missed notifications, not bothering to look at him when she finally added, "But that's just for right now. Everything will change when the baby gets here."

Dante's throat constricted. Even though he'd thought the same thing when they'd initially started dating, he didn't like the way that sounded coming from her. He didn't like it one bit. Which was why he reached into his back pocket and pulled out the folded ad. "In that case, you should know that they left you another note. On this."

He handed her the circular for a chain department store. The page advertising baby goods was folded down at one corner and the note attached read, *Lots of good Black Friday deals on baby gear. You and Dante should swing by for some shopping and then we can grab lunch.*

"Oh, boy," Eloise said when she read it.

"Yep." Dante rocked back on his heels. "I had a feeling you might say that."

"That thing that Winona said last night…" Eloise started.

"Which thing?" Dante asked. Uncle Stanley's girlfriend was prone to making offhanded comments that took everyone aback. It really could've been a number of things.

"About this being *our* baby. Nobody really corrected her. Do your parents think…" Eloise trailed off.

Dante's ears began ringing, like his brain was sending out a warning. He didn't know why, but suddenly, he didn't want to hear her say that it wasn't his baby.

Nor did he want to admit it aloud. It was obviously the truth, but he didn't think it would do anyone—especially him—any good to hear the actual words right now. "The only thing my parents think is that nobody should pay full price for something. And before you bring up how successful you are with your own money, you should know that they also keep Jordan updated whenever his favorite tea tree shampoo goes on sale at my mom's salon."

Eloise's cell phone buzzed in her free hand. She dropped the store ad on the counter. "Sorry. Charlotte just sent me a text. Let me read it really quick."

To occupy himself, Dante started thumbing through the ad.

Eloise sighed. "It looks like she and Allison are already on their way to the airport. They lasted longer over there than I did, but I guess we're not doing brunch anymore."

Dante held up the circular. "Maybe we should hit this sale, then. There are some pretty good deals in here. Fifty percent off a Diaper Genie. I don't know what that is, but we might as well go look at them."

"Did you say *fifty* percent off?" Eloise asked, then stepped closer to Dante to look with him. "How far away is that store?"

"About sixty miles. We probably won't see anyone we know if that's what you're worried about."

She patted her stomach. "I'm not the one people would be surprised to see shopping in the baby aisle."

Dante wasn't sure if it was a challenge or a warning, but he wasn't as concerned about the gossip as he had been the first time they'd been seen together. In truth, it wasn't like they were hiding anything at this point.

"Well, nobody's going to be surprised to see *me* in the sporting goods aisle. So, we might as well get two shopping carts while we're there."

It turned out they only needed one shopping cart. And it was mostly for the new basketballs Dante was buying for his rec league. They stood in the baby department for what seemed like hours, but Eloise was too overwhelmed to decide on anything.

"How am I supposed to know which pacifier to get? There's a million of them."

"This one looks cool." Dante picked up a green one with a soccer ball on it.

A dad wearing a baby strapped to his chest reached for a neon orange one and handed it to Dante. "My little guy likes this brand better. And the brighter the pacifier, the easier it is to find when they lose it in their crib in the middle of the night."

The man added a couple to his own cart, then continued on. He wasn't the first parent who'd offered unsolicited—and sometimes contradicting—advice as Eloise and Dante helplessly wandered the aisles.

"You want the blanket that wraps all the way around and then snaps closed," one woman had said.

Another woman passed by a few minutes later and said, "You don't want the blanket with the snaps. They're only good for swaddling. You can't use them in a car seat or stroller."

If Eloise thought everyone had opinions about her pregnancy and marital status, it was nothing compared to the strong recommendations they had concerning baby-wipe warmers. All the well-meaning comments were starting to give her a headache.

"Maybe we should come back another day," Eloise suggested.

Or not at all. She could have her assistant look at reviews online and order whatever Eloise was going to need. She really hated shopping.

Dante jerked his thumb at the overhead sign suspended from the ceiling. "But the sale is only for today."

He had a good point. She hadn't been lying when she'd embarrassingly confessed to him at the car dealership that she could afford whatever she wanted without her parents' money. Yet, there had been a time when she was supporting herself through graduate school and had to live as frugally as possible. Eloise had learned to appreciate a bargain and it was hard to pass up 50 percent off.

"Fine. But if we go with everyone's recommendations, we're going to end up with one of everything. That's not exactly a money-saving strategy, either."

"Okay. Let's think about this logically," Dante said. "What stuff are you going to need right away? Diapers. Wipes. Probably these baseball pajamas in newborn size, and maybe this cool beanie with the snow skis."

"Why do you keep picking out all the sports-themed stuff?" Eloise asked.

"Because sports are gender neutral," Dante replied as though he were explaining a foreign concept to her.

"The circus animals are neutral, too," Eloise pointed out.

"Yeah, but the clowns are kinda creepy. How about this one with the stripes?"

"I like the stripes. But what if the baby's diaper leaks? We might need more than one."

"Good call," Dante said, throwing in an extra, as

well as a matching package of six onesies. "What else? The baby isn't going to be eating right away, so we can probably skip the high chairs and the food section."

"You'll need a car seat," a woman wearing medical scrubs said. "They won't let you drive the baby home from the hospital unless you have one installed."

"Hey, Tamara." Dante smiled at the lady. "This is Eloise Taylor. El, remember how I mentioned Jace Abernathy delivered his son himself? This is his fiancée, Tamara Hanson. She's the maternity nurse at Bronco Valley Hospital I told you about." He turned back to Tamara. "Did you just get off your shift?"

"I'm heading in after this. I wanted to get ahead on my Christmas shopping and saw the sale on diapers. We need to stock up for Frankie." Tamara then extended her hand for Eloise to shake. "Nice to meet you, Eloise. Forgive me for saying so, but you look really overwhelmed."

"Is it that obvious?"

Tamara chuckled. "Jace had that same expression when he found out how much stuff Frankie was going to need. There's this great website that breaks down lists of recommended items according to the baby's age. That way, you don't buy a bunch of stuff you don't need right away and then have no place to store it."

"Oh, my gosh. I didn't even think about where I would put everything." Eloise forced herself to blink to avoid remaining in a state of perpetual wide-eyed shock. Her suite at the hotel was large, but not for a crib and a jogging stroller and the swing set and the jumping thing and... She gulped. "There's just so much stuff."

"If you want some other free advice," Tamara said as she patted her shoulder gently, "don't do any of this on an empty stomach. Go out to lunch, read over the list. Make your own list. And then come back when you've had time to let it all soak in."

"I love that advice," Eloise said. In fact, she'd been living by that advice her entire pregnancy, but she wasn't sure she could ever absorb so much in such a small amount of time.

As if reading her thoughts, Tamara said, "No matter how much stuff you buy in advance, you'll never be fully prepared. So take your time and remember that the most important thing your baby is going to need is a caretaker who loves them. And more diapers than you ever thought humanly possible." Tamara tilted her head. "Who's your obstetrician?"

"Well, it was Dr. Kimball," Eloise said, getting an I-told-you-so look from Dante when Tamara widened her own eyes. "But he's retiring this week and I haven't met the new doctor."

"He's definitely earned his retirement after all these years," Tamara said diplomatically. "He's a nice guy but with his eyesight, it's not a bad idea for him to pass the reins onto the next generation. Stop by the hospital some time for a tour of the maternity ward. If I'm free, I'll introduce you to some of the labor and delivery nurses. That way, you'll know some friendly faces already before your due date."

Eloise pulled out her phone to open her calendar app.

"Oh, you don't need to schedule an appointment or anything," Tamara said. "We never know when things are going to be chaotic so just show up whenever and if I can't leave my station, I'll find someone to take you around."

"That would be great," Eloise said, then thanked the woman before saying goodbye.

She and Dante left everything else behind and paid for the basketballs, then found a nearby restaurant. It was already too late in the day to meet Aaron and Denise Sanchez, who'd texted that they'd finished their shopping and were heading home.

Instead of going over the list of baby items, Eloise started talking about her job and what she needed to get done before the baby arrived and then they discussed Dante's job and everything he needed to do before winter vacation.

She was very careful not to bring up their attempted shopping trip. Not only was it a reminder of how unprepared she was, but it was also a reminder of how none of this would last once the baby arrived. After the amazing night they'd just shared together, Eloise was desperate to keep things between them as normal as possible. To enjoy these last few weeks as a single woman and not a single mom.

She spent the entire weekend at his apartment, waking up each morning with Dante pressed against her back. Even in sleep, they were drawn together.

Sunday afternoon, she went grocery shopping with him and then his parents' house to make dinner. She really wasn't much help besides cutting up vegetables for the salad, although she did keep his parents entertained with a story about a client's commercial for their very expensive collection of kitchen knives and how many tomatoes they went through before the model finally stormed off the set when he couldn't get the perfect slice. Desperate to finish the shoot and not go over budget, Eloise had impulsively walked into the closest restaurant—a delicatessen—and asked if any of the cooks could be a stand-in. She put an apron and a chef's hat on the first guy who volunteered and the commercial did so well, the Food Network offered the man his own show.

Thankfully, none of Dante's family brought up the fact that the two of them spent the past couple of nights together. Nor did they say anything when she and Dante got in the same car together to leave. Although, as soon as the engine started, Dylan texted his brother to say that he was done staying out on the ranch and would be back in the apartment tonight. Dante read her the message.

"Oh," Eloise said, a knot already forming in her rib cage. She'd been warning herself all weekend that this was temporary, that spending their nights together wasn't going to last forever. "I guess I should probably start sleeping in my own bed before the housekeeping staff notice that I've only been coming by to pick up different clothes."

They were still parked at the curb. Once they drove to the intersection ahead, he'd have to turn the car right to continue on to his apartment or left to take her back to the hotel.

"I'm sure they've already noticed, El." The familiar way Dante said her name made the ache in her chest worsen. Until he added, "Just like they'll probably notice if twice as many of the extra fluffy towels are being used all of a sudden."

Her heart soared at what she thought he was suggesting. But he could just as easily have been warning himself against staying the night at the more public hotel.

Either way, Eloise was relieved that she wasn't the only one thinking about the possibility.

The longer they stared at each other across the dimly lit interior of his car, the more Eloise wanted him to stay with her tonight. "We can hang up the towels after you use them. And set our alarms so you leave before—"

Dante didn't even let her finish. He'd already put the car into gear. "I just need to swing by my place superfast to get some clothes and my lesson plans for tomorrow."

Anticipation raced through her, and she refused to think about how she was only delaying the inevitable. At some point, they would have to face reality, but not tonight.

Nor would they for the next five nights.

Just as they'd quickly settled into a weekend routine, they easily settled into a weekday routine. Dante left for school in the mornings and Eloise threw herself into her own work. Dante did his after-school rec league in the afternoons and Eloise took a Pilates class, although her mom had been right about the need to ease her aching back muscles. By Thursday, she was about one phone call away from heading out to the Triple T to use their hot tub.

After their respective workouts, Dante would pick her up and take her to his apartment to make her dinner—for the first time in her life, Eloise was getting sick of eating out—and they'd end up back at the hotel before Dylan came home.

Dante even insisted Eloise use the washing machine at his apartment instead of sending her clothes out to be laundered by the hotel. It almost would've felt as though they were playing house, if it hadn't involved all the driving back and forth between both of their places.

By the time the realtor called on Friday morning with a new listing for a home that was located right on the invisible border of the Heights and the Valley, Eloise had to remind herself—for the millionth time—that it was all too good to be true. She was going to have start making some decisions on her own soon.

Chapter Twelve

The Bronco tree lighting ceremony was on Saturday, the second of December, and Dante had never missed a year. Even when he'd been away at college, he'd driven home for the annual event. The park and the surrounding streets were all decorated for the season with their twinkling lights and hanging wreaths, and local restaurants set up booths to showcase their menus and sell food.

For Dante, it was the official kickoff to the holiday season. It also meant the Heights Hotel was at full capacity and he had to park a few blocks away because the valet was turning away cars.

Eloise was finishing up a video call when Dante let himself into the suite with the extra keycard Eloise had given him on Monday morning. She smiled at him and lifted her forefinger in the universal sign that she needed another minute. This past week with her had been surreal, but also very, very ordinary. One minute Dante would be racing across town, butterflies in his stomach like a lovesick teenager, because he couldn't wait to see Eloise. The next minute, he'd be kissing her hello with a passion he'd never known existed. And less than an hour after that, they'd be standing together in his kitchen as he cooked and they talked about their days as if it were the most normal thing in the world.

Dante flung open the curtains and was staring out at the park across the street, watching crowds of people bundled up in coats and colorful scarves, when Eloise finally ended her call.

She came up behind him and hugged his waist. "You're like a kid on Christmas Eve looking out this window in hopes you'll catch a glimpse Santa and his reindeer flying past."

He grinned, not bothering to contain his excitement as he pulled her around in front of him so she could see what he was seeing. "I can't help it. I love this time of year. Ask any of the teachers at school and they'll tell you I'm almost worse than the students when it comes to these three weeks before break."

"I'm guessing we'll see a lot of people we know down there," Eloise said, her tone hard to read. She definitely didn't seem as excited as he was, but she was probably worried about running into her family.

"Everyone in town usually goes."

"Which means my parents will no doubt make an appearance. I remember coming a few times when I was a child, but we never got to run around and play like the other kids. We had to sit with our parents on those cold hard chairs and listen to the mayor give a boring speech."

Most of the town VIPs sat in the reserved rows while everyone else crowded around, drinking hot cocoa—or sometimes adult beverages brought from home—and talking amongst their friends until the mayor flipped the symbolic light switch and the tree lit up.

"In that case, I don't blame you if you're not as excited as I am about it. But trust me, it's way more fun experiencing it my way."

"And you don't think it'll be weird if we're seen together?" Eloise looked up at him. Her eyes seemed to be asking a lot more than just that question.

Dante wasn't sure if he had the right answers. The only thing he was sure about lately was that he didn't want whatever this was to end. "At this point, El, it'll cause more gossip if we're *not* seen together."

She nodded. "Okay, then let's do this. But I want a hot cocoa and some of those cinnamon-and-sugar donuts from that booth the concierge keeps telling me about."

"Come on." Dante pulled her toward the entry and helped her into her coat. "I promise we can do all of the things you didn't get to do when you came to the lighting ceremony as a kid."

Thirty minutes later, after the sun went down and the mayor flipped the switch, Dante was regretting his promise.

"You said I could do all the stuff I missed growing up," Eloise reminded him as she blew on her hot cocoa.

"I did. But technically, they didn't have the sledding hill back when we were kids." The early snow from Thanksgiving had already melted and the town had rented a snowmaking machine to create a fun winter wonderland spot for kids. "So it doesn't count as something you ever missed doing."

He tried to offer her one of the fresh donuts from the bag he was carrying, but she wasn't distracted. "It looks like a fifty foot run at the most, and it's not even that steep. There's toddlers doing it. How dangerous can it be, Dante?"

"The fact that you don't even know the answer to that tells me that you've never fallen off a sled before. What would Dr. Kimball say?"

"He's officially retired this week, remember? I'll ask the new doctor when I meet her on Monday. But I'm not going to fall off."

"You don't have a sled," Dante pointed out, hoping to end the discussion once and for all.

"Here, Mr. Sanchez." Mason, the student they'd run into at LuLu's, handed Eloise a red plastic disc. "Your girlfriend can use my sled."

"Thanks, Mason. I'll take good care of it." Eloise looked at Dante. "Are you coming or not?"

He glanced at the top of the hill, then at the base, where it was more icy from all the little feet packing down the man-made snow. He was going to have some strong words for the councilperson who'd come up with this idea to draw in more tourists for the tree lighting. "I think I better stay down here and get ready to catch you."

"In that case, hold this for me, please." She passed him her hot cocoa cup, then rose onto her tiptoes and kissed his nose. "I'll be back down super quickly."

"Not too quickly," he yelled as she followed the other children marching up to the top of the slope, which looked higher than it had a few minutes ago. "And keep your feet out in front of you so you can use them to slow down."

She turned around to wave, but Dante wasn't convinced she'd heard him. He found a nearby bench to set down the hot cocoas in case he needed to run to Eloise's rescue. His heart was racing, but he held his breath as he watched her awkwardly lower her pregnant body onto the round sled.

"What in the world is she doing?"

Dante heard the deep voice behind him and though he'd never met the man, he knew exactly who was speaking. Dante felt a growl build in the back of his throat and forced himself to inhale through his nose.

"You're not going to allow her to do this, are you?" Thaddeus Taylor seemed to be talking to Dante. "Not in her condition."

"I'm not sure if you've ever met your daughter, sir," Dante replied, not taking his eyes off the woman in question. "But Eloise doesn't take no for an answer when she's determined to do something."

"She gets that from her father," Imogen Taylor said as she stepped between the two men. Then she held out a leather-gloved hand in his direction. "You must be Dante Sanchez."

Dante managed to give Eloise's mom a brief nod and a quick handshake before returning his attention to their daughter, who was now sliding right toward them before veering quickly to the left. Thankfully, she landed only a few feet away without so much as a scratch. Although she was laughing so hard that she lost her balance as she tried to stand and ended up rolling off the sled. Dante was by her side in seconds, helping her get upright.

"That's not determination," Thaddeus said, apparently just as quick to respond to his daughter's struggle. "That's stubborn recklessness."

Dante saw something flash in Eloise's eyes and he braced himself for the joy to leave her face. But her expression remained the same. "Hi, Mom and Dad. Have you met Dante yet?"

"Your mother has, but I was too busy trying not to have a heart attack as I watched you and my first grandchild almost die on that contraption."

"Geez, Dad, it wasn't even a bunny slope. Nobody was going to die." Eloise brushed the powdery bits of snow off her backside, but continued to smile. "You sound just like Dante."

Dante was about to point out that he in no way sounded as dramatic as Thaddeus Taylor had. But before he could, the man said, "Well, I'm glad at least one of you has some good sense."

As much as Dante appreciated the recognition as being the sensible one, he was also insulted on Eloise's behalf. He was about to defend her honor when Imogen again intervened. "Thad, dear, Dante is Jordan's brother-in-law. He's the teacher with the after-school program at one of the local elementary schools. Remember, Jordan talked to you about making a donation before the end of the year for tax purposes?"

Great. Now Dante was going to have to swallow his pride and be indebted to *two* Taylor men for contributing to his school and his students. Although, he noticed Eloise's mom had deftly avoided mentioning that the donation wasn't for the better-funded Heights Academy.

Eloise and Imogen were both looking at him expectantly, so Dante extended his hand as his manners overrode his defensiveness. "Nice to meet you, Mr. Taylor."

The older man shook his hand briefly. "Tell me, Dante, has my daughter been eating right and taking care of herself? Other than this little stunt, of course."

Eloise raised her hand. "Your daughter's right here and you can ask me."

"I *could* ask you," Thaddeus said. "But you never tell me anything. A man has a right to know about the health of his only grandchild."

It was the second time Thaddeus had mentioned Eloise's baby and although his tone was gruff and judgmental, he also couldn't hide his concern. Especially not after he'd matched Dante stride for stride to assist Eloise at the bottom of the hill. Dante doubted he'd ever be on Team Thaddeus, but it was refreshing to see Eloise's father show some human emotion.

"Well, I'm not Eloise's doctor or her spokesperson so I can't speak for her. I will tell you, though, that your daughter strikes me as being very smart and very capable. I've only seen her make the best decisions and I have no doubt that she will continue doing so."

Thaddeus pulled a card out of his pocket. "This is my number, Dante. I want you to call me if she needs anything but is too stubborn to ask. Also call me when she goes into labor. I donate enough money to that hospital, the least someone could do is notify me when visiting hours are."

"Still over here, Dad." Eloise wiggled her fingers again. "If you want to come see the baby after they're born, then just say that. To me."

"Of course I want to," Thaddeus announced, as though it should have been obvious. "Why would you think otherwise?"

Dante could think of a million reasons Eloise would

think that, but he didn't trust himself not to list them all right here in the park where everyone could hear.

"How wonderful that we got all that settled," Imogen said as though years of hurt and resentment had somehow been erased just like that. Her mom then leaned toward Eloise's belly. "Hi, Baby, it's your Imo-Gram. I'm here with your Grandpa Taylor and we can't wait to meet you."

"I told you that I'm not going to be anyone's Grandpa Taylor," Thaddeus told his wife, and Dante felt his own fingers curl into fists at the implication. "That's what our kids called my dad, and I hated it. I've decided when this little one gets here, I'm going to be a Pop Pop."

Dante would've spit out his hot cocoa if he still had it. Eloise's eyes couldn't be any wider as she looked at her father as though he'd lost his mind.

"Um, Dad, why don't we discuss names later? Much later when we're all... When we've all..." Instead of finishing her sentence, Eloise looped her arm through Dante's. "Anyway, we have to get going. Dante and I were just about to go check out the shops."

"It was nice to meet you both, Mr. and Mrs. Taylor," he said again, but her parents seemed to already be distracted.

"Imogen, the mayor is on his way over here. Under no circumstances are we letting him have his anniversary party at the ranch again so..."

Eloise was pulling Dante away before he could find out why Thaddeus wasn't keen on hosting the mayor. Although, to be fair, she didn't have to pull too hard. Dante was relieved to get away from all that awkwardness.

"Are you okay?" he asked when they were out of earshot.

"I think so. Was that weird or was it just me?"

"Which part? Your dad getting all panicky about you injuring yourself sledding? Or the part when he wanted me to give him a report on your overall health?"

Eloise rolled her eyes. "I can't believe he gave you his business card. You can throw it away if you want."

"Are you kidding? I'm putting his number in my contacts list. Under the name Pop Pop."

Eloise threw back her head and laughed. "Okay, so it wasn't just me who thought that was odd."

"It's definitely a one-eighty from how he reacted at that party." Whoa. Dante couldn't believe that had only been a month ago when he'd first met Eloise. He felt as though he'd known her forever. Yet, there was still so much he didn't know. "That's a good thing, right? Your dad was definitely concerned tonight about you and especially about the baby."

"I guess. My mom predicted he'd come around and maybe she's been working on him. It's possible that all my siblings standing up to him on Thanksgiving was like an intervention of sorts. But I think it's going to take a team full of experts to address his tendency to jump straight into overbearing and controlling mode when he thinks he's simply being protective."

Eloise paused before they crossed the street toward the rows of shops that were open and decorated for Christmas with their seasonal window displays. "We don't really have to go shopping. I was just throwing that out there as an excuse to get away before my dad brought up baby names again."

"Going to the local shops is also part of the Bronco tree-lighting experience, so we should probably stop into a few before grabbing more hot cocoa. Now tell me about his suggestions for names."

As they talked, they wandered in and out of the shops and picked up half a dozen cupcakes from Kendra's Cupcakes to have after dinner.

"Oh look, Sadie is doing a pop up shop for her Holiday House tonight. Did I mention that I love Christmas? Let's check it out."

One of the first things he saw when they stepped into the themed store, which was half the size of Sadie's permanent store on Commercial Street, was a display rack with matching family pajamas. But he resisted the urge to walk toward it. Eloise was looking at ornaments and Dante saw a candy cane–shaped serving platter that would be perfect for his mom, who made the best chocolate peppermint cookies. But his gaze kept going toward the pajamas.

It was ridiculous, he told himself. Themed family pajamas were for…well…families. Or people who woke up together on Christmas morning. Who was going to wear a matching set with him? Dylan? Not only would that be incredibly sad, it would also be unlikely since his brother was spending most of his free time out on his new ranch.

Unable to avoid the display, Dante saw the tiny white velour one-piece that was no bigger than the length of his two hands side by side. There was an embroidered Christmas tree on the front with a big gold star and gold letters that said Merry and Bright.

He couldn't stop his hand from taking it off the rack.

Sadie Chamberlin, the owner of the shop, said, "Those have been selling faster than we can keep them in stock at the main store. We only have that newborn size left.

If the baby gets here before Christmas, it should fit perfectly."

"I'll take it," Dante said.

"You'll take what?" Eloise asked.

"The baby's first outfit." He held it up. "We never finished shopping the day after Thanksgiving. This is gender neutral, right? And not sports-themed."

Just then, three more people entered the already busy shop. Sadie kissed one of the men on the cheek. "Dante, this is my fiancé, Sullivan Grainger."

Dante's parents had already received an invitation for the couple's wedding on Christmas Day. It was taped to the front of their fridge, possibly as a nudge for Felix and Shari who were supposed to be setting a date soon.

"Sullivan, this is Dante Sanchez. He's the teacher that all the kids hope they get assigned to at the beginning of the school year."

"Nice to meet you." Sullivan shook Dante's hand. "This is my brother Bobby Stone and his girlfriend, Tori Hawkins."

Dante thought about his friendly dinner with Tori's cousin Corinne, which felt like ages ago. Before anyone could bring up whether or not that had been a date (it hadn't), Dante in turn introduced everyone to Eloise. He was still holding the baby outfit in his free hand when several things happened at once.

Tori pointed to the bright star on the front of the outfit and said, "Oh that's adorable."

Sadie squealed and pointed to the ring on Tori's left finger. "When did you get *that*?"

Sullivan pointed at his brother Bobby and said, "It's about time."

Bobby cleared his throat. "I guess I should've mentioned earlier that Tori's not my girlfriend anymore."

Tori beamed up at him. "He just asked tonight. I said yes, obviously."

"Congratulations." Eloise smiled at the newly engaged couple.

"Congratulations right back at you two," Bobby said, gesturing to the baby outfit in Dante's hand. Bobby Stone had recently returned to Bronco after being presumed dead, so it was likely the man didn't want to draw any extra attention to himself and was trying to change the subject.

Dante should've corrected Bobby, but before he could, Tori and Sullivan were offering their congratulations as well. Even Sadie, who'd always lived in Bronco and knew Dante's reputation, didn't say a word. Or maybe she was just caught up in the moment with all the happy news.

"Thank you," Eloise finally murmured in response, but didn't bother clarifying that Dante wasn't actually the father. It was possible she hadn't heard them over the carolers singing outside. Although it was more likely that she was too mortified and didn't want to make things more awkward.

Since Dante couldn't just stand there and not respond, he said, "Thanks," then handed the tiny outfit to Sadie. "I'll take this and, uh…" He looked around the store in a last ditch effort to pretend like they weren't only buying baby items "…I'll take that candy cane platter over there for my mom."

The three newcomers moved on into the small shop and he and Eloise didn't talk as Sadie rang up his purchase. Dante took the bag and was surprised by how heavy the package was. Or maybe that was just the guilt weighing him down for pretending that the child Eloise was carrying was his.

As they exited the shop, they ran into Robin Abernathy who wanted to show Eloise a display at the fancy bath and beauty store next door. "They have a line of pet shampoos and I'm thinking Rein Rejuvenation could do a similar line for manes and tails."

"Go on ahead to the next store with Robin," Dante told Eloise, who looked way more comfortable discussing business than she had discussing baby clothes and wedding announcements. "I'm going to run over to my car and drop this off so I don't have to carry it around the rest of the night."

Thankfully, when Dante returned without the bulky package, Eloise didn't bring up anything that had been said earlier at Sadie's pop-up Holiday House. They stopped by the food booths and ate their way through the park, stopping to chat with people they knew. When they finally made their way to the massive pine tree in the middle of the park to see the lights up close, Corinne Hawkins was there with Mike Burris, the ex-boyfriend Dante had heard so much about. Mike had his phone camera out and Corinne was laughing about his selfie-taking skills. Eloise offered to take a photo of them together and then Corinne insisted on returning the favor.

Later that night, after Eloise fell asleep in the hotel bed beside him, Dante was restless and replayed every conversation they'd had that evening for some sort of clue to what Eloise was thinking in terms of their future. He picked up his phone and opened the recent picture, staring at their smiling faces on the screen. No matter what happened after the baby came, Dante would at least have this. The memory of him and Eloise together on one of his favorite nights.

Eloise had been trying not to think about how quickly Christmas was approaching because she didn't want to think about how much different the holidays would be for her this year. But seeing Dante's excitement at the tree-lighting ceremony forced her to realize that she couldn't keep avoiding the inevitable.

She turned up the heat on the water in the shower and sighed as it eased her aching muscles. Looking back, maybe sledding down the hill last night hadn't been the smartest decision. Her mom was right; Eloise was reactionary. Particularly when someone told her she couldn't or shouldn't do something. But it had been fun and she'd felt like a kid again. Up until the moment when Dante and her father had run to her with matching expressions of worry across their faces.

She'd never thought the two men would have anything in common, but apparently, she was the common denominator. Or at least her baby was. When her father had assumed that Dante would be with her when she went into labor, Eloise held her breath, not knowing how he was going to respond. When everyone at Sadie's pop up shop assumed Dante was the father and congratulated both of them, she'd held her breath again, not sure how he was going to respond.

Eloise lathered her hair with shampoo and scrubbed her scalp harder than she needed to. She was tired of holding her breath. She was frustrated that she'd put herself in the position of waiting for Dante to respond first. Hell, he'd even bought the baby their first outfit—

their first anything—last night when Eloise had been too indecisive to buy so much as a blanket before now.

So then why was she allowing him to get this close? Why was she holding on to some kernel of hope that he might want to stick around and play the role of daddy? Why was she letting down all the guards she'd carefully put in place and doing what she'd never done before?

Why was she starting to rely on him?

"Hey, El," Dante said as he cracked opened the bathroom door. "I'm going to call downstairs and order room service. You want the Belgian waffle and the sunny-side up eggs?"

See? she told herself, unable to stop the tears from filling her eyes. The man even knew her damn order before she did. He paid attention to so many small details and noticed everything. There was no way he hadn't known exactly what he was saying when he'd accepted congratulations from those people last night. And Eloise had allowed it.

Because she was already falling for him. Because she'd already let things go too far. She'd been holding onto hope that he'd been feeling the same way, but even as she convinced herself that he did, she suddenly wanted to put a stop to it. She couldn't let him take on such a huge responsibility. He had no idea what he was getting himself into. Not that she did.

"Actually, I'd prefer the oatmeal this morning," she said, trying to keep her tone as happy as possible. Thankfully, the shower spray covered the fact that she was having one of her morning cry sessions.

"Are you sure?" Dante asked, taking a step inside the huge marble-tiled bathroom and staring at her through the glass enclosure. He was bare chested, wearing only his jeans from last night. "The last time you ordered that, you took three bites and then asked to trade me for my pancakes."

"Well, today I'm craving oatmeal. Tomorrow I might be craving something else. Who knows how many times I might change my mind and want something totally different." She was trying to tell herself that she could be talked out of her desire for Dante, yet she ended up sounding contrary instead.

As she rinsed her hair, the spray of the water muffled her hearing, but she was pretty sure she heard him say something about craving her. The next thing she knew, Dante was opening the shower door and stepping inside to join her.

Her body responded to his as it always did, even though her brain knew that this couldn't keep happening. When she was with Dante, his arms around her like this, she lost all rational thought. And that wasn't good. She needed space, she needed distance so that she could think clearly. It was finally time to figure out some sort of plan.

His thumb traced the hardened tip of her nipple as his mouth trailed kisses along her neck. She moaned his name and instead of pushing him away, she pulled him closer. When he sat on the tiled bench and angled her gently onto his lap, Eloise told herself that this would be the last time. Just once more and then she'd insist that they take a break. They couldn't keep going on like this. By the time he slid inside of her, though, she didn't want him to ever stop.

When they finished making love in the shower, Eloise found herself ordering the waffles, after all. It was Sunday morning and there was no sense in ruining the weekend at this point. Monday would be soon enough to tell him that they needed to take a time out and think about what they were doing.

Except the rest of the day, when they weren't touching each other, the doubt wouldn't go away.

It crept back in when she was watching Dante cover for his dad by refereeing a youth basketball game later that morning. Eloise sat in the stands surrounded by all the other parents and couldn't escape the fact that someday she'd be the one cheering on her own child. Where would Dante be then?

The doubt popped back up when they stopped by Dylan's ranch with bags of burgers and fries for lunch because Dante was worried about how much extra time Dylan was spending out there, working himself to distraction and leaving two new employees in charge of the dealership. As Dylan gave them a tour and talked about all the repairs he planned for the ranch, Eloise wondered if she would ever get to see it fixed up.

By Sunday evening, Eloise was getting downright antsy. His parents had called to cancel dinner because his dad was still fixing a broken sink at his mom's salon and didn't want to call a repairperson. The weekend was almost over and she didn't know how she could wait until tomorrow to have the conversation she knew was inevitable.

They were at his apartment and Dante was in the kitchen cooking dinner while Eloise sat at the small table, trying to focus on her laptop. She needed to get a presentation ready for a new client and all her ideas were proving to be garbage. Needing a break, she stood up and rubbed her lower back.

"Are you feeling okay?" Dante paused, holding a wooden spoon in his hand.

"Except for the baby doing some extra kicking and stretching lately, I feel fine physically. I think I'm just a little off my game these past few days." There. She'd opened up the door for "the talk."

"What do you mean?"

"I'm starting to have doubts."

"About my spaghetti? I don't have to use as much garlic if you're worried about heartburn again."

Even hearing the word *heartburn* made her wince. She'd rather suffer from that kind of pain than the heart sicknesses she was about to put herself through.

"Dante, remember that first night I met you and when you walked me up to my room it was like a dam had burst open inside of me and I couldn't stop talking?"

"Yes?" Dante drew the word out slowly.

"I'm about to do that again."

"Okay." Dante shut off the stove and set down his spoon. "I'm ready."

"I should've made a list, but oh, well, here it goes." Eloise stood up straighter, trying not to wince at the muscle spasm near her hip joint. She inhaled and then continued. "I can't stop thinking about everything I still have left to do before the baby comes. I know I've been avoiding it up until now, but it's time I force myself to handle it once and for all. And as much as I've enjoyed our time together, I feel like I should be concentrating more of my energy on preparing for the due date."

"Like buying a car seat? I've actually been looking at a few online and was going to—"

"It's not just the car seat, Dante. It's all of it. Everything is going to change and I need to get on top of those changes now."

"Are you referring to changes with work? Changes with your body?" Dante narrowed his eyes, yet held her gaze. "Or changes with me?"

"I don't know. All of them, I would imagine. I'm not Winona Cobbs. I can't predict the future."

"But if you *could* predict the future, what would you want to see?" he asked.

"I want to see stability."

"Am I not stable enough for you?"

"I think that in your heart, you might want to be. But when faced with the reality, you might decide that it's more than you signed up for." Like her ex-boyfriend had. Unlike Wade, though, Eloise didn't think she would recover as easily if Dante let her down.

"Are you trying to break up with me?" His voice was low, tense, and she couldn't meet his penetrating gaze. "Or is this some sort of preemptive strike because you think I'm going to eventually break up with you?"

Whoa. He was intuitive, she'd give him that. But the way he'd said it made Eloise feel like she was being a coward. So she snapped back. "It's hard to break up from a relationship that was never actually defined."

"Yeah, I know what we told ourselves when all of this first started, Eloise. But let's not pretend as though it was just some meaningless fling."

"I'm not saying it was meaningless. In fact, being with you this past month had more meaning to me than I ever thought possible. But we both knew it was bound to end."

"Why?" Dante crossed his arms in front of his chest. "Why does it have to end?"

"Because in a few weeks, it won't be just me and you anymore. There will be a whole other person that will need to come first."

"I'm pretty sure I've been the one pointing that out to you this whole time and you've been the one avoiding the topic because you didn't want to overthink things and be controlling like your parents."

She hated it that he was right. "I know. But all that nesting I've been avoiding? All those lists of baby items I haven't bought? Something clicked in my brain the other day and now I can't shut it off. I need to focus on becoming a mother right now and I can't do that if I'm too focused on being with you."

"Why can't you do both? People have babies all the time and still stay in lo—" He cut himself off just before saying the word she desperately wanted him to say—but was just as terrified to hear. Dante ran a hand through his hair before continuing. "All I'm saying is that you make it sound like everything ends as soon as you give birth. Like our relationship can't survive a tiny baby."

At that exact moment, Eloise didn't trust herself not to reach for him and tell him that she hadn't meant it. That it was just the hormones and her insecurity talking. She needed to put some distance between them so she could think and not react. Turning to her laptop, Eloise said, "I don't know what it can or can't survive because I've never experienced this situation before."

She began packing up her briefcase and Dante asked, "Are you leaving?"

"I think I should stay by myself tonight." Subconsciously, she must've anticipated something like this happening because she'd driven herself over earlier today and her car was, thankfully, parked outside.

He looked out the window. "The snow is coming down pretty hard. I don't think you should be driving in this. Stay and we can talk about things. You already have your notepad. We can make one of your lists."

She shook her head, not realizing how hard it would be to resist him. "I need to go. Don't push me on this, Dante."

"Push you?" Dante asked. "How can I be pushing you when you've been too busy pulling away this whole time?"

"I haven't been pulling away, I've been protecting myself. You're the one with the reputation for not being able to commit."

As soon as she said the words, she wanted to take them back.

"And you think you're the expert at commitment, Eloise? Ever since you stepped foot in Bronco, you've had the other foot halfway out the door. And it's not just where I'm concerned. You've been living out of a suitcase for the past month instead of looking for a permanent home. You're leasing a car, despite the fact that you have the money to buy it outright. You won't even put the baby's due date in your little calendar app because you don't want it affecting your work schedule."

This time, it was his words that hit their mark. She snapped her head up, then grabbed her phone off the table and opened the app to December 15. She began typing furiously, then showed him the screen. "There. Are you happy?"

Dante read aloud what she wrote. "'Baby arrives. Everything changes. Call Dante so he can say he's having second thoughts.'"

He pulled out his phone and did the exact same thing.

But instead of letting her read it, her device pinged with the invite notification. "Baby arrives. Dante is by your side. You have to apologize and buy him all-you-can-eat ribs at LuLu's. And banana pudding."

Eloise made an awful snort that was part laugh and part sob.

It was one of the hardest things she'd ever had to do, but she had to leave. She needed to think and not react. She couldn't even bring herself to say goodbye because that would've been too final. Instead, she managed to say, "We'll see. Only time will tell."

She hitched the strap of her purse on her shoulder and walked out the door.

Chapter Thirteen

Dante knew better than to try to talk Eloise out of something when she already had her mind made up. If she needed space, then he'd give her space. But he wasn't about to let her convince either one of them that what they'd shared these past few weeks wasn't meant to last.

He also wasn't about to let her put herself in danger proving her independence. He told himself he'd give her ten minutes before going after her. Just to make sure she made it back to the hotel in this weather.

He lasted five.

There was something nudging him, telling him that he shouldn't wait. It was that same pull that he had the night they met. He hadn't been able to shake it then, and it certainly wasn't going to ease up on him tonight. Grabbing his keys and his coat, he hurried outside, and his feet sank into several inches of snow on the sidewalk as he jogged to his car.

Luckily, his windshield wasn't iced over yet, and the wipers made quick work of the layers of powdery snow. There weren't many drivers out on the road in these conditions and he only saw one set of tire tracks. Relief washed through him as he realized that as long as he could see her tire tracks, he knew she was safe. It was when those tracks swerved suddenly to the left that Dante's heart went from pounding to racing. He pulled over and left his engine running as he sprinted across the street. Eloise's car had swerved into a ditch and it was clearly stuck. The interior light was on and from here he couldn't see any airbags deployed. But he also couldn't see any movement.

"Eloise!" Her name wrenched from his throat. His phone was already out of his pocket and he was calling 9-1-1 as he made his way to the driver's side door. "Eloise," he yelled again and nearly dropped to his knees when she turned her face toward him.

"Dante?" she asked, rolling down the window. "How'd you know I was here?"

"Are you okay?" he asked, ignoring her question. "What happened?"

"There was a moose. It just came out of nowhere. I swerved a little too hard and now I think my tire's stuck. Or flat."

He looked down at his phone, not surprised to see that his call hadn't gone through. "There's no reception."

"I know. I already tried calling for an ambulance."

"An ambulance?" He opened the door so he could inspect her for injuries. "Are you hurt?"

"No." Her seat belt was still on and he didn't see any blood, but it was dark. Just when he was about to breathe a sigh of relief, she added, "But I'm pretty sure my water broke."

"Already? But your due date is the fifteenth," he said, then immediately realized how ridiculous he sounded.

"I guess some things can't be scheduled."

"Okay, I'm going to walk back up to the road and see if I can get a signal. Are you okay if I leave you here?"

"I'm having a baby, not dying." She swung her legs out of the car. "I can walk."

He put his arm around her. "Let's at least get you to my car. It might be quicker to drive you straight to the hospital."

They only got a few feet before Eloise was doubled over with pain. When it passed, Dante asked, "Was that a contraction?"

"I think so," Eloise said. "I've never had one before."

They made it to the road when another one hit, lasting longer than the first. "Are they supposed to come back-to-back like this?"

Eloise's face was pale in the glow of the streetlight and she shook her head. "I don't think so. I was going to ask my new doctor tomorrow to recommend a birthing class. But now I guess I'll have to try to remember those Lamaze videos that I watched when I was back in New York."

Dante had his phone back out and saw that he had one bar. He pushed Send and almost shouted when the operator came on the line and asked what his emergency was.

"We're having a baby," Dante started. Then clarified. "I mean my girlfriend is having a baby."

It was the first time he'd actually called Eloise that, but he couldn't enjoy it. He was too busy trying to help her across the street to his car. "The contractions are only about two minutes apart. We're on the side of the road."

He opened the rear door but Eloise shook her head and pointed to the back hatch. "I need to lie down."

"It sounds like she's in transition already," the emergency operator said. "Give me your location."

He was able to tell the operator where they were right before Eloise yelled again in pain. Dante held her hand and whispered to her as she panted in short gasps.

"Sir, are you still with me?" the operator asked when Eloise took a shuddering breath and eased her head back down. "I timed that one and it was ninety seconds."

"What does that mean? Should I drive her to the hospital?"

"You probably won't get there in time. I already have an EMT dispatched to your location and they should be pulling up soon."

"I see them," Dante shouted when the flashing red lights came around the curve. "They're here."

Jace Abernathy, who volunteered with the fire department exited the vehicle with an EMT and Dante reached for Eloise's hand. "It's going to be okay."

"Hey, you two," Jace said as he came striding up, as calm as he would be walking into Doug's or a coffee shop. "I hear we're going to have a baby."

"I can't have a baby yet," Eloise lifted her head to tell him. "I don't have a car seat."

"We'll get you one before you leave the hospital," Jace said. "But let's get you to the hospital first."

His partner arrived with the gurney and Eloise had another contraction before they could get her loaded onto it. Dante grabbed a bag out of his back seat, then caught up to them just as they got her settled into the ambulance.

Not wanting to leave Eloise's side, but seeing how tight the space was, Dante asked, "Should I follow you guys in my car?"

Jace relayed a bunch of numbers to the medic, who passed Dante a pair of latex gloves. "Nope. I'm going to drive. My partner's going to need you back here with him. Eloise, it's time to push."

Ten minutes later when they arrived at the emergency room, Dante was holding a tiny baby girl in his arms and Eloise could barely keep her eyes open.

"Eloise, I know you're exhausted and your body just went through an entire marathon in record time," Jace's partner said over the chatter on the radio clipped to his belt. "But I need you to listen to me. Hospital staff are already out here to meet us. They need to get you checked out and they need to take the baby to NICU for a screening. It's all very routine in situations like this, so I don't want you to be nervous."

"Dante," Eloise said softly, her voice hoarse.

"I'm right here," he said, squeezing her hand.

"Stay with her, okay?"

"I promise," he told Eloise. "I won't leave her side."

"And if someone already called my dad and he's here, don't let him name her Delores."

Before he could ask what she meant by that, the back of the ambulance doors opened, and chaos ensued.

When Eloise woke up, she was in a darkened hospital room. There was a light blinking on a monitor by her bed and an IV line connected to her arm. She sat up in a panic, looking around, and nearly cried in relief when she saw Dante in the recliner across the room, holding her sleeping daughter.

"Are you okay?" he asked, his voice a whisper.

"Is *she* okay?" Eloise replied. She had a vague memory of a doctor examining her and some bright lights and loud beeps. Every time she'd asked someone about her baby, they'd told her that she was all right. But Eloise needed to see for herself.

Dante stood and carried the newborn to her, carefully transferring the bundle, then moving Eloise's IV cord out of the way. "She's perfect. Just like her mom."

Eloise marveled over the sight of her tiny daughter, tears filling her eyes and relief filling her heart. "I can't believe she's mine. That she's here."

"You were a champ earlier in the ambulance," he said, his fingers brushing the hair from her face as she studied the tiny human in her arms and wondered how she'd gotten this lucky.

"It's all been such a blur. When I woke up, I thought it might have been a dream. But she's real, isn't she."

Dante nodded. "Very real and very healthy. I stayed with her in the NICU while they checked her out. She was twenty inches and weighed in at six pounds, eleven ounces. All of her tests came back normal, and she was ready to come to the room before you were. The on-call doctor was concerned about your heart rate and they wanted to watch you for signs of hypothermia since you forgot your coat at my house and were exposed to the elements for a while. They gave you some fluids and some meds to get your blood pressure back to normal. The doctor said it can cause grogginess, but that you should be feeling better in the morning. The baby and

I were down here when they wheeled you in, but we didn't want to wake you."

The baby let out a little yawn, her lips settling into a suckling motion. "Should I feed her?"

"They had me give her a bottle already, so I don't think she's hungry. The lactation specialist already stopped by but said you should wait to nurse until after the meds wear off."

"Thanks for staying with her." Eloise felt the dampness at the corner her eyes. When she wiped away her tears, she noticed the swaddling blanket had shifted. "What's she wearing?"

"The outfit I got her. It was still in my back seat from last night and I grabbed it before we got into the ambulance." Dante pushed the blanket open wider to reveal the golden letters right above the tiny Christmas star. "The nurses upstairs commented on how she barely cried when I put this on her, so they started calling her merry and bright."

"Merry," Eloise repeated. "I like it."

She settled back into her pillows and felt her eyelids growing heavy.

"Here," Dante said. "I'll take her while you get some sleep."

When Eloise awakened again, there was sunlight streaming through the windows and she was much more alert and oriented. She also wasn't surprised to see Dante sitting in the recliner chair, holding the baby in front of him as he talked to her about how much she was going to love Christmas in Bronco. "What do you think, Merry? Are you excited for your first Christmas?"

Merry.

Eloise remembered calling her that last night after

seeing her in the outfit Dante had bought. Her first breath, her first outfit, her first bottle, probably her first diaper change judging by the smell coming from the wastebasket. Dante had been there for all of those. What would it be like for him to be there for the other first moments?

"You're the first grandchild and the first niece on both sides, Merry, so don't be surprised to see a lot of gifts under the tree for you. Let me know if there's something special you want from Santa and I'll put in a good word, as well." When the infant only responded with a wide-eyed stare, Dante continued. "You know what I want for Christmas? I want your mommy to love me as much as I love her. She's not ready to yet, and I get that. But I hope that someday she will."

Eloise's chest expanded and all the worries and doubts she'd been clinging to fell away. She lifted her arms over her head to stretch, and to let Dante know she was awake.

"Look who's finally decided to join us." Dante smiled at Merry. "It's Mommy. We won't tell her that her timing is perfect now that you've already had your first diaper blowout. Let's go show her your new outfit."

When Dante passed the baby to her, Eloise burst out laughing. "Really? You went back to the store and bought her the baseball pajamas?"

"No. My parents did. Apparently, they hit the sale before we got there and I guess great minds think alike."

Eloise scanned the room, but the door was closed. "Were your parents here?"

"They were, but they didn't come inside. I texted Dylan to let him know where I was and to arrange a tow truck for your car. It's back at his dealership and his mechanic is replacing one of the tires. He told my parents and they dropped off my car in the parking lot and left a bag of stuff for us at the nurse's station. There's cookies in there and some banana nut muffins. Well, one muffin. I ate the other three. It's been a long night."

"You have to watch your food around him, Merry," Eloise said as she rocked the baby in her arms. "Especially the baked goods."

"Don't listen to her, Merry," Dante replied as he sat on the edge of the bed. He ran his finger along the baby's cheek. "I'll share everything I have with you. If your mom will let me."

Eloise's throat constricted and she reached for Dante's hand. "I'm sorry about last night."

"No, Eloise. *I'm* sorry. I shouldn't have pushed for you to stay when you weren't ready."

"I needed to hear it. You were right. I was so busy trying not to be overprotective like my father, I didn't realize that I was avoiding confrontation like my mother does. Instead of staying and fighting for what I want, it's always been easier to start over with something new. Instead of staying in town and fighting for my spot in the company business, I ran off and did my own thing."

"But you have a great career and a beautiful daughter because of that decision."

"True, but I also want to raise my daughter to face her fears, no matter how uncomfortable that can be. Being around you and your family, I've learned that there are healthy ways to challenge each other instead of running away from confrontation." Eloise squared her shoulders and looked Dante in the eyes, ready to finally tell him what she truly wanted. "I want my daughter to have a family like the Sanchez family."

Dante bit his lower lip as he thought about her words, then gave her that knowing grin that melted her heart every time. "You know, the best way for her to have that would be for her mommy to marry into the family."

"Well, there's only two single Sanchez brothers left. You and—"

"*Me* or *me*," Dante quickly interjected. "Those are your only two choices."

"In that case, I think I'll pick you. But keep in mind, *you'll* be marrying into the Taylor family. And that might prove to be a lot less fun."

"Trust me, I know." Dante winked at her playfully. "I still have your father's card in my wallet and I've had the whole night to rehearse how I was going to tell him that he has a new granddaughter and soon-to-be son-in-law."

Eloise smiled back at him. She loved the way he could handle the trickiest of situations with a great sense of humor. "I might need a couple more hours of peace and possibly a shower before Pop Pop and Imo-Gram show up. I have a feeling I look worse than I feel."

Dante brushed a kiss across her forehead. "God, Eloise, you had me so terrified last night. First, when I thought you were leaving and never coming back. And then when I saw your car down the ditch, I was afraid it was too late to tell you how much I love you. I knew you weren't ready to hear it, but I don't want to hide it anymore. I love you so much, Eloise Taylor."

"I love you, too, Dante. And thank you for being stubborn enough to come after me last night." Eloise paused. "Wait. You never told me how you knew to follow me. How you knew where to find me."

"I found you because I saw your tire tracks go off

the road." Dante glanced up at the ceiling before continuing. "But why I went after you in the first place? I don't know. Something told me I needed to. It was like this pull, this voice that I couldn't ignore. I've never felt anything like it until I met you."

"Do you remember when Winona Cobbs said that thing about us having a magnetic attraction and if we had met earlier, we'd have had many more kids by now?"

"I remember thinking that she was probably right. Because I'm ready to have more kids with you right now." In response, Merry passed gas loudly, her bottom vibrating in Eloise's arms. Dante chuckled. "Or maybe once we get this one out of diapers. I don't know how many blowouts I can handle just yet. Why? What did you think of Winona's comment?"

"I thought she was just being whimsical. But maybe there's a reason why none of the guys I've ever dated felt right. My mom told me that I'm the type of person who loves deeply and I thought she had me confused with Charlotte. Then after Winona said that, I realized that I always wanted to love deeply, but any time I ever tried to fall in love, I just couldn't. Until I met you. Everything clicked into place, even though I didn't want to trust it."

"From now on, let's always trust whatever this is between us. When you said things would change once the baby was born, you were right. As of last night, I could never go back to the way things were. Not when I have all of this."

Merry got her fist free from her swaddling blanket and grabbed onto Dante's finger. He smiled at their daughter, then leaned forward and brushed another kiss on Eloise's lips.

For the first time in her life, Eloise felt like she was home.

* * * * *

Look for the next title in the
Montana Mavericks: Lassoing Love continuity

A Maverick's Holiday Homecoming
by Brenda Harlen

On sale December 2023, wherever
Harlequin books and ebooks are sold.

And don't miss the previous titles in this series:

The Maverick's Surprise Son
by New York Times *bestselling*
author Christine Rimmer

A Maverick Reborn
by Melissa Senate

A Maverick for Her Mom
by USA TODAY *bestselling*
author Stella Bagwell

Falling for Dr. Maverick
by Kathy Douglass

Available now!

SPECIAL EXCERPT FROM

HARLEQUIN
SPECIAL
EDITION

Sparks fly when beautiful PR expert Georgia O'Neill brings an armful of stray kittens to veterinarian Mel Carter's small-town animal shelter. Mel has loved and lost before, and Georgia is only in town short-term, so it makes sense to ignore their mutual attraction. But as they open up about their pasts, will they also open up to the possibility of new love?

Read on for a sneak preview of
The Vet's Shelter Surprise,
the first book by debut author Elle Douglas.

Chapter One

"Now, you keep those claws away from my sleeve. This is cashmere," Georgia murmured to the first adorable, yet inconvenient ball of fluff that she gently separated from the rest of the kittens, all cuddled up beside their plump mother cat. She deposited it in the banker's box lined with dish towels as the little creature mewed and glared at her, then went in for the second, her hands protected by red oven mitts.

"Okay, okay, you'll all get your turn. I'm trying to help you here. Something tells me your fur likes water almost as much as my shoes do," she said, eyeing the soft brown suede of her brand-new ankle boots and shifting the umbrella wedged between her neck and shoulder. One by one, she moved the six kittens, the mother helping her by leaping into the box unassisted, nuzzling her babies and licking their foreheads as they jostled to be next to her.

Despite the rain, Georgia paused for a moment, taking in the sight of the mother cat's fierce love and protection, and her kittens' desperate battle for her affection and attention. While Georgia was no animal person, it was hard to deny how cute the little fluff balls were. They were adorable, but it would only get them so far. They'd soon realize they'd have to claw their own way forward in this world.

Only an hour ago, Georgia had discovered the cat and her kittens while taking the garbage out to the bins housed in the shed behind her aunt's lakefront cottage. Their gentle cries guided her to the dugout under the stairs leading to the shed, where the furry brood was nestled in a pile of dried-out leaves and twigs. The mother didn't appear to be feral; she was well-fed with a healthy gray coat. She was just a bit out of her element.

Just like Georgia.

Georgia had promised herself she would keep her phone confined in her aunt's old wooden bread box until at least 4:00 p.m. (happy hour—or not so happy, depending on what messages had come through in the meantime), but this was an emergency, right? What kind of person would she be, leaving those poor, defenseless animals out in the rain? Talk about bad press. And it wasn't like she was about to take them inside. Just the thought of vacuuming all that fur was all the permission she needed to free her phone. She'd braced herself for an onslaught of messages on her home screen, and was surprised to find that none had come through. Was she already irrelevant?

After a quick online search for the local animal shelter and a message left on their voice mail, Georgia had a purpose for the day. It wasn't glamorous, and it required her to drive in the rain, which she hated, but it was a welcome event; Georgia didn't do downtime. "Let's get you somewhere safe," she whispered to her box of kittens as she navigated around puddles to get to her car.

She placed the box in the back seat of her rented Audi, shut the back door, then paused. She opened the door again and strapped the seat belt across the box, congratulating herself on how well she was executing this small heroic act.

The GPS guided her the ten minutes it took to navigate the winding, tree-lined roads to reach the Sunset County Animal Shelter, where she planned to deliver her rescued strays, then get back to the business of her day, which so far included waking up early after yet another terrible sleep, drinking too much coffee, resisting looking at the news, getting dressed and made up for no one, and looking out the window waiting for something to happen. The rest of the day promised more of the same, so really, this little adventure might be the highlight.

The shelter, a small limestone structure with a steep gabled roof, sat at the top of Sunset County's Main Street, which led down to the shore of Hollyberry Lake, one of the four sparkling lakes in the charming but very dead Northern Ontario town. Out front, a sprawling garden of mums in every shade of red, yellow and orange were like a mirror reflection of the large red maples flanking the building, their branches swaying in the breeze overhead. The sign outside needed a fresh coat of paint and the windows were on the dustier side, but, for all its flaws, it exuded the same homespun charm that oozed from every pore of Sunset County, a stark contrast to the traffic jams and bright lights awaiting Georgia's return to Los Angeles. Whenever that would be.

The mother cat eyed Georgia warily as she unbuckled the seat belt and gathered the banker's box in her arms. "Trust me, you're better off here," Georgia said as she kicked the back door closed with her boot. She scolded herself for forgetting the umbrella in the car as she turned toward the front entrance, eager to shield the little kittens from the rain. She was capable, sure. But no one would ever mistake her for the nurturing type.

As she let herself in through the front gate, a red van across the street caught her eye, emblazoned with a Channel 4 News logo. Georgia froze as she watched a petite woman with long braids emerge from the front seat, and a camera operator pull his gear out from the back of the truck. Impossible. How had they found her? No one was supposed to have the slightest clue who she was in this teeny-tiny town in the middle of nowhere. Wasn't that why she'd taken a five-hour flight and driven north, to the last place on earth she'd ever be recognized? She'd only been there three days, and had barely left Nina's cottage.

With her heart in her throat and the box in her hands, Georgia bolted up the path and let herself in through the shelter door, then peered out the window past the Help Wanted sign (Help wanted? More like help needed!). The camera operator was fiddling with the mic on the reporter's lapel. Georgia gasped, her mind racing. As if she hadn't suffered enough of an invasion of her privacy over the last few weeks.

She stared intently at the news crew across the street, then almost jumped out of her skin when she heard a throat clearing behind her. "Can I help you?" a voice sounded from what felt like inches away.

Georgia spun around, colliding with a woman, causing her to tip the box sideways. She felt the mother and babies slide to the side of the box, and narrowly saved them from tumbling out by quickly shifting her arm to block them. Before she could even look up at the source of her surprise, she felt the box level in her arms as the woman in front of her helped steady it. "Whoa, whoa," she said. "Easy there."

One of the little kittens, a miniature orange-and-white puffball the size of a teacup, had gotten loose and had its claws stuck in her sleeve. Georgia allowed the woman to take the box while she cupped the kitten in her hand, gently dislodging its teeny-tiny claws from the threads of her sweater.

"Nice save," the woman said. Georgia cradled the kitten in her hands, steadying herself, and took in the stranger in front of her, a woman with the most intense brown eyes she'd ever seen and perfect wavy chestnut hair that fell just above her shoulders. She wore a white lab coat over a hunter green sweater and jeans, and looked at Georgia with a curious and amused expression. She peered inside the box. "Ah. I see someone didn't heed public health advice."

Georgia narrowed her eyes. "Excuse me?" The kitten moved in her hand. She looked down at the baby animal, who rubbed his little head on her wrist, then yawned, revealing a pink tongue not much bigger than a pencil eraser.

"Looks like he likes you," said the woman, as the mother cat made a squawking mewing noise. "But Mom's not too happy."

"Here," Georgia said. She placed the kitten back in the box in the woman's arms and looked up at her. "So, here they are."

The woman raised her eyebrows.

"I left a message earlier?" Georgia said.

"Not that I know of," the woman said, looking back in the box. "Seamus isn't here right now. He's the manager. He would have told you that you have to keep them."

"Well, these aren't mine. I found them."

She looked at Georgia quizzically. "Found them?"

"Under the porch out back of my aunt's house. I don't live here. I mean, I'm just in town for a bit. I don't know who these belong to." For someone who coached others in speaking for a living, Georgia felt her speech getting all muddled up in the woman's deep brown gaze. "And why would you be surprised?" She looked around the room. "You're an animal shelter, right?"

The woman looked away, then furrowed her brow. Georgia followed her gaze out to the street where the news team was still standing and remembered why she'd flown in there like a tornado.

"We're currently an animal shelter. We might be without a home soon, though." She studied the reporters, then looked at Georgia. "The county's plans to cut funding were just announced yesterday, and our regular fundraising won't be enough to cover the shortfall. Looks like the local news is reporting on the story."

A wave of relief washed over Georgia. Of course there were other things going on in the world other than her own personal, and very embarrassing, drama. For example, the undeniable electric charge pulsing through her from standing so close to this incredibly alluring woman. She steeled herself. If there was anything Georgia O'Neill was good at, it was keeping her cool. One recent lapse didn't negate that, right? "Okay, well, I'm very sorry to hear that, Doctor…"

"Melanie Carter. Mel. Don't apologize to me. I just check in on the animals once a week or so. It's my uncle Seamus who's losing. This place has been his life's work. Not to mention the animals." Mel was a tad cool in her demeanor, but at the mention of her uncle and the animals, Georgia thought she detected her expression softening.

"I'm Georgia O'Neill. What will happen to them?" Georgia asked. She looked behind Mel's shoulder to see a hallway that led to a series of rooms where she guessed the animals were kept.

"Nothing's set in stone yet. But we'll try to move them to another place a few counties over. So," she said, looking down at the box of kittens, "we're in no place to take in any new animals."

"What am I supposed to do with these?" Georgia asked, straightening her posture. The kittens were cute. But seeing Mel Carter, with her broad shoulders and narrow waist that suggested a regular fitness regimen, holding on to the box, inspecting the contents—well, that just about made her knees buckle.

Georgia felt Mel's eyes studying her. Was she sizing up her ability to care for another living thing? Or was that flicker in her eye something else? Georgia was suddenly glad she'd taken the time to get herself together that morning rather than giving in to the temptation of spending the rest of her day in her pajamas. Being locked in Mel Carter's—*Doctor* Mel Carter's—

gaze was poking some serious holes in her trademark cool confidence.

"You'll have to take them with you," Mel said, and for a moment Georgia wanted nothing more than for the doctor to lay out more orders. She'd pretty much do anything Mel wanted her to, and maybe then some. "There's really no—"

Mel was interrupted by the door to the shelter opening behind Georgia, and a small gray-haired man coming through the entrance. His glasses were crooked and the laces on one shoe were untied, though it was unclear as to whether his disheveled state was situational or just a general way of being. He bumbled past Georgia without acknowledging her. "Melanie," he said. "How's my Checkers?"

"Just fine, Seamus. I gave her a dose of vitamin E mixed with selenium. She should be back to her old self before you know it."

"Thank you, Doctor. Now, what have we got here?" Georgia watched as Seamus peered into the box of kittens that she was apparently about to inherit. He let out a shout of glee. "It's Molly! Oh, the Harris family is going to be overjoyed. They've been worried sick about her. And look at these kittens. Beautiful."

Seamus turned and did a double take when he noticed Georgia. "Oh. Hello. Where did you find them? Not sure if you've noticed the posters all around town, but there are two young girls who have been beside themselves for weeks. Seems that they'd been trying to keep her inside, with her delicate condition and all, but one of them left the back door open after burning a batch of sugar cookies and Ms. Molly here couldn't resist an adventure. She's an outdoor cat, but she must have been chased or scared by something and lost her way."

Lost her way. Georgia and Molly had more in common than she'd initially thought. She was about to answer, when Mel cut in. "Georgia here found them under her porch and wanted to dump them off," she said.

Georgia's face went hot. "I found them under my aunt's porch. And I wasn't dumping them off. It's an animal shelter."

Mel's expression changed from skeptical to amused. "You're right." She smiled, and Georgia instinctively touched her neck, something she'd trained her clients not to do. It showed vulnerability. Weakness. Which was what Mel was making her feel. Mel peered back in the box. "It's just frustrating how many people don't neuter or spay their cats and aren't willing to care for the kittens."

"The Harris family will take good care. Now, why don't I call them?" Seamus said. "Finally, some good news today." He pulled back the curtain to look at the news truck driving away.

"I heard you might be losing some funding," Georgia said. "I'm really sorry." She paused, looking back at the kittens still in Mel's arms, and again had to gather herself. Someone gorgeous holding kittens? Come on. They made calendars out of this, didn't they? "I'd be happy to deliver them to the family. My day's pretty open." Another task. She was starting to feel like herself again.

Seamus nodded. "Wonderful. I'll go call them now." He looked at Mel. "They live just up on Russell Road. You're heading that direction, right? Why don't you show Georgia the way there?"

"Happy to," Mel said, but Georgia failed to detect any happiness in her response.

"Thanks," said Georgia. Dropping off a lost cat and her kittens to a family who thought they were gone forever? If only she could get that news crew to come back to get some footage of this. And maybe a shot or two of the gorgeous vet cradling some very adorable animals.

She watched as Mel grabbed her jacket from behind the reception desk. This was supposed to be a break from work. But all of a sudden, Mel Carter had Georgia's mind on overdrive.

Mel knew very well she should have thanked Georgia. Probably profusely, for going out of her way like she did. Heck, she'd been in the business long enough to know that some people were downright cruel to animals. It tapped into an anger deep inside her that propelled her to go to work every day. Taking care of those animals that were turned away, who were so humble and so brave despite their circumstances. Nothing deserved her attention more than that.

She'd once thought of going into oncology, or even dentistry, but she thanked her lucky stars every day that she'd had the instinct to pursue veterinary medicine. There were lots of great humans, but there were lots of downright rotten ones too. Mel knew that well enough, and every day tried to silence the voice in her head that told her she attracted the bad ones. So, she was more than fine to devote 100 percent of her energy to those beings that were 100 percent deserving of all the attention and care in the world.

Mel had never seen this Georgia woman before. She'd grown up in Sunset County and knew the whole town, as well as the seasonal cottagers. Not only had she never seen or heard of her, but she stuck out in a way that was intriguing but set off more than one alarm bell. Firstly, her smooth skin had a hint of a summer glow that wasn't common in these parts toward the end of October. Then there was the fairly impractical nature of her attire, which, granted, caused Mel's eyes to linger maybe a moment or two too long, but didn't align with the usual jeans and fleece pullovers sported by most in the area. Georgia appeared as though she'd stepped right out of the pages of one of those fashion magazines her sister Andie always had lying around her place, the ones Mel teased her for with their headlines of "How to Own It in the Bedroom and the Boardroom!" or "Get Clear Skin from the Inside Out!"

She held open the shelter door for Georgia, then followed her to the street. "You can follow me in your car. It's only a few minutes up the road." She looked at Georgia's Audi, which had a sticker from the car rental company on the bumper. "Hope you're not planning on staying in town too long. Those tires won't cut it up here once the snow comes."

Georgia fished her keys out of her purse. "The guy at the rental company told me they're 'all season.'"

Mel knew her last comment came across as unwelcoming. She'd been brought up better than that. "Where are you from?" she asked as Georgia unlocked her door and slid into the driver's seat. The car was definitely impractical. But she looked great behind the wheel.

"LA."

Now the tan made sense. "So, not much experience with winter."

"Actually, I grew up right outside of Chicago. I know

the drill. I'll be gone by the time the bad weather comes."
She flashed Mel a quick smile.

So she was just passing through. Most Sunset County
cottagers came from Toronto, but every now and then
someone visited from farther afield. "That's me," Mel
said, nodding to her silver pickup truck. "I'll lead the
way."

Through her rearview mirror as she buckled her seat
belt, Mel watched as Georgia applied lipstick, for whatever reason, and ran her hand through her silky, toffee-
colored hair. Mel cleared her throat and shook her head.
She'd lead Georgia to the Harris place and then be on
her way. One thing Mel had always shared with animals
was a strong sense of instinct. And her instinct was telling her that Georgia might be drop-dead gorgeous, but
she was trouble. And when it came to fight, flight or
freeze, Mel knew enough by this time in her life that
flight left you with fewer problems in the long run.

She guided Georgia through the winding roads just
outside of the Sunset County downtown, then pulled
into the long gravel driveway leading to the Harris
home. The family, clearly having received Seamus's
call, were all assembled on the front porch, waiting to
welcome home their cherished pet. Hopefully they'd
be ready to house six more. Mel slowed to a stop at the
side of the driveway, and rolled down her window as
Georgia pulled up beside her.

"Here we are," Mel said. "Take care."

"What, you're not coming up?" Georgia asked.
"What if they have any questions? I have absolutely
no idea how to care for kittens."

Mel considered. Georgia was right. She sighed, then
shifted back into Drive. She'd stay for a few minutes

to make sure the family was all set up to care for their new pets, then head back to her clinic in town to finish the pile of paperwork waiting for her. A tall, boring pile of paperwork. It felt like exactly the solution to how hyperaware she'd been feeling since Georgia O'Neill burst through the doors of the shelter, her magnetic energy awakening something in her that Mel had worked to stow away for the past three years. Ever since everything she believed in and the life she thought was a happy one turned out to be a complete sham. She had to get away from Georgia, despite a nagging desire to be closer to her side.

Mel navigated the rest of the way up the path to the house. The two little girls were jumping up and down on the front porch, huge grins on their faces. She sat for a moment, watching as Georgia removed the box from her back seat— did she have a seat belt around it?— then proudly handed the box over to the girls, who at their parents' permission had run down from the porch, almost attacking Georgia. It was a pretty great scene. Mel struggled to keep herself from grinning, then got out of her truck.

"Molly!" the younger girl said, hoisting the mother cat out of the box and into her arms, as the other twin enveloped them both in a giant hug. "We thought you were gone forever."

One of the girls separated herself from the hug and peered into the box. "Mommy, Daddy, look at the kittens! They're so cute!" she exclaimed, carefully lifting one out of the box. "We're keeping them, right?"

"We'll see," said the dad. "Seven is a lot of cats in one house."

"Might be a bylaw infraction," Mel said. Georgia

shot her a look. Well, someone had to be the practical one, right?

"I'm sure we can find a home for a few of these cuties," Mrs. Harris said, peering into the box. "We can't thank you enough for finding Molly. There've been a lot of tears around here."

"I'm just glad she found her way home," Georgia said, her eyes sparkling. Mel swallowed hard as Georgia trailed her hand through her hair, allowing it to cascade down her back in a perfect thickness that Mel could easily imagine running her fingers through.

Georgia reached in and picked up the same orange-and-white kitten that had gotten stuck in her sweater earlier. "You're home, little one," she cooed, nuzzling the miniature animal against her face. Mel breathed in sharply at the idea of touching her perfect, tanned skin. It was time to leave.

"He likes you," said one of the little girls to Georgia.

"Let us know if you want dibs on him. You can visit in the meantime," their dad said.

Georgia laughed. "Oh, not me. I'm just in town for a bit. Good luck finding homes for them, though."

After another minute of small talk and thank-yous, and a few instructions for care from Mel, the family waved goodbye and carried the box into their home, leaving Mel and Georgia standing outside together.

"There you go. Your noble deed for the day," Mel said. "Collecting some good karma."

"Ha!" Georgia said, rolling her eyes. "Don't I need it."

Mel didn't know what that meant, and had no intention of probing, but it confirmed her instincts about Georgia O'Neill. *Trouble.*

"All right, well, you enjoy your time with your aunt," Mel said, turning toward her truck.

"Actually, she passed last month. I'm just here—well, I'm helping sort a couple of things out with her estate."

Mel turned back. "Nanny?" she asked.

Georgia looked confused. "Her name was Nina. Nina Miller."

"We all—" Mel took a moment to gather herself. "Everyone in town called her Nanny. She was like everyone's grandma."

"I didn't know that." She looked to the side when she said it. Had Georgia and her aunt been close? Maybe she just wasn't telling the truth. Mel had never been good at detecting a lie, a crucial flaw that had only resulted in her getting burned. Torched, actually.

Georgia's eyes flickered with sadness, and Mel softened. "Well, I'm sorry about your aunt. She was an amazing woman." Georgia's eyes welled up a bit. Mel had to get out of there. "Lots of helpful people in this town if you need anything." It was the truth. Mel had only left Sunset County for a while to go to university and then vet school, and the familiar workings of the small town, and the way people took care of one another, were close to Mel's heart.

Georgia was quiet, and Mel felt the pressure of her waiting for a better response, but she said nothing. She might have been raised to be polite, but she was no therapist.

"Okay, well, thanks for bringing me out here," Georgia said. "Good luck with the rest of the animals at the shelter." Once again, Mel felt the strong pull of the vulnerability that was showing through the cracks of Georgia's confident, self-assured presentation. She watched as Georgia got in her car, and Mel returned the quick wave she offered as she drove away.

Mel heaved a big sigh as she got back into her truck, forcing herself to relax. But the way she was feeling? It might take a bit more than some deep breathing to recover from being around Georgia. She was a spark. The type that Mel knew could blur her judgment.

If Mel had learned anything in the past few years, it was that there were all sorts of ways that life could pull the rug out from under you. And she needed to stay on solid ground.

Chapter Two

A small package was propped up at the door on the front porch of Aunt Nina's cottage. It could only be from one person. Despite Georgia's desire to remain as under the radar as possible for the next few weeks, she thought it prudent to let at least her best friend, Paulina, under strict secrecy, know the exact location of her hideout lest some terrible accident befall her.

So far, so good. She hadn't counted on being a hero in her first few days in town, but she had to admit she'd enjoyed seeing the looks on the young girls' faces when she'd returned Molly and the kittens.

And then there was Mel Carter. The veterinarian looked as though she'd walked out of a casting call for the role, every bit the "I'm not a doctor but I play one on TV" stereotype. Seriously. The woman was a knock-out, and it irritated Georgia to no end that her attempt to do a good deed went so unnoticed. Punished, even!

That comment about her being too irresponsible to neuter her cat? If it weren't for her disarming, penetrating gaze, and the subtle swagger of her detached demeanor, Georgia might have had the wherewithal to bite back. It was a capacity that she was rarely without.

She sighed, picked up the package and brought it into the redwood-shingled cottage her aunt had lived in for the last thirty years, the one she'd left behind every time she'd traveled to visit Georgia and her parents in San Diego in Georgia's early childhood, or Evanston in her teens. Georgia's calendar had never afforded her the time off to travel to Nina's place, when summer enrichment programs, SAT prep and competitive tennis all began to take over her life, all in the name of following the carefully laid-out path her parents had designed for her. But she'd loved when her aunt visited. Nina was younger than her sister, Georgia's mother, by ten years, and took an interest in Georgia's life beyond her schoolwork and extracurricular achievements. A visit from Nina always promised frivolous fun, like trips to the soft-serve ice cream truck in town for breakfast, or hours-long games of Monopoly. Georgia could only imagine that there were some negotiations behind the scenes and some disapproval from her parents, who only put up with Nina's disregard for Georgia's usual routines because it allowed them to leave on research field trips without too much guilt.

Standing in the entrance of Nina's cottage, she felt the same sense of calm that her aunt had brought to any space she entered. It was a small structure, but immaculately maintained. The wood-paneled living room looked out over a small, tree-lined inlet of Robescarres Lake, which afforded some privacy from the passing speedboats, canoes and kayaks. A bedroom sat to the left side of the living room, and to the right of the entrance was a small, bright kitchen edged with countertops that offered forest views wherever you were cooking.

So they called her Nanny. The fact that Mel knew her aunt wasn't surprising—Nina was very social, and could barely walk ten meters down the street without striking up a casual conversation with whoever happened to be walking by—but the way that Mel dropped her aunt's nickname so casually, as though Georgia should have known, summoned a lump in her throat that she was having a tough time swallowing.

She plopped down into the worn green corduroy couch that wasn't about to win any design awards, but felt like a perfect hug—the kind of couch you could spend a whole day on, reading paperback mysteries and drinking hot chocolate. She examined the box in her hands, laughing to herself at the name Paulina had addressed the box to: "Hurricane Georgia." Only Paulina could get away with that. With anyone else, it would be too soon.

Georgia winced when she recalled, for the millionth time, the event that had earned her that nickname. How could a mere thirty seconds threaten to tear down everything she'd worked for all these years? How long would she be the laughingstock of the industry, the bringer of the greatest irony: the PR rep who earned the worst PR of all time?

It had all happened three weeks earlier. Georgia had known the red-carpet gala fundraiser would be a challenging evening, but thought she could manage. Days before the event, she'd received notice that Nina had finally lost her battle with cancer. And that there were

strict instructions that she didn't want any kind of fu-
neral or end-of-life celebration. Georgia was griev-
ing, hard, crumbling inside but doing everything in
her power to hold it together for her job. She'd always
been able to compartmentalize.

What she hadn't anticipated was the combination
of that grief paired with the incredible amount of pressure she'd been feeling in the first three months of her
new role as Brand Reputation and Issues Response
Specialist at Herstein PR, one of the world's leading
agencies—with offices in LA, London, Miami, Toronto
and New York—and the company to which she'd committed every last ounce of her time and energy over the
past several years.

Not only was Georgia starting to handle the major
flubs of some of the firm's top clients, but by special
request, she'd continued to rep a huge tennis star who
loved Georgia and insisted she'd employ another firm
if Georgia wasn't on her team. The athlete was one of
the marquee guests of the charity event that evening.
Georgia was accompanying her on the red carpet, and
stuck by her side during interview after interview until
one of the journalists had veered off of the agreed-upon
script. Instead of being asked about her athletic prow-
ess and many amazing achievements, both on the court
and in her philanthropic work, the star athlete was questioned about her love life and her weight, which had recently gone up and was the subject of massive tabloid
speculation—was she pregnant? Was she not? Georgia
knew very well that she was not, and had been scram-
bling to figure out how to shut down the interview without causing a scene.

The pivotal moment came when the journalist asked

an even more insulting question, insinuating that the tennis star's weight was the reason behind her recent catastrophic loss in the finals of the US Open.

Georgia didn't remember much, but the videos that went viral on social media immediately following the event quite easily filled in the memory gaps. Georgia first used her elbow to jostle the tennis star out of the way, preventing her from answering the question. Not only did she then proceed to give the reporter a piece of her mind (filled with expletives that Georgia had no idea were part of her vernacular), but in her expressive delivery she sent the tennis star's glass of red wine flying toward the journalist, who, as it turned out, was a former college badminton player and boasted tremendous reflexes, the type that allowed him to duck prior to being hit by the projectile refreshment.

As luck would have it, the multiple-Academy-Award-winning starlet who was hosting the event, Aurelia Martin, was wearing a stunning white Valentino gown and happened to be directly behind the journalist, engaged in an interview of her own, and was splattered from cheek to hip with Georgia's assault. And it was all. On. Video. From multiple angles. In a way that allowed news outlets to create a humiliating, almost 360-degree compilation of the footage, which then traveled to TikTok and Instagram and beyond, where millions of people had viewed the dramatic event, and Georgia's complete and utter humiliation.

And then there were the memes. Objectively, some of them were quite clever, and if Georgia hadn't been the subject of the jokes, she might have admired the tidal wave of fun at her expense. She'd always been in awe of the power of social media.

Her meltdown had resulted in the VP of the company mandating that Georgia take a "wellness pause" from her work. Once she'd wrapped her head around the forced exile, and the impact on what, until recently, had been a promising career trajectory, Georgia weighed her options. The company owned a villa in the Turks and Caicos, but the island would be teeming with their clients on holidays. She briefly toyed with the idea of one of those silent retreats in Colorado, or even just hiding under her duvet for a good long while, but when she received the call from the lawyer handling her aunt's estate, informing her that Nina had left everything to her, hiding out in the small Canadian town felt like the perfect move.

Her aunt wouldn't be there, but maybe being in her home, surrounded by her things, would give Georgia the assurance and guidance she needed to get back on her feet and recover from this fiasco. Nina had always been her guide, and as gutted as Georgia was that she was no longer there to lean on, she longed to at least feel her spirit. Not to mention that handling her aunt's estate would give her something productive to work on, even though in typical Nina style, everything was so well organized, and her place was so tidy and clutter-free, that there really wasn't much to do.

Georgia's parents, as always, were off in some far-flung location—was it Krabi province in Thailand this time?—conducting research on infectious disease ecology and evolution, and were happy to leave the task to their only child, who had seemed to gravitate to Nina more than them anyway.

Georgia's goal was to get the cottage on the market in the next week, in the sweet spot before the fall ended and the beginning of what she'd read was a slow winter real-estate market in Sunset County. By then, she'd be welcomed back to the office and could pick up where she'd left off, helping the brightest stars and athletes in LA manage their public personas.

She picked up the box she'd found on the front porch, peeled back the packing tape, then laughed as she opened the top flap to reveal the contents. Paulina knew her well. Nestled into some shredded paper threads was a bottle of her favorite red wine from the vineyard they loved in Sonoma, as well as a jar of Dr. Barbara Sturm face mask, a pair of furry hot-pink Gucci slippers and a note reading "Hope you find your zen place! xoxo—P."

She instinctively reached for her phone to text her friend and remembered that she had returned it to the bread box and vowed to keep it shut away until 4:00 p.m.

It was only one thirty.

Georgia contemplated the living room of the cottage, trying to decide her next move. She needed to do a bit of staging before putting the cottage on the market, but that could wait.

The energy that she'd been feeling since being in the presence of Mel Carter hadn't gone anywhere, and one of the first things she planned on doing once she freed her phone was going to be looking her up on the internet to see what she could find. Despite Mel's less-than-perfect manners, Georgia predicted she'd have a squeaky-clean online presence. But Georgia had a few more tricks up her sleeve, with a forensic accountant's level of scrutiny from working with her clients.

If anything, she could spend a few minutes studying any profile pictures she came across. Her pink lips. Those deep brown eyes that could make you forget it was a human necessity to breathe, and the easy way she tucked her dark, glossy waves behind her ear. Georgia shivered.

She had some serious energy to expend.

After changing into her running gear, she did a few stretches, then set out to the backcountry roads around Nina's cottage. She settled into a comfortable pace, inhaling the cool fall air that carried a faint hint of bonfire smoke but felt cleaner than any air she'd ever breathed. Georgia was used to hills near her place in Hollywood and found a sudden burst of energy that she gave in to, finally settling into her favorite part about jogging: the moment when her mind went completely blank, and her only focus was getting to the next imaginary goalpost she set for herself on the path ahead.

The roads on the outskirts of Sunset County had a wide gravel shoulder on each side, so Georgia felt safe even when the occasional car or motorcycle whizzed by. Every time a nagging thought or a flash to the last few weeks threatened to enter her consciousness, Georgia picked up the pace just a bit more, and the increased challenge helped to keep the intrusions at bay.

Her watch alerted her that she'd hit the five-kilometer mark. She slowed to a walk in front of a unique, modern-looking home that was a touch out of place compared to the other houses and cottages in the area. The wide glass windows reflected the trees around it in a way that allowed the forest to continue uninterrupted, as though the house was trying to camouflage itself.

She'd stopped to examine the building further when a big fluffy dog with black, white and golden fur came bounding across the yard to greet her at the fence. Georgia crouched down and extended her hand through an opening between the fence posts, allowing the dog to sniff her. Then she petted its soft head. Seemed she was becoming quite the animal whisperer.

"What's your name?" Georgia asked quietly, as the dog panted and licked her hands. The dog had the gentlest eyes she'd ever seen, as though it could peer right into someone's soul. The earnest, sweet animal in front of her gave her a small window into why people loved being in the presence of dogs.

Then again, they didn't necessarily smell terrific.

"I didn't peg you as an animal person," a voice called from closer to the house. A familiar voice, which was unusual in an unfamiliar town.

Georgia stood up, and her heart, which had just started to slow down in the brief break from running, immediately sped up again at the sight of Mel Carter, who was emerging from the front entrance of the house holding a dog leash and making her way toward Georgia. A hot blush burned her already red cheeks. "You live here?" Georgia asked. "Nice place."

"You seem surprised," Mel said, her eyes traveling over Georgia's tight running top and pants, sending a heat wave of desire coursing through her body as though Mel's gaze was a laser beam. Mel had also changed since Georgia had last seen her and was still wearing her faded jeans, but she'd swapped out her lab coat for a red-and-black houndstooth wool button-up, rolled up at the sleeves.

Georgia had to consciously resist the urge to touch her neck, or fix her shirt, or smooth her hair. "Well, it's a bit surprising. I mean, not that you live here. Just that of all the places in the area I could have stopped for a break in front of—"

"Franny here has that effect on people," Mel said, opening the gate and leashing up Franny before she could bound toward Georgia. "She's a bit of a neighborhood ambassador."

"She's very cute," Georgia said, taking a tentative step forward to pet Franny again. Franny leaped up, trying desperately to lick her cheek. Georgia laughed and scratched the dog behind her ears when she settled down. "Rescue, I'm assuming?"

"Yeah," said Mel. She squatted down to Franny's height, and immediately Franny turned back to Mel for more pets. "She's a Bernese mountain dog. A farmer down the road got really badly injured in a trailer accident. He's not walking anymore, so he had to give up the farm. I took her in a couple years ago." Mel stood up, and Franny immediately jumped up again, almost hugging her, then licked her cheek. "Okay, okay," she said. "We're going for a walk. Don't worry." She looked at Georgia. "So—how's it going at your aunt's place? I'm sure that's a big chore. Going through everything."

Georgia nodded. "Luckily she was a minimalist. And a bit of a neat freak. So, it's really not a lot of work. Just—" Despite herself, she found the words coming out of her mouth. "Just a bit hard to say goodbye. We were close."

Mel's expression softened, telling Georgia that she knew something about her pain. And for a moment, Georgia saw an opening, as though Mel was about to offer her help. Or invite her to walk together. There was a shimmer of warmth, a genuine connection.

"Well, good luck with everything. Let's go, Franny," Mel said, taking a step away from her, and suddenly the spell was broken and Georgia felt foolish for entertaining the idea that a woman she had met mere hours ago would have any interest in doing anything to help her. "You know your way home, right?"

"Yeah, for sure," Georgia said, adjusting her watch. Had she done something wrong? She knew some people didn't like to talk about death, but surely someone in the health-care profession would know very well that it was a fact of life, wouldn't they? And what about that current of electricity between them? There was no way Mel didn't feel it too.

She glanced over her shoulder to check the road before crossing and give a quick wave before resuming her jog, but Mel had already turned her back and was walking the other way. "Take care," Mel called, without turning around.

Georgia stared for a moment, then started back toward Nina's cottage. Mel had clearly missed the class on bedside manners at vet school.

Try as she might to get back into the same zone she'd found so effortlessly at the beginning of her run, Georgia had no luck. That look in Mel's eyes—the one that for the very briefest of moments made Georgia desperate to know what she was thinking—was burned in her brain, and no amount of pushing herself and letting the fatigue overtake her would make it go away.

She'd come to Sunset County seeking a quiet place to hide out while she settled her aunt's affairs, and where she could find some way back to being the woman she was: a kick-ass PR agent, on top of her game. An achiever. A woman who could hold it together in the most challenging of situations.

So far, Mel Carter and her strong frame, and her deep, penetrating eyes, were *not* helpful in this endeavor.

Not one bit.

* * *

As soon as Mel knew Georgia was long gone, back toward Robescarres Lake, she stopped for a moment and took a deep breath while Franny sniffed a fallen branch at the side of the road. She looked out into the thick forest to her right and shook her head.

She knew she'd been incredibly rude. And should have asked Georgia if she needed anything. Her aunt had just died, an aunt she was close to, and now she had to pack up her place. Of course, that would be a hard thing to do. Heck, extending a hand, even to a stranger, was the essence of living in a small town, and she'd had more than her share of offers to help after everything that had happened to her three years ago. Not that she'd asked for it, but there was something reassuring in knowing there were good people looking out for you.

Even knowing this, she couldn't bring herself to do it. Because as soon as Mel offered help, and as soon as Georgia said yes, well, then she was in trouble. Georgia O'Neill was the first woman since Breanne who'd made Mel feel as though she was no longer standing on solid ground. She'd given in to that feeling for Breanne, big-time, and was still raw from the ache of that loss. A loss on two counts, and it was sometimes hard to know which was worse.

In the first few days, it was Breanne's death. The agony of losing the woman she loved and the future she'd envisioned, a future that was so vivid and so promising that it seemed impossible that something so alive and real could be snuffed out in a moment.

And then the details of the car accident were confirmed, and her best friend since childhood came clean with what was going on. Mel learned the reason why

Breanne was rushing to get home, on a rainy night, when the roads were slippery. Mel had called her to say she'd just landed a day early from a conference and was going to take her out for dinner. Knowing the truth turned her sorrow, which was infused with a deep disappointment, into fierce anger.

Instead of going home from the airport, Mel had traveled by taxi to the hospital, where Breanne was about to take her last breath. Mel would never forget running through the hallways of the ICU ward, dodging wheelchairs and beds and nurses muttering at her to slow down, moments away from getting to the love of her life, with her suitcase trailing behind her and a ring in her pocket.

She'd missed saying goodbye.

It hadn't even for a moment struck her as strange that her best friend, Lauren, was there. Given what they'd been through together growing up, from skinned knees, soccer championships and failed math tests as kids, to supporting Lauren through her mother's Parkinson's disease and Lauren seeing Mel through the stress of vet school, of course she'd be there when Mel needed her most.

It was days later, over a bottle of whiskey, in a moment when she felt like she had her best friend, basically her sister, by her side to help her through what would be an impossible road ahead, when Mel learned the truth.

Lauren had called on the way over. "Can we talk?" she'd said. Her voice was timid, restrained. Nothing like her usual easygoing, affable self.

"Yeah, sure," Mel had said, not in the mood for conversation but grateful for her friend's company. She was working on her speaking notes for Breanne's celebration of life, and was terrified by the idea of standing up in front of a crowd and trying to make it through the speech without losing it.

When she opened the door, Lauren stood holding a bottle of Jim Beam, dark circles under her teary eyes, which were avoiding any contact with Mel's.

Mel had pulled two rocks glasses from the cupboard and poured them each a measure. "I might need you up there with me," she said. "In case I can't make it all the way through."

When she'd turned back to look at Lauren, her head was in her hands, her body shaking with guttural sobs. "I'm sorry. Oh, God, Mel, I hate myself."

Without Lauren even saying another word, the pieces of the puzzle started to click together. They'd always gotten along well when the three of them hung out, which Mel loved. Lauren would sometimes bring dates when they went out for drinks or to the movies, but she'd never suspected that the easy banter and affection between Lauren and Breanne was anything more than her girlfriend and her best friend getting along well for her sake.

"It just…happened," Lauren had whispered.

Just *happened*. Like the sunrise. Like the tide going out. Like a sneeze you couldn't control. Mel's stomach lurched, her anger clouding and shaking her vision at the same time.

She sat stiff and humiliated as Lauren choked out the hideous details of the affair. It had started during the trip the three of them had planned to take to Algonquin Park. Mel came down with strep throat the day they were supposed to leave. She'd encouraged them to go on without her. Then Mel's late nights getting the clinic up and running had apparently facilitated future meet-ups. She listened as Lauren tried to absolve herself of her guilt. *We felt so terrible. We were planning to tell you the truth.* And again: *It just happened.*

When she'd looked down at the table in front of her, she could barely make out the jotted-down notes she'd been working on of ideas for what she was going to say about Breanne. The words staring back at her re-arranged themselves, accusing her of being a complete fool. "How could you?" she managed.

Lauren continued to sob silently.

Minutes passed as Mel let the truth sink in. "Leave" was all she could think of to say. It was the last word she'd ever said to Lauren.

Her life had seemed perfect. Then. The person who mattered to Mel the most was gone, and the other, while still alive, was dead to her. Lauren had begged for her forgiveness, and in the weeks that followed, persisted in trying to convince Mel that their friendship could be mended. It took a while, but Lauren finally relented.

Over the past three years, the pain and anger had gradually turned to resignation, and a commitment to never get duped again. She'd tried therapy, but there didn't seem to be much of a point. It couldn't help her go back in time.

Small-town life suited her. She had a purpose, peo-ple knew her enough to respect that she liked to keep a polite distance, and there was the steadiness that very little changed, save for the cottagers and the weekenders passing through—mostly couples on a short getaway.

It had been a long time since she'd faced that same feeling she'd experienced when she first met Breanne on their university campus, when life seemed kind and it was conceivable that she could be happy. And although Mel knew nothing about Georgia O'Neill, how long she'd be in town for or what that meant for her, that familiar feeling was undeniable and set off every signal in her body to get as far away from Georgia as possible, as quickly as possible. Georgia thinking Mel was rude was way better than the alternative.

Franny sniffed, and Mel realized she'd been standing still for several minutes, staring out into the crimson-and-amber tapestry of the forest. "Come on," she called, then whistled, which made Franny leap up, wagging her tail in a fit of excitement.

Mel let Franny off her leash and watched her bound down the forest trail chasing a chipmunk, blissfully living in the moment. Animals were simple. Uncomplicated. They gave you all their love, unconditionally, and wanted nothing in return.

But most of all, they were loyal.

Chapter Three

"Hurricane Georgia, huh?" Georgia said, flopping back onto the couch with her phone.

Paulina's big grin filled the phone screen, and her booming laugh rang through the speaker. The sight of her best friend immediately brought up Georgia's spirits. Paulina was wearing a fluorescent yellow button-up with a black lightning bolt print and sparkly red-rimmed glasses, which fit her self-ascribed "fabulous Indian Ms. Frizzle" aesthetic. "Come on. That was at least a category four," Paulina said.

"With the wreckage of a five. How are you?"

"Oh, you know. Grant's on the road right now. So I'm sleeping really well."

Georgia rolled her eyes, laughing. Paulina was in a new relationship with a semipro basketball player and loved to brag about his stamina, both on and off the court. "Miss you, though," Paulina said. "How are things there?"

"Well. I just finished organizing the apps on my phone by color, and I've watched at least two hours of dance videos on TikTok, so safe to say you might need to get up here ASAP."

"Wait, so what you're saying is you're actually taking a break?"

Georgia tilted the phone down so Paulina could see her outfit, a purple tie-dyed lounge set.

"Wait," Paulina said, "are you still in your pajamas? This is bad. I'm on my way."

"Yeah, right," Georgia said. As a senior associate at her law firm on a fast track to partner, Paulina was just as devoted to her job as Georgia. "It's been all right. I'm just... I'm restless." Georgia sighed and stared out the window to the lake, which was sparkling in the early-evening light. Two loons bobbed close to shore, slowly paddling through the green lily pads dotting the surface of the water. At least she wasn't the only one in town with nothing to do.

"You're a workaholic. Makes sense. But you need this time."

"I'm not a workaholic."

"And I'm not a coffee addict."

"Fine. I'm finding it a bit challenging. But these slippers are definitely helping." Georgia pointed her feet in the air and wiggled her toes.

"Why don't you sign up for an online course or something? You've always talked about learning Mandarin."

"Nah."

"Scrapbooking?"

"Stop."

"Part-time job?"

"Ha. I might be needing one. Maybe I'll update my résumé."

"Volunteer? I know you love to work. But what about putting in some hours somewhere, just because it's a good thing to do? And good for your mental health."

"Maybe. Anyway, thanks for calling. I'm going to go organize my cosmetics bag or something. I'll call you tomorrow."

"Don't forget to relax. Miss you!"

Georgia tossed her phone on the coffee table and stared up at the ceiling. Where had she put that wine Paulina sent?

After pouring herself a generous glass of cabernet sauvignon (she was here to relax, wasn't she?), Georgia threw a couple of logs on the fire and sat back in front of the crackling flames, the light and heat comforting her while the pink evening sky began to fade to dark.

Maybe Paulina was onto something. She didn't need a work visa to volunteer. And doing something productive that contributed to society would look really good to her bosses and show them she was ready and able to work again. Maybe she could volunteer at Nina's old school. She could handle a few hours of playing with kids, couldn't she? Entertain them with a few celeb stories?

A quick Google search of the school board's website quashed that idea. All volunteers were required to provide a vulnerable sector check, which would take time to come through.

Maybe there was some kind of charity race or big event in the area she could help promote. Another few minutes of Google searching revealed a fundraising bingo that was happening at the local Legion, but it was scheduled for that evening.

Georgia sipped her wine. She'd figure this out.

Ever since she was a child, she'd been trained to be calculated and confident in everything she did, every decision she made. She was the one friends came to for advice. Other parents used her as an example for their own children: "Why can't you be more like that Georgia O'Neill?" She wore it as a badge of honor. And lived in a state of perpetual fear that the badge could be stripped away at any moment.

The truth was, Georgia liked being on top. She loved working hard, and her parents might have laid out the expectations, but Georgia happily met them.

It wasn't until she was in her first year at university that she felt the full weight of her parents' grand plan, each step in her life carefully mapped out for her, likely before she was even born.

College prep school. Violin lessons. Summer enrichment programs at campuses across the country. An exchange in Spain. And right into premed at Northwestern, where her parents were professors and researchers and could meticulously advise her on her course selections, professors most likely to write her a glowing reference for med school, and volunteer jobs and research positions at Chicago's top hospitals.

A bigger curveball had likely never been thrown their way when, without telling them, Georgia had switched into modern languages with a minor in art history early in her second year. Georgia wasn't sure what had surprised them more: the one-eighty on her academic plan or her bringing home her first girlfriend at Thanksgiving.

And as always, Nina had been there to guide her through, taking her phone calls late into the night, talking for hours and helping her figure out the right thing to do. Not right for anyone else, but right for her and her alone.

And here she was, at a time when she should have been working to advance her career righting *other people's* wrongs, trying to figure out how to wipe her own slate clean and get back to the steady trajectory of success that was true to her heart and that she'd set in motion years ago.

Paulina was right. She should take this time here, in Sunset County, to rest and move beyond what had happened. It was a small part of her story, and it was time to get over it. She remembered that morning, when she'd thought the news truck was following her. When she'd peered out the shelter's window, past the Help Wanted sign.

The Help Wanted sign.

If there was anything the past twelve hours had taught Georgia, it was that she was an unexpected hit with animals. And how hard could it be, petting and cuddling kittens and puppies, racking up some volunteer hours and making a few well-curated social media posts that her bosses would hopefully see?

The shelter manager—what was his name? Samuel? Steven? Seamus. He seemed like a nice man. And someone who likely hadn't seen her video.

And then there was Mel Carter. She had to admit that the idea of seeing Mel again wasn't an entirely unpleasant one, even if she seemed a bit odd and prickly.

Either way, she could put up with Mel and her moods. Plus, she'd told Georgia she only worked there once a week.

She scrolled back in her call history and dialed the

shelter's number. It was past business hours, so she left a voice mail. "Hello, Seamus, we met this morning," Georgia said. "Georgia O'Neill. I saw your Help Wanted sign when I came by with the kittens. And I'm ready to help." She concluded the message with her phone number and a promise to follow up if she didn't hear from him by noon the next day. It was always good practice to exert a little control over the situation.

Her dampened mood was slightly lifted by the idea of having something productive to do (the wine didn't hurt), and she sat back on the couch, watching the dancing flames in the fireplace, and for the first time since arriving in Sunset County, she felt something approaching relaxation.

It was so quiet at Nina's place, and so warm and comforting. No wonder her aunt was always calm.

She'd lock in the volunteer job in the morning, and then do some work organizing her aunt's things later in the day. For now, she was going to enjoy the moment.

Right after she did some internet searching for Dr. Mel Carter.

"You mean that woman who was in here yesterday? Who's clearly never held an animal in her life, never mind has no experience whatsoever?" Mel said, moments after Seamus shared that he'd hired a new volunteer, and she'd be coming by momentarily to fill out the volunteer information form. Through gritted teeth, Mel was trying to manage her tone; she hated speaking to her gentle and kind uncle in a confrontational way.

"We've had that sign up for weeks, and no luck," Seamus said. "My back is giving me so much trouble, I can't keep up with all the extra work. And she seems nice."

Mel clenched her jaw. How was it that the one person she was eager to avoid was now about to invade her workspace? To be fair, most of Mel's time was spent at her clinic down the street, but still. What was Georgia up to? She was supposed to be dealing with her aunt's estate, not volunteering on a whim to make Mel's days more difficult.

"Fine," Mel sighed. "Hope she knows what she's getting into, though. It's not glamorous work. And she seems a bit—" she thought about the sheen in Georgia's thick, shiny hair, the expensive-looking outfit she'd worn to the shelter, the pristine Audi "—high-maintenance."

"I'll give her the benefit of the doubt. It's not like anyone else is knocking down the door to help out."

Before Mel could respond, the door of the shelter flung open, and in strode Georgia, looking like a complete knockout in a pair of royal blue high-heeled shoes, a black leather jacket and oversize tortoiseshell sunglasses. Mel's annoyance melted away, and she steadied herself.

Georgia removed her sunglasses, revealing her hazel eyes framed with long lashes—eyes like a doe, but Mel wasn't sure she had the animal's trademark innocence.

"Georgia, welcome," Seamus said, rushing to the door to greet her and shake her hand. "We're so happy that you're interested in helping us out." Seamus looked at Mel expectantly.

Mel cleared her throat, trying to recover from Georgia's sparkling entrance, which had all but bowled her over. "Hey, Georgia" was all she could muster.

Georgia didn't seem fazed. "I printed out the volunteer form at my aunt's place. So, here it is. All filled out." She grinned and passed the paper to Seamus.

"Thank you," Seamus said, surveying the form. "Now,

let me just pop this in a file folder. Then I'll give you a tour of the facility."

Mel saw her chance to make an exit. "All right, then. I'll see you around," she said and turned to her uncle. "I'll be back on Thursday. Just call if you need anything." She watched Seamus stand up on a chair to open the top cabinet, then stop, bending over and crying out in pain.

"You okay?" Mel asked, rushing to Seamus's side.

"My back," Seamus said, groaning, then accepting Mel's hand to help him off the chair. "I've really got to get to the chiropractor."

"Slowly, slowly," Mel said as Seamus got back on solid ground, wincing and holding his lower back.

"Can I call someone for you?" said Georgia, her big eyes shining with concern. She was right there with Mel, holding Seamus's other hand.

"No, no, I just need to rest for a few minutes," he said. With both of their assistance, he sank into the office chair, then looked at Georgia. "This is why we need you here. I'm getting too old to manage things on my own." Mel bristled.

"Well, I'm glad to be of service," Georgia said.

"Melanie, you don't mind giving Georgia a quick tour of the facility before you leave, do you?"

Mind? Of course she minded. Every moment she spent in Georgia's presence was another moment she felt herself losing her bearings. The woman was bewitching.

"I can come back tomorrow, if you're busy…" Georgia said, and Mel saw an out, until she looked down at Seamus's expectant expression. The old man knew her all too well.

"Not at all," Mel said through gritted teeth. Fine. The

universe was testing her. She'd take Georgia on a quick tour, make sure Seamus was okay to get home on his own, then get the heck out of there.

She glanced at Georgia's impractical, albeit incredibly sexy footwear. Was she trying to torture her? "Have you got any other shoes you can wear? A number of our animals are out back. It's dirty."

"Ugh, what was I thinking?" Georgia laughed. "Sorry. In my line of work, heels are pretty much the uniform. I'm sure I'll be fine."

Despite herself, Mel couldn't help but smile. This would be interesting. What line of work did she mean? Cocktail waitress? Runway model? Pageant queen? Not that Mel was a fashion expert, but in her mind, any job that required a woman to wear heels was woefully behind the times. And Georgia O'Neill didn't seem like the kind of woman to be coerced into doing anything she didn't want to. So, the heels had to be a matter of personal preference.

"All right. Follow me," Mel said, leading Georgia down the bright hallway toward the back room. Time to see how she'd do with their resident reptiles. "Right in here," she said, motioning to the open door at the end of the hall. "After you."

Heels clicking against the linoleum, Georgia breezed by, leaving the floral scent of her shampoo in her wake and causing Mel to take a deep breath before following her into the room. How was it that something as inane as hair soap could make her heartbeat rev up to double time, and make her palms sweat like a cold glass of lemonade on a hot day? It really had been too long.

Mel surveyed Georgia's reactions as she walked between the reptile tanks, silently peering into each one with a curious expression.

"Who's this one? What's his name?" she asked, pointing to the iguana.

"That's Sherbet. And she's a she," Mel said.

"Okay. Cute. And who's this?" Georgia pointed to the turtle.

"That's Pixie. Careful with that one. She almost took my finger off last time I fed her," she said. She followed Georgia to the gecko tank. "Lollipop is the brown-and-white one, and Gummy Bear is the yellow one." She waited for Georgia to approach the final tank, which housed a ball python snake named Slinky. Slinky was mellow and gentle, as well as nonvenomous, but Mel knew very few people who liked being in the presence of his sort. Time to see how much Georgia really wanted to volunteer at the shelter.

To Mel's surprise, Georgia scanned the tank and tapped quietly on the glass. "A snake," she said matter-of-factly.

"Slinky," said Mel. Georgia was full of surprises, she was starting to realize. "Most people don't want to go near him with a ten-foot pole."

"I lived outside the desert for a few years as a kid. Place was teeming with snakes," she said. "Okay, next stop?" Her sparkling hazel eyes ratcheted up Mel's heartbeat from double time to a full-on Ginger Rogers tap dance.

Next stop was the bunny room. Mel was doomed.

Georgia followed Mel through the animal shelter, meeting the different residents and trying to solicit the little information Mel seemed willing to share. Mel was curt with her explanations and checked her watch several times, and when Georgia asked her about her vet clinic and how long she'd been operating it, Mel made Georgia feel as though she'd asked for her blood type and password to her online banking account. Wasn't politeness supposed to be a thing in Canada?

She sensed that Mel had introduced her to Slinky the snake to get a rise out of her. It had taken everything in her to maintain her cool. The truth was, she hated snakes. As a child, when her parents were visiting professors at UC San Diego, she refused to go on hikes with them to Joshua Tree or Anza-Borrego because of what she'd read about the local residents of the parks, and on any trip to the zoo she'd skip the reptile pavilion. But she wasn't about to give Mel the satisfaction of seeing her as anything less than an animal lover in her first thirty minutes at the shelter. She needed this position.

Mel led her through the shelter's back door to the fenced-in outdoor space, where a series of pens with plywood roofs housed a variety of farm animals: a few goats, a potbellied pig, some ducks and a few others who must have been hiding in their homes.

"This is the outdoor crew," Mel said. "You'll mostly be feeding and watering them." She motioned for Georgia to follow her to the back pen. Dammit. The heels were definitely a mistake. Mel must have noticed her taking careful steps through the uneven gravel and sand, and extended her elbow for Georgia to grab on to. She paused for a moment, unsure about the sudden kind gesture, then placed her hand on Mel's forearm, grateful for the support and appreciative of the soft strength of it.

"She's not as cute as Slinky, but..." Mel pointed to a sandy-colored miniature horse with white hair, tucked in the back corner of its pen, with eyes so sad that Georgia instinctively wanted to take the animal into her arms. Snakes? No way. Horses? Now they were getting somewhere. "This is Taffy," Mel said, then whistled and grabbed a carrot from the bucket outside of Taffy's pen. The little horse trotted over slowly, looking up at Georgia with curiosity.

"She's beautiful," Georgia breathed, then looked around at the collection of farm animals quietly going about their business in their pens. "Wouldn't a local farmer want to take them in?"

Mel passed Georgia the carrot, and she accepted. Their hands brushed together, and the warmth of Mel's skin felt like her California sunshine on the most perfect of days. Georgia clutched the carrot, then looked sideways at Mel to find the woman examining her, chocolate-brown eyes pensive and deep, as though she was being tested. Georgia straightened her posture, and despite her heels digging into the gravel, took a few steps closer to Taffy's pen and extended the carrot to the horse, willing her to come closer.

"Some do," Mel said. "Depends on their backstory. Some of these were collected by the SPCA after a report of mistreatment. Others had to be given up by their owners once their farms were sold to developers. Lots of reasons why animals end up here," she said. "That one," Mel said, motioning to Taffy, "is infertile. Wouldn't sell at market. Not worth it for the breeder to house and feed her, so she got unloaded here." Mel's words carried a sharp sense of protectiveness.

"You poor thing," Georgia whispered, lightly running her hand over Taffy's soft head.

"She's gentle," Mel said. "Seamus is training her to be a therapy animal."

"I can see why."

"You're good with her," Mel said.

"You sound surprised." Georgia looked up to see if Mel's expression had changed, but it was still all business. She was a tough one to crack. But it wasn't Georgia's style to back down. "I was always jealous of the girls in my class who grew up on ranches," she said, remembering her peers who showed off their ribbons from horseback riding events during show-and-tell, or who spent their weekends riding the trails of the nearby canyons. In contrast, Georgia's weekends were spent doing reach-ahead math sessions with tutors and practicing the violin while her mother sat in the adjoining sitting room, tut-tutting every time Georgia made an error.

The idea of spending her day on a majestic horse, galloping beside a stream or across a palm oasis (high up and out of the reach of any snake, of course), was the stuff of many a daydream, and something she knew her mother and father would never go for.

"And you never went riding as a kid?" Mel asked.

"No," said Georgia. "My parents had my time pretty mapped out. But I plan on it, someday." She looked into Taffy's eyes, charmed by the animal's innocence and gentle nature. Maybe she could convince Seamus to keep her on Taffy duty.

Mel hadn't said a word, and Georgia looked to her side to see if she was still there. What had moments ago been an untrusting expression was now the slightest bit tender, as though she actually cared what Georgia had to say, and maybe, just maybe, was interested in hearing more.

Georgia paused for a moment, then opened her mouth, ready to continue, when Mel cleared her throat loudly, then checked her watch. "Well, gotta run," she said, looking away from Georgia, then starting back toward the shelter. She stopped, then turned back. "Need my help getting back?" she said, gesturing toward her heels, which were now covered in dirt.

"I'm okay," Georgia said. What had she done wrong? "I'm just going to spend a few more minutes out here looking around. You go ahead."

"All right. I'm going to help Seamus out and lock up, so you can exit through the gate. See you around," Mel said, beelining back to the building.

"Wait," Georgia called, just before Mel could leave. She turned around, and Georgia took in her tall, lean body and the way her jeans hugged her hips perfectly. "You haven't told me which one is your favorite."

Mel raised her eyebrows, then chuckled. "I don't play favorites," she said. "You look long enough in any of their eyes and you'll find something to love." With that, she disappeared through the door, leaving Georgia outside with her new charges.

She stood in the quiet of the shelter's outdoor space and considered what Mel said, and the notion of having to look for something in someone to love. Was that how it worked? Didn't love come easy, effortlessly, not like something you set out to do?

Not that she was looking to Mel Carter as the authority on all things love. The woman didn't exactly have warm and fuzzy written all over her.

But that intent, searching look in her eyes, quietly observing, was leading Georgia to believe that there was a lot more under the surface, and maybe something that she was keeping hidden from the world. Georgia prided herself on her ability to read people. To know when they were telling the truth, when they were lying, when they were afraid. It was part of why she was so good at her work. But with Mel? It was challenging.

Now she was working with her. Would Mel ever reveal anything about herself to her? The idea was intriguing, and just a bit nerve-racking.

You're here for a few weeks. A month, tops, she reminded herself. In that amount of time, how much of someone could you really know?

Don't miss
The Vet's Shelter Surprise *by Elle Douglas,*
available November 2023 wherever
Harlequin Special Edition books
and ebooks are sold.

www.Harlequin.com

Get 3 FREE REWARDS!

We'll send you 2 FREE Books plus a FREE Mystery Gift.

FREE
Value Over
$20

Both the **Harlequin® Special Edition** and **Harlequin® Heartwarming™** series feature compelling novels filled with stories of love and strength where the bonds of friendship, family and community unite.

YES! Please send me 2 FREE novels from the Harlequin Special Edition or Harlequin Heartwarming series and my FREE Gift (gift is worth about $10 retail). After receiving them, if I don't wish to receive any more books, I can return the shipping statement marked "cancel." If I don't cancel, I will receive 6 brand-new Harlequin Special Edition books every month and be billed just $5.49 each in the U.S. or $6.24 each in Canada, a savings of at least 12% off the cover price, or 4 brand-new Harlequin Heartwarming Larger-Print books every month and be billed just $6.24 each in the U.S. or $6.74 each in Canada, a savings of at least 19% off the cover price. It's quite a bargain! Shipping and handling is just 50¢ per book in the U.S. and $1.25 per book in Canada * I understand that accepting the 2 free books and gift places me under no obligation to buy anything. I can always return a shipment and cancel at any time by calling the number below. The free books and gift are mine to keep no matter what I decide.

Choose one:
☐ **Harlequin**
   Special Edition
   (235/335 BPA GRMK)

☐ **Harlequin**
   Heartwarming
   Larger-Print
   (161/361 BPA GRMK)

☐ **Or Try Both!**
   (235/335 & 161/361
   BPA GRPZ)

Name (please print)

Address   Apt. #

City   State/Province   Zip/Postal Code

Email: Please check this box ☐ if you would like to receive newsletters and promotional emails from Harlequin Enterprises ULC and its affiliates. You can unsubscribe anytime.

Mail to the Harlequin Reader Service:
IN U.S.A.: P.O. Box 1341, Buffalo, NY 14240-8531
IN CANADA: P.O. Box 603, Fort Erie, Ontario L2A 5X3

Want to try 2 free books from another series! Call 1-800-873-8635 or visit www.ReaderService.com.

*Terms and prices subject to change without notice. Prices do not include sales taxes, which will be charged (if applicable) based on your state or country of residence. Canadian residents will be charged applicable taxes. Offer not valid in Quebec. This offer is limited to one order per household. Books received may not be as shown. Not valid for current subscribers to the Harlequin Special Edition or Harlequin Heartwarming series. All orders subject to approval. Credit or debit balances in a customer's account(s) may be offset by any other outstanding balance owed by or to the customer. Please allow 4 to 6 weeks for delivery. Offer available while quantities last.

Your Privacy—Your information is being collected by Harlequin Enterprises ULC, operating as Harlequin Reader Service. For a complete summary of the information we collect, how we use this information and to whom it is disclosed, please visit our privacy notice located at corporate.harlequin.com/privacy-notice. From time to time we may also exchange your personal information with reputable third parties. If you wish to opt out of this sharing of your personal information, please visit readerservice.com/consumerschoice or call 1-800-873-8635. **Notice to California Residents**—Under California law, you have specific rights to control and access your data. For more information on these rights and how to exercise them, visit corporate.harlequin.com/california-privacy.

HSEHW23

HARLEQUIN
PLUS

Try the best multimedia subscription service for romance readers like you!

Read, Watch and Play.

Experience the easiest way to get the romance content you crave.

Start your **FREE TRIAL** at
<u>www.harlequinplus.com/freetrial</u>.